RELATIVE DANGER

RELATIVE DANGER

JUNE SHAW

FIVE STAR

An imprint of Thomson Gale, a part of The Thomson Corporation

THOMSON

GALE

Detroit • New York • San Francisco • New Haven, Conn. • Waterville, Maine • London

LIBRARY OF CONGRESS CATALOGING-IN-PUBLICATION DATA

Shaw, June.
    Relative danger / June Shaw. — 1st ed.
        p. cm.
    ISBN 1-59414-531-8 (alk. paper)
    1. Grandmothers—Fiction. 2. Granddaughters—Fiction. 3. Louisiana—
Fiction. I. Title.
PS3619.H3936R45 2006
813'.6—dc22   2006021334

U.S. Hardcover:
ISBN 13: 978-1-59414-531-5
ISBN 10: 1-59414-531-8

First Edition. First Printing: December 2006.

Published in 2006 in conjunction with Tekno Books and Ed Gorman.

Printed in the United States of America on permanent paper
10 9 8 7 6 5 4 3 2 1

ACKNOWLEDGMENTS

I thank relatives who have offered their support to my writing, especially these most important people and their families: Nora Shaw, Bob Breaux, Al and Sharon Naquin, Dawn Naquin and Allison Fakier, Scott Naquin, Debra and Mike Blanchard, Nolan and Becky Naquin, Billy and Delta Shaw, Ronnie and Janet Shaw, and Lois Naquin. Thanks to special friends Chuck and Margaret Giroir, Billy and Deanie Sevin, Irma Daigle, Irma Arceneaux, Jeanette Nannie, and my T-LaLa Red Hat Society queen and princesses.

Thanks to many who helped critique *Relative Danger,* especially outstanding authors Lonnie Cruise and Dorothy Bodoin. More assistance and support came from members of my writers' groups: SOLA (Southern Louisiana chapter of Romance Writers of America in New Orleans), Mystery Writers of America, Sisters in Crime, Kiss of Death, and Guppies.

I owe much gratitude to Major Roland Caillouet, Head of the Criminal Department for Lafourche Parish Sheriff's Office, Keri Clark, Jonette Stabbert, and Mark Nannie for information about their professions. If any mistakes were made, they were my own.

I thank Alice Duncan, a fantastic editor who championed my book to publication. Special thanks to John Helfers of Tekno Books for first noting the merits of *Relative Danger,* and to everyone at Five Star for doing such an exceptional job.

Acknowledgments

I'm grateful for my mom's friend, Odette Seely, who gave me the delightful knowledge that some women only dust their stoves instead of cooking on them.

And huge thanks to all of my former students for letting me know how various teenagers act. No, none of YOU behaved like some of the rowdy kids in this book.

For my hunk,
Bob

CHAPTER 1

I drove across town following Chicken Boy, anticipation fluttering in my chest like the big yellow feathers flapping through the open window of his truck.

We headed west on the freeway, and people in oncoming cars laughed at the chicken driving ahead of me. I was glad the guy I rented from the costume shop brought pleasure to so many—until a half-dozen feathers flew off his wing and stuck to my windshield. A small boy in a passing car pointed and laughed like crazy, but all I could see was a wing full of yellow coating my vision. I turned on my windshield wipers, and feathers floated off to the right, making me notice the tops of nearby buildings and billboards. The colors of one made me catch my breath.

I spied only part of the sign, but even without my bifocals, knew the cayenne-colored letters on a muted green background would spell Cajun Delights. And that would mean Gil Thurman, my ex-lover, was in town to open another of his restaurants. I hadn't been to Chicago in a while, but family members would have told me if Gil had a restaurant here before now.

To stop thinking about him, I turned the radio volume up until golden oldies vibrated in my head, and I had to lower the window to let some sound out. A warm breeze whipped in like a hot flash, engulfing me in exhaust fumes from five-fifteen traffic.

The teen in costume chugged ahead toward the suburbs, and

I backed my foot from the gas pedal to keep from ramming him. Twisting my shoulders to my music, I followed until finally we rolled into a neighborhood holding modest brick and stucco houses with clean lawns. I parked at the curb and hurried up the steps of the red-brick home I hadn't visited in six months.

Chicken Boy waddled up, and I stepped back while he rang the buzzer near the front door. I remained hidden by his bulk, waiting to see my granddaughter Kat and her reaction. She was seventeen, old enough to try to maintain her cool, but still enough of a kid to be thrilled by the arrival of an eight-foot chicken.

Chicken Boy mumbled through his beak, "Nobody's answerin', Mrs. Gunther."

"Try again, please," I said.

He smashed in the doorbell with a feathered wing.

The door was yanked open. "Yes?" Kat's voice sounded upset. "Oh, you must have the wrong place," she said, her tone softer.

Chicken Boy sang, "Happy graduation to you. Happy graduation to you. Happy grad-u-a-tion—"

He faltered for the next words, so I picked up his tune and finished the song I'd composed. "—to the girl who's about to finish near the top of her cla-ass. Happy graduation to you." I sprang out from behind the chicken, spreading my arms.

My grandchild peered at my face. She stared at the fellow in costume. Kat's hands covered part of her eyes and tears hit their outer rims.

"Baby girl," I said, cringing, "what's wrong?" She fell into my arms, her head leaning down to my shoulder. Kat's thin body trembled. I caught my breath, not prepared for this response, and held her close.

She drew back and her lips lifted at the edges, but she wiped dampness from her eyes. "Hi, Gram."

"Hello, sweetie."

She sniffled. "We never know when you'll pop up in town."

"I like for my visits to be surprises."

"They always are."

Chicken Boy stood beside us, watching. I handed him a tip, and he lumbered off.

Kat's hand brushed russet hair off her face and I noticed that even with no makeup, her cheekbones stood out like her daddy's. Her nose remained slim like her mom's. She had forest-green eyes and had sprung up much taller than my five feet, two inches. Her once budding curves now blossomed beneath a blue shirt and navy slacks. My grandchild had grown into a slender young woman, one with striking beauty.

"It's always great to see you, Gram. And that was really sweet." She nodded to indicate the boy heading for his truck. "But I doubt if I'll be graduating near the top of my class."

My stomach clenched. How could things have changed so much so soon?

"Come on in," Kat said. She led the way through the living room that appeared dark, even with sunlight falling through lace curtains. Her tennis shoes squeaked on the polished wooden floor, and my mules made a sucking noise through the space that still felt like a shrine. Framed pictures of the dead lined the walls and tops of shiny tables, strangling life from the room. Each picture showed my daughter-in-law Nancy excited about life. She had been dead two years.

I lifted a snapshot of her on a swing in a playground. "She always looked so happy."

Kat nodded, her face somber. We walked off to the kitchen filled with the scent of roasting meat. "Sit down, Gram. I'll just be a minute." She opened the broom closet door, and I sat at the table. Mauve curtains hung in the bay window, and a cheerful print with skinny piglets rimmed the walls. At least the kitchen retained Nancy's spirit. She'd had a knack for lifting people's moods. Her laughter was a salve for my son. She created a nurturing life for Kat. But Nancy needed a new heart, and nobody had died in time to give her one. She would have wanted Kat laughing now.

A squat ceramic pig with a smirk sat in the center of the table. I lifted his head and grabbed a cookie. "Hm, homemade chocolate chip. And still slightly warm." I shut my eyes and savored warm melting chocolate, the experience involuntarily making me think of Gil Thurman. He'd often baked these after we had a tumble in bed, his special treat to say *Love you, Cealie.* I shrugged away thoughts of him and watched Kat.

"When the doorbell rang, I dropped the salt," she said. Using a broom and dustpan, she attacked the spilled salt and its box on the floor. Before I could offer to help, she scooped up the mess and put everything away. Steam bubbled from pot covers on the stove, and Kat scurried to lower the heat. She yanked covers from pots, releasing aromas that made my stomach growl. "The water almost boiled out of the potatoes I planned on mashing."

She was cooking real mashed potatoes. No wonder she'd been so upset. Kat tried to do everything, and she did it perfectly.

"Come sit and relax," I said, recalling a major lesson I'd learned from maturity. The constant attempt for perfection caused stress. Learning life's lessons was one of the few positives I'd gleaned from aging. Kat settled beside me, and I said, "What happened? Your grades were always terrific."

Her gaze shifted to the table. "A problem just changed everything."

"Problem? Well I doubt if I could help with most of your honors classes, but I was pretty good in some subjects." I thought about pulling out the papers I'd shoved into my purse. I'd brought one of my high school report cards and my college

12

transcript, thinking Kat would laugh while comparing her grades to mine. Math had given me some problems; so did some of the sciences. I didn't think she had difficulty with any subject. But this didn't seem the right time for trying to get her to chuckle. "Let me look at your books. Maybe I could call out some things for you."

"It's not that, Gram. Somebody from school died."

"Oh Kat, not a student?" She shook her head, and I exhaled with relief. Clasping her fingers, I still dreaded. "A teacher?"

"No, a custodian. His funeral's tomorrow."

"Oh, the poor man. And you were close to him?"

Again she shook her head. "He'd only been at school a few months. I didn't know him well."

An acquaintance's death caused her grades to plunge? Confusion settled inside me, offset by a rumble in the driveway. Kat jumped up. She darted to the stove and turned knobs. "Dad's here."

"His truck sure is loud."

"He brings a lot of customers' cars and trucks home to work on. It gives him something to do in the evening."

I glimpsed my son through the bay window. Roger wore khaki clothes coated with grease stains. He had his father's height of six feet, but the build on my departed husband had substance. Roger's shoulders hunched. His face wore a pinched expression and aimed toward the ground as he passed the window, giving him a more wilted look than someone in his thirties should have.

He watered sprightly flowers I couldn't name that stretched in profusion along his wooden fence, and my heart ached for him. At one time he'd gained cheer from the colorful tract he created, but now my son kept a dismal expression. Kat and his friends and I had worked so hard to pull him out of the melancholy. We'd brought him to different places, and he began to put forth effort. He started that garden, growing beautiful things, and returned to being an active parent for Kat. But he seemed unable to sustain the effort and gradually faded back into this lethargic state. I had suggested therapy and offered to take him, but he refused.

Pain for him jabbed inside me. "Doesn't he ever do anything fun?" I asked Kat.

She peered out the window, her eyes sad. "Never."

"I'll be back in a minute," I said.

I walked out the back door, crossed the yard, and stopped beside Roger. "Hi, Son."

His head jerked. I'd startled him. "Mother," he said in greeting. I stifled the urge to wrap him in my arms and cuddle him in a rocker. "I saw a car and thought Kat might have company," Roger said before he bent to let me peck his check. I hugged him, and he gave my back a stiff pat. My pop-up visits seldom drew much response from him any longer, another source of my sorrow.

He turned off his hose and looked me over. "You're dyeing your hair orange now?"

My hands flipped up to my waves. "This isn't orange, it's burnt sienna. And it's natural."

Roger grunted. I considered asking about work and what he'd been doing but knew he'd answer "The same," as he usually did on the phone.

"I came for Kat's graduation," I said.

He nodded. Roger then studied the newly mowed grass. There had been a time when this young man had been lively, though I had to work hard to recall it. He'd once been a happy child, playing without reservation. The vacant gaze of his pale blue eyes made those years difficult to remember. Creases cleaved the tanned skin near his eyes, and strands of white salted his black hair.

White hair on my child? Time had swept by more quickly than I'd imagined.

"It's good to see you," I said, wanting to tell him how much better it would be to see him content. But I'd said that during my last visit, and he assured me such comments didn't help.

He made momentary eye contact. "You, too." Roger shifted his eyes toward the grass.

I clasped his arm, satisfied to find it more muscular than it appeared. "Have you given any more thought to getting counseling?"

"I never needed that. I'm fine."

Sure. "And Kat?" I asked, wondering if he actually knew.

"She's good, too."

Oh, of course. "I could stay longer," I said. "I don't need to be anywhere else soon."

His gaze met mine. "And you'd take me to more places? Thanks, but I really don't need my mother looking after me anymore."

Let me look after you, I yearned to scream, but his body shifted away, letting me know that more attempts at conversing now would increase his discomfort. "Pretty flowers," I said.

Roger glanced at his garden as if he had never seen it. When I walked back to the house, I heard pipes shudder as he resumed his absentminded watering.

I had observed his initial grief with sadness but understanding, and satisfaction emerged when I watched him gradually appear to have renewed interest in life. But I didn't know how to deal with this setback. I wanted to scream, to shake away all of his misery and have him get on with living. I knew the anguish of losing an adored spouse. I'd cried out in my bed at night when my husband Freddy was in some hospital, the relentless needles stuck in him. Around him, I'd made myself act cheerful. I even told him he'd get better. But dammit, just like Nancy, he didn't.

I understood Roger's grief. But now I wanted my child to know joy again. I yearned to soothe the creases from his forehead and see brightness return to his eyes. But I had tried all the suggestions I knew, and until I determined more ways to help, I could offer only my support.

Kat was spooning food into serving dishes when I returned to the kitchen. "Have dinner with us," she said.

The anxiety twisting in my belly wouldn't let food pass. "Please invite me another time. Today I just wanted to see you and your dad and let you know I'd arrived."

"I did like the chicken guy," Kat said, escorting me through the house.

On the front stoop, I told her where I was staying and gave her the phone number. Then I returned to our halted conversation. "Tell me about that custodian. Why should your grades be dropping if a man that you barely knew died?"

Her eyes took on a sheltered cast. She didn't want to discuss the subject.

"I promised your mother," I reminded. "I said I would stand in her place to watch you graduate. I'd be at your wedding. And I'd be near when you have every one of your babies."

Kat awarded me a grin. "How many babies will I need to have?"

"We'll see."

Our lightened mood lasted only a moment. She grew silent, the air surrounding us heavy. "If something went wrong to change your future, I need to understand," I said, not mentioning how much Nancy wanted to see her only child wearing a cap and gown. No one in Nancy's family had finished high school. Nancy had planned to, but she became pregnant with Kat and never went back for her diploma. How she wanted to see this child take a diploma in her hand.

Kat released a deep sigh. "I didn't really know the man who died. Mr. Labruzzo seemed nice. When I saw him in the halls, he and I told each other hello."

"Then why would a stranger's death affect you so much?"

She stared at the concrete floor. "I've had this great teacher, Miss Hernandez."

"I remember you mentioning her." Kat had spoken the woman's name with the same reverence as she reserved for Nancy. "But what does your Spanish teacher have to do with a custodian dying?"

"He died in the auditorium. And the police have been acting like they think Miss Hernandez killed him."

"Somebody *murdered* him? At your *school?*"

"He died after our classes were over. Mr. Labruzzo was cleaning the balcony and fell over the rail. He hit his head."

"Falling doesn't sound like murder," I said.

"At first we heard it was an accident. Now the police are saying his death remains unclassified, but they're treating it like a homicide."

"Why would they suspect Miss Hernandez?"

Kat looked away. "I don't know."

I understood her concern about her favorite teacher but wasn't sure if she knew why the woman was under scrutiny, or if she just wasn't ready to tell me. "So why would your grades drop?"

She peered down. "Because I quit going to classes."

"You've *what?*"

Splotches sprang to her cheeks. A passing car honked. More vehicles rumbled by while I managed to absorb that Kat had stopped attending her classes. She said nothing else and only stared out at the road.

My memory of how to relate to sullen teens had long ago

vanished. I'd taught some of them briefly way back when, and, of course, reared my own. But if I were graded today on how to understand teens when they didn't want to reveal themselves, I'd probably earn a D-minus. But Kat wasn't a belligerent troublemaker. She was tenderhearted. Sensitive. Maybe too much so. And maybe too attached to a murderer? I shuddered.

My favorite teacher then came to mind: Mrs. Tabor, with her warm smile and hug for us students near the door of her fourth-grade classroom. I knew everybody had a special teacher who helped direct her life. "Miss Hernandez has been really important to you," I said, trying to prompt more information from her.

Kat's face brightened. "She's been like a mom. I always go to her room before classes start, and she sits down and talks to me. She really listens."

"I'm glad you found someone like that, but I'm sure Miss Hernandez wouldn't want you to let your grades go."

The cloudy eyes returned. "Lately she's been ignoring me. I try to talk to her, but she's always too busy. She seems to be constantly looking over her shoulder."

"Maybe she knew the custodian well, or she's concerned about what his death is doing to students. Especially one of them." I watched my granddaughter tighten her arms about her small waist. Maybe she knew more about her mentor's involvement than she was saying. "Kat, you have to go to school."

"I can't think, I can't study, it's miserable over there."

"But you're about to start finals, and your senior year is almost over. Your average could drop tremendously if you don't show up for exams."

She shook her head. What had gotten into the child? A horrible thought occurred to me. "The police haven't implicated *you?*"

Kat's arms jerked. "I didn't do anything wrong."

Alarm spiked from my heels up to my scalp. I stepped closer to hold Kat, but she backed away.

Fearing for her, I knew my arguments weren't going to counter her resolve or get answers to my questions. She loved going to malls. We could probably make more progress with girl-talk in a clothing store. "Let's go shopping tomorrow," I suggested. "You can pick out treats for yourself and help me find something special to wear while I watch you march across that stage."

"You don't have to. I might not even show up for graduation."

I locked my knees to keep from falling. How could she choose not to attend? Maybe some kids received diplomas without taking part in the ceremony—but I'd promised Nancy—I would see Katherine in a cap and gown. We needed a stage and her hand reaching out, accepting a diploma.

But she wasn't willing to talk now, and I couldn't think. I kissed her cheek. "I'll talk to you soon."

"All right." She spoke without emotion

By the time I started my car and drove past her house, the front door was shut. Kat had disappeared inside.

Throughout her school years, she'd made top grades her mother was proud of. Kat couldn't let that all go now. I needed to get her back into classes.

Who in this town could help me?

CHAPTER 2

My heart pounded while I steered down streets, wanting Kat's problem to disappear.

She'd been through pre-K, kindergarten, and twelve more years. Her grades had been excellent, and she'd hardly missed any days. Now someone she didn't know had succumbed, and everything she'd worked for all those years would vanish? These final days of high school, which should have been so much fun, would be ruined?

No, that couldn't happen. I had to keep her in classes, and I'd probably need assistance.

"Dad's always grumpy," Kat had told me once when I phoned. Roger remained mired in his world of memories, surely waiting for cheerful Nancy to come home. Kat and I knew she wasn't returning, but did he? While I was in town this time, I'd have to push harder to bring him out of his misery. But the most pressing problem was Kat.

Roger was in no position to notice her withdrawal, let alone try to help her work her way out of it. I lived states away, and Kat's final exams were about to start. Whatever I could do, I needed to do quickly.

Who else did I know in this town? I wondered, trying not to consider the sole answer.

After Nancy's death, Kat had naturally been mournful at first but had gradually taken up her life again. She'd joined clubs and always excelled in classes. A cute boy at school liked her.

Then another. She'd recently broken up with a boy named John Winston.

While I drove aimlessly, I tried to imagine murder connected in any way to my grandchild. My mind couldn't set them both in the same scene. Kat had said that at first everyone believed the custodian's death was accidental.

"That's it," I said, my statement letting the image sink in. "The man tripped and fell." And police ordinarily treated deaths as homicides until they determined otherwise. That's all that was happening at Kat's school.

Tension left my shoulders. Kat and her mentor teacher probably had a misunderstanding. Kat was upset because Miss Hernandez wasn't giving her attention. The woman could have distractions from her life or job—too many papers to grade, a breakup with her boyfriend? If she was so kind to Kat, she couldn't possibly be a murderer—could she?

I shook my head, noting that I merged into thickening traffic. Kat wouldn't like Miss Hernandez so much if the woman could be violent. And Kat had said the custodian's funeral was tomorrow. If she quit going to classes, she'd probably only missed a day or two. With a little nudging, she would make more effort to talk to her friend, tell her how she felt, and life would resume as before. All I had to do was make sure Kat returned to her high school.

I breathed easier. Life was much simpler without worrying about a murder, especially one connected to my family. I felt almost positive that Kat's anxiety stemmed from the disruption of her relationship with the teacher. Still, a nagging doubt remained. I needed to be sure. Ever since I'd adjusted to being a widow, I'd learned to make decisions on my own, but this extrasensitive issue concerned my grandchild. I needed to discuss what happened with someone else.

Roger was too detached for analyzing disturbed tender moments Kat had shared with her mentor. But I did not want to see Gil Thurman. He was the only other person I really knew in this city, but I was driving in the direction opposite his restaurant.

The feel of Gil's warm hands enveloping mine returned. I recalled the rich texture of his voice and, especially, his wisdom. I forced my rental car into a sharp turn.

Gil had been out of my life for almost a year, and I didn't plan to open it to him again. He'd been my shoulder to lean on throughout too many happenings and almost got me pregnant when I was certain I was past all of that. In those fretful days my breasts felt fuller, my lower abdomen tender. "I'm afraid we might have created a baby," I told him the night we snuggled in his den listening to a downpour.

Gil's head fell back with the deep-throated laughter I admired. Until that moment.

"What's so funny?" I asked, anger heating me.

He rubbed thick fingers through my hair—which was then natural strawberry blond—and said, "That's wonderful, Cealie. Us, new parents. Just think of it."

I had thought of it. I wanted to shove his hands out of my hair and punch his arm till it throbbed. I wanted to scream about all my plans. I'd expected to tell him I had toiled for decades with my husband to create a successful business. Managers now ran all the offices of my Deluxe Copyediting agency. I'd worked hard to learn to live without a mate and was no longer needed as a mom. *My* time had finally arrived.

The morning after my announcement, Gil drove me to the doctor, who assured me I could no longer conceive. My body carried only a urinary infection. The tingling in my breasts? Gil was surely connected.

Later he snuggled me on his lap on the recliner, rubbing his big hands in circles on my back, saying, "Oh baby, it'll be all right."

And that's why I needed to avoid him. Instead of letting me make my own way, Gil almost made me want to settle down again and try to start a new family. And I couldn't. I just couldn't!

"No way," I reaffirmed, tapping my brakes now on the freeway. The cars I drove past all seemed stopped. I needed to slow with them to find his restaurant.

Gil was certain of everything he wanted from life. Sometimes he pushed too hard to press his assuredness down on me. I needed to find my own certainty. I'd mourned about life making me a widow long before those golden years that I had planned to spend comfortably alongside my husband. Without him, my house felt empty. Humongous. Like my friends, I'd started to become dowdy. That's when I read about a woman's speech called "Changing Your Inner Underwear." Exactly what I needed! My inner panties and brassieres underwent a major upheaval. It was still okay to want to feel sexy. I could enjoy washing clothes for just one person. I wasn't only my past, I was me—Cealie Gunther. I needed to tend to my spirit and rediscover myself.

What made me happy? What did *I* like to do?

That concept seemed foreign. Guilt popped up, that same guilt a mother experiences when she wants to do something for herself instead of putting everyone else first. But my husband had died and my family was grown. Nobody wanted me to cling to them anymore. I was inching toward my golden years alone.

A while after I decided to make some attitude changes, my friend Jo Ellen made that momentous phone call to me. She was a few years older than I, but while she moaned about hoping her kids would call and when she'd start receiving retirement benefits, Jo Ellen made me realize I was heading down the same path. I had also often waited to hear from family members. And even though I hadn't planned to retire any time soon, I was getting older, and more of my friends were choosing Social Security as their main topic for conversation. Was that all there was? My face developed more wrinkles, my eyesight worsened, and I could no longer hold in my stomach no matter how hard I tried—and that's all I had to look forward to? Jo Ellen's call made me aware that I'd been settling for routine existence and never considered what I really wanted from whatever time I had left. Well, I *had* thought about it just a little before I subscribed to those newsletters on sexual behavior. But her comments had made me determine my days were whittling away, influenced by anything or anyone except me. That's when I took control.

On that fateful day I chose to start a new search for me. I strode through my house shouting, "I am woman! Able to make my own way alone." I took off from my house and started locating the path. I'd even begun to feel comfortable traveling without a partner. And then I met Gil.

I couldn't hand him the independence I worked so hard to achieve. I had told him I was leaving to continue searching for me, and he said, "Happy hunting. You're mature enough to know what you want, Cealie. I'll miss you."

Dammit, I finally got over missing Gil and didn't want to run to him again. But Kat was in need. He might help.

I pulled into his parking lot, assuring myself all I wanted from him was feedback. His thought-provoking insight. And if my stomach quit jumping, his chef's food.

The grand opening sign was out front, the paved lot next to the restaurant filled. A Jeep backed out, and I took its place. I walked alongside the building built like his others, tall in front and sloping to the rear, and couldn't resist the urge to run my hand along its gray cypress to feel the rough texture. The tin roof would plunk-plunk during downpours, its extension in front sheltering guests when they walked underneath.

I drifted across the bridge that crossed a pond and spied swimming ducks. Gil and I met on a bridge such as this. At his second restaurant, in Vicksburg. I was the one tossing crumbs to the ducks, and he stood near. Gil Thurman was a presence. He spoke in that husky tone, and with no hesitancy came close. Gil looked and sounded better than anything in that restaurant or anywhere else.

We lost touch after I left Vicksburg. While I continued looking for me, he'd headed for Denver to open Cajun Delights number three.

My gaze skimmed the water, and I wondered about Kat. How could I help?

Laughter came from people exiting the front door, the scent of fried seafood wafting out with them.

I passed a swing beneath the tin overhang and reached the door with stained-glass panels, where a sign said *Treat yourself to another Cajun Delights.* My heart surprised me with its flutters.

Gil might or might not be inside this place. He might have come to inspect the building and hire great cooks and friendly people, then flown off to start another. One way or another, the familiar setting would let me feel his presence. Answers might come. Gil usually had good ones. Besides, I was hungry. My stomach had settled, and the food in his restaurants made it happy. Once I ate, my brain would work much better.

Inside the door an enthusiastic young man with a handful of menus greeted me. I didn't let my gaze stray while he led me to a table and drew back my chair.

"I'd like Eggplant Supreme please," I said without opening a menu. The eggplant would be stuffed with shrimp and crabmeat and topped with crunchy buttered breadcrumbs. "And smothered potatoes. A Caesar salad on the side."

He went off, and I saw smiling faces everywhere enhancing

the décor. Pictures in rough-hewn frames depicted wildlife and swamp scenes. A wooden floor with swirling knots shone, and waiters carried scrumptious-smelling steaks and tangy boiled seafood to cozy tablecloths with black and white squares. High-backed seats at booths blocked my view of many people. So did the string of diners selecting items from the central seafood bar.

My waiter returned with tea and crackers. I thanked him, took a crispy square and ate it with sips of the icy drink. Fiddling began, making me and others turn toward a small stage.

On it a trio used a fiddle, accordion, and washboard to play a foot-stomping Cajun tune. I grinned, recalling how Gil and I had danced to a similar ditty. Customers looked pleased, even those lining up near the door to wait for tables. The music lowered enough for conversations to take place. The waiter brought my salad and I ate, as always, swept up in the atmosphere of Gil's restaurant. He'd delighted in the fact that his mother had been Cajun, which made him decide on the name of his establishments. I'd have to bring Kat and Roger here before I left town.

Again a death had altered Kat's life. I had to do all I could to prevent this new death from damaging her future.

"We're happy that y'all are here tonight," a man said into the mike once the band stopped playing. He wore a tie, confident attitude, and friendly smile, certainly the new manager.

I watched him while eating my greens. The space in my stomach began to fill, and my thoughts tried to jell. A custodian killed, possibly murdered. By Kat's Spanish teacher? The question stuck in my mind, and no matter how hard I tried to dislodge it, the horrendous thought stayed.

"We hope you enjoy the food and come back again," the manager said. People clapped, and he added, "We're pleased to have Cajun Delights in your city. We want to thank the proprietor, Mr. Gil Thurman, for bringing us this restaurant."

I applauded. The man onstage pointed beyond me, and my heart lurched.

There, at a corner table, sat Gil. The gunmetal gray of his sports jacket matched his thick hair, teased now with silver streaks. The top button of his white shirt was open. He stood, and I saw that he wore dark jeans. Colorful jockey shorts would be underneath.

Applause rang in my ears. Or maybe it was blood rushing.

"Thank you all for coming," Gil said, the deep richness of his voice sending molten urges through my body.

People at his table raised their hands toward him and clapped. At the chair beside Gil's sat a young woman with a bronzed cherub face. Hair like liquid ebony draped around her face, and a black knit top revealed mega cleavage. She gave Gil an expansive smile, her eyes sparkling like those of a woman in love.

Gil's gaze fell to the woman. He grinned and then peered at his customers. "Please enjoy yourselves. And don't forget to tell your friends where we are." He began to sit when his gaze located mine. Gil sprang to his feet, mouthing, "Cealie."

Somersaults bounced through my belly.

Gil strode to me, saying, "You're here." He leaned and kissed my lips. Gil's lips were warm, his scent manly. I let my mouth linger.

Behind him, someone snickered. The waiter stood, holding my entrée. He set it down and left. Gil stared at me. "What a treat."

I didn't speak, enjoying the marvelous twinges in my torso.

"Cealie, I can't believe you're really here."

I struggled to draw my gaze away from his mesmerizing dark gray eyes. Gil's neck filled his open collar, and chest hair sprinkled the V above his top button. That same chest hair had often tickled my cheeks. I felt a rush of passion no lady should feel while out in public.

"Nice to see you, too," I said, willing my voice normal. I slid my left hand into my right palm and pinched, an action I'd discovered was more discreet than slapping myself. *You are woman, remember? You want to do your own thing.*

"I don't know what brought you, but I'm glad it did." He cocked his head and gave a smile that made me sizzle. "Would your visit have anything to do with me?"

Kat's horrid situation sprang to mind. "No," I said.

"I didn't think so." Gil looked disappointed. He indicated the place where the pretty woman sat watching us, her red mouth now puckered in a pout. "Come over to my table and join us."

"Why don't you just join me for a minute," I said, pointedly adding, "if you can?"

Gil sat and drew his chair close. My gaze flickered toward his table. Surely that young woman's skirt was black and clingy. Black pantyhose would probably run beneath that tiny skirt the entire length of her long legs.

Her gaze locked with mine. We gave each other appraising stares.

My skin had more sag than hers, and my waist was surely not as tapered. I was a decade or two (okay, maybe three) older. Was Gil dating a child now, I wondered, my teeth clenched.

Well that was his decision to make. Still, I wished I'd worn something sassier than the boxy lime-green pantsuit made of crinkled fabric. It was a wise choice in some ways, loose and comfortable with an elastic waistband. The cropped pants were fashionable but made my legs appear shorter. Comparing me in this outfit to the woman staring back, I looked about as chic as Chicken Boy.

She shifted her eyes toward the man seated opposite her.

I turned toward Gil. "Kat's graduating."

"Little Kat? Already?" With a hearty chuckle, he squeezed my hand.

Forget Legs, I thought, grinning. Gil's here, holding my hand. "I'm only in town until the graduation," I told him. "I'll take Kat downtown for some shopping, maybe catch a play or a concert. I have a condo on Tyndale."

"Those are nice. Good location."

"And not too far from Kat and Roger's house."

My granddaughter's name drew a fresh smile from Gil. "I'd love to see Kat graduate. Cealie, I know you didn't want our relationship to continue, but would you be my escort?"

I felt like the last girl to be asked to the prom. Now I had another major reason to want to see Kat's graduation. I'd absolutely have to see about that death at her school.

Reason set in, offsetting what felt like the headiness of new romance. I didn't want to fall in love with this man again. No, I didn't love him any longer. *I didn't.* "We'll see," I said.

Gil leaned back in his chair. "How's Roger getting along?"

"Not much improvement. He still won't see a therapist. I think he needs new interests, something to get him excited."

"Has he dated?"

"Dated? I doubt it. Kat would've told me." I drew in a breath. "But now Kat has a problem. She might not graduate."

"Not graduate? Why?"

I shook my head, still unable to believe it myself.

"What happened?" Gil said. "Can we help her with something?"

I explained and he remained intent, holding on to every word I said. "And I don't know," I completed, "maybe she's scared to go back there. You know horrible things take place at some schools."

Gil's pensive eyes told me he was mulling.

A fellow with oversized eyeglasses stood at the microphone

and began a joke for the joke-telling contest.

Gil stared at me. "So what do you think?"

"I think I have to do something. Roger's no help to her, and I can't have Kat not going to classes. She can't give up when she's so close. That girl has got to walk across a stage and get her diploma."

Gil gripped his chin like he did when in deep thought.

"Of course," I said, "since the man's funeral is tomorrow, he died recently, so I imagine Kat only missed a day or two of classes."

Customers clapped politely while the man on stage spoke too quietly, finishing his joke. A woman scooted up to take his place. Her body was round, her thin hair frizzed. She started her joke with much animation, making people chuckle.

Gil's focus remained inside, and I waited for him to decipher how he'd assist me. I glanced at my entrée. Crab lumps poked out beneath a toasted coating. Flecks of roasted peelings decorated my potato. Saliva filled my mouth.

Belly-laughter erupted from people at tables. The jokester woman rushed back to her seat, and the MC asked if anyone else had a joke to tell. No one stood. By audience applause, the MC declared the plump woman a winner. He said she'd get her meal gratis, and she yelped.

Gil drew nearer, his mouth close to mine. I withheld the urge to press my lips there. The jokes always made me cheerful. And having Gil help me consider Kat's dilemma allowed me to be in a lighter mood.

He wasn't smiling. Gil waited until whistles of approval for the winner quieted and then asked, "What does Kat want?"

My smile faded. "What do you mean, what does she want? She wants to graduate, of course."

"Is that what she told you?"

"No, she said she might not. But that's just because her idol

30

teacher is suspected of murder. Once that's cleared up, everything will be okay."

"Who was murdered?"

"A custodian. Or he might have only fallen."

Gil grinned. "I see."

He glanced toward his table near the wall, where Legs was staring at us. Her look told me, "Get your eyes off my man!" I knew the look. I'd used it often when I was with him. Gil checked the date on his watch. "That doesn't give the police many days to solve the mystery, if there is one. I imagine graduation is getting close."

"It is. So I need to hurry and do something."

He gave the laugh I usually liked, but not at the moment. "From what you've told me, Kat might have sensitive issues with a teacher friend to deal with. She might want some help with that, or she might not."

"Oh, she certainly needs help," I said, nodding.

"And the other trouble," he said, his gaze making direct contact with mine. "You have no business getting mixed up in what might have been a murder. Let professionals investigate that situation."

Protests struggled along my tongue. "But I have to do something," I said.

Gil clasped my hand. "Cealie, you like to control situations. You're really good at some things, but—"

"I'm good at leaving," I said, shoving myself to my feet and turning. I left Gil's restaurant. Let him go back to his new girlfriend, I told myself, driving away.

My shoulders tightened. Sure, let him.

I'd solve Kat's troubles by myself.

CHAPTER 3

I hurled myself into the condo and slammed the door, then realized I hadn't paid my restaurant bill. Hadn't even offered. A smirk registered on my lips. Good. Let Gil do it. I hadn't eaten any of his food anyway, except for a few greens and a cracker.

"What does he mean?" I asked Minnie, my new cactus, in the kitchen. "I do *not* try to control!" I planted the palms of my hands apart on the counter and bent over the pink-headed plant as though waiting for her to give me a sassy response.

Minnie was smart and didn't answer.

I took deep breaths to squash my angry thoughts. Still hungry, I filled a plastic glass with water and gulped it. Minnie's prickly head tilted a little, so I filled another glass and dumped it on her. I flung the glass at a trash can.

"That man!" I yelled, slinging myself across the den. "No wonder I left him. How dare he tell me not to get involved in Kat's problems!" I paced through rooms, fuming, and made ugly comments about Gil to Minnie. I touched her prickers. Not stiff. I considered purchasing another cactus, one with really hard thorns, and setting it down on Gil's chair.

After a while I felt better. Much calmer. Who cared what Gil thought? I knew Katherine and was certainly aware of what she needed. She needed graduation. Cap and gown, the whole bit. I'd do something. And I could do it without Gil Thurman's assistance.

What was he telling that young woman with long legs at his

table? That I was only an old friend visiting in town?

Old. *Me?*

I swiped a dry towel across the stovetop. My anger-venting produced more sheen on its flat black surface but did nothing to brighten my mood. I tossed the towel. Trying to think, I circled through rooms that looked pretty to me yesterday but not today. I dropped to a chair in the den and powered up my laptop. I could surf into cyberspace to get my mind off worries. First I'd check e-mail. I slapped that button.

Hey Cealie, a subject line said.

I clicked that one. Somebody knew me, and I could use a cheerful message.

Are you still in San Francisco? I've been trying to find you and hope you still have the same e-mail address I came across. What's been happening? I miss you, Cuz. Hey, I have a big problem. Please write or call. Luv, Stevie.

Groan. I didn't need another relative's problem to solve. My cousin Stevie hadn't contacted me in years. She used to yank my pigtails when we were small and took great pleasure in watching me cry and then calling me crybaby. Stevie now thought she was psychic, but I knew she only told people all the ridiculous thoughts that popped into her ditzy head.

I hit the delete button and switched off the power. Let Stevie conjure my image to find out where I was.

"I'm sorry," I said, again in the kitchen with Minnie cactus. "My dilemma isn't your fault, and I don't need to take out my frustrations on you." She seemed to accept my apology. Her head looked a little pinker, her two-inch high stem straighter. I told her goodnight and turned off the light. I'd recently purchased her when a wave of nostalgia swept through me and held on, making me feel a need for a living companion. Animals wouldn't be great for all my travels, but plants lived. I knew next to nothing about real plants, and the only thing I knew about cactuses was that *cactuses* and *cacti* were both correct plurals, with dictionaries seeming to prefer *cactuses*.

I preferred *cacti*.

And I knew these plants didn't require much upkeep. Perfect. At the nursery Minnie's pinkish head with matching topknots captured my attention. And she didn't prick. Now I was trying to make her my friend, but I'd need to be much kinder.

In my bedroom I kicked off my mules, reconsidering Legs. Surely she'd been wearing spiky heels with ankle straps. I shrugged out of my wrinkled pantsuit. It was supposed to be that way. A woman must have designed the fabric, and she had been wise. How many wrinkles she must have fussed with in her own garments. I liked my outfit—until I saw that woman with Gil. Her black skirt probably only wrinkled where its skimpy bottom creased underneath her.

I lay in bed, deliberation not letting me sleep. What did Gil mean, I tried to control? I'd help Kat, even if she hadn't asked. I promised Nancy. The diploma. Then the wedding. Whether Kat liked it or not, she'd have babies!

In the morning the image of Gil's sexy new girlfriend stuck in my brain, so I dressed in a more revealing outfit than the matronly one I'd worn yesterday. I phoned for directions and drove through streets, confused. Gil's comments made me almost depressed, and I loathed depression.

"I want information about substitute teaching," I told the woman seated behind the front counter at the school board office. She looked older than I was and wore whitish makeup and a tan buttoned blouse. She gaped at my bosom. If I were shy, I'd have covered myself. My sexy clothes felt out of place in this dark-paneled environment, making me recall that most teachers dressed conservatively. Why hadn't I used my brains instead of my emotions to select an outfit for this mission?

Two men wearing suits strode out from the offices behind her. They walked beside the counter and gave me admiring stares.

"I taught briefly. That was quite some time ago," I told the receptionist, "but I've been a professional woman for years."

Her eyes lingered on my little clothes, letting me know what profession she thought I was in. After much hesitation, she said, "You'll have to talk to someone in Personnel to see if you qualify for a certificate. Our schools always need subs." She peered at the cleavage I'd shoved up above my chamois-colored sweater.

"And I know what school I'd like to go to," I said.

Her gaze located my face. "Then you might talk to an administrator there, too. But the board will be doing a background check on you."

Did she also think I used drugs? I met with a snobbish man in Personnel, let him copy the transcript I'd brought to show Kat, filled out his papers, and paid a fee. He gave me a letter and told me a certificate would arrive in the mail.

Reconsidering my purpose for the day, I swung back around to the condo and changed into something more school-like, a high cut periwinkle dress. The stiletto red heels came off. I grabbed tan pumps from a box on a pantry shelf, slipped them on, and went out, making a quick stop near the airport at Dickers Rent-to-Own.

"You decided to buy this beauty?" Rick Dickers asked, his plastered salesman's smile growing. "Your rental time's not up yet, but I can't blame you for wanting to keep her." He patted the hood of the PT Cruiser I'd driven. *Done deal, sale made,* his pats said.

"Nope, she's not quite right, although I do like her sassy rump." I'd chosen this model because its odd shape seemed a cross between an old Volkswagen and a gangster's car. Driving it gave me a sense of being naughty. I'd thought Kat would enjoy that image, but she hadn't been in a laughing mood.

Now that I was going to her school, I wanted my vehicle, like my clothes, to make a professional statement. I always liked to rent cars from large lots like this, with new and used vehicles, whenever I could find them because I'd have so many choices. I wanted a different car now but didn't want to take long to decide which one. I had a purpose. A mission. I skimmed the massive lot. "I want that one," I said, pointing.

The owner's eyes flashed. "The Lexus?"

"Yep."

In two scoots he'd departed and returned with the keys. I had him rush to change the paperwork, and then I paid the larger fee.

The car's leather-scented seat caressed my hips and back. The Lexus drove better than the similar ones I'd owned. A temptation stuck to buy this lovely piece of machinery, but I remembered I wanted nothing that would chain me down. I'd been anchored by possessions too long. Who wanted to squander time deciding which tires would be better than others, which you had to do when you owned a car? I was free to do my own thing now. Whenever I flew to new destinations, I didn't want to lug around an automobile.

I pulled into the paved parking lot in front of Sidmore High School. I would check out the school's atmosphere, see if there was any truth to what Kat was hearing. Was her mentor suspect?

Pounding in my chest made me pause. What if someone in that chunky building ahead of me really did kill the custodian? Hell, I was chicken. I wanted nothing to do with murder. I stood outside the Lexus, apprehension making me light-headed.

But Kat needed me. She said the custodian's funeral was today. Why did a custodian die at this school? And if he was murdered, who did it? How did the people in this place like my grandchild? Most important, I needed to discover how to get her back here again.

Trucks, cars, and Jeeps jammed together in a parking maze. Every child in the school must own a vehicle, and some might have brought two. I left the Lexus in the only spot I found, near the road. The lone soul outside, I sauntered toward the building that looked fairly new but not impressive. In cold institutional oyster gray, it stretched in a broad expanse, leaving little grass exposed. They should have left more space outside for growing things. Kids needed to see flowers and trees. The slightly darker section tacked on to the building's extreme left must house the swimming pool. When it was added last year, Kat had enthused about her diving classes.

I hadn't been in a school in years but had certain expectations. I expected order. Polite children, like Kat. Fairly pleasant, boring teachers. I expected many people to be out for the funeral.

I trotted up the stairs to the landing. *Home of the Mighty Cougars* was plastered above double doors, along with painted cougar paws, eyes, and whiskers. A sign with a slash across a pistol said *No Weapons Allowed.* I wondered how many people that note frightened.

I reached for the door just as someone inside shoved it out. Three large boys hustled through. The huskiest one slammed against my shoulder. "Oops," he said, grinning while he glanced back at me. He wore a thick sports jacket that advertised some team, and he scrambled down the stairs with the other boys.

"An apology would be nicer than 'Oops,' " I said.

"Right, Grandma."

"If I were your grandma, I'd have taught you manners!"

The big guy stopped. With a slow turn of his head, he peered over his shoulder. The mean-eyed gaze he speared me with made my knees weak. The other boys hooted. They all turned away and headed for the parking lot. I still held my breath. This was what high school was like? What was I doing here?

I exhaled, drew in deep breaths, and stood straighter. Opening the heavy door, I expected to find mourning. The door hissed and slammed shut behind me.

I witnessed bedlam.

No wonder those rough boys rushed out the school. I'd entered during a riot. Screams bounced off the walls, and huge kids shoved each other. A bulky mesh bag flew across a mass of thugs. I shrank back, ready to dash out the door.

"Can I help you?" a quiet voice said. The young woman stood almost a head taller than I did, and her kind expression gave me hope. She didn't look anxious about the riot. My gaze flitted to the students. Didn't she realize what was happening?

She glanced toward where I looked. "It's lunchtime," she said wearily, readjusting the stack of papers in her arms. "Did you need the office? It's right this way."

I followed where she led, not letting my gaze stray from students. If this was how they acted for lunch break, what did they do during their actual riots?

And I wanted to make Kat come back here?

Grateful to find the office located away from sweaty teens and musty book odors, I entered a large room with two sides covered by plate-glass windows. Surely the glass was bulletproof, and this was the viewing area where guards stood to watch the inmates. Signs blocked a portion of these windows. One sign mentioned graduation, another, senior rings. I appreciated the long stick wrapped in lagoon blue and yellow that leaned inside one window. Probably used to beat down any rioter who attempted to come in.

Near the door I walked through, a newspaper obituary had been posted on the wall. My glance at the article showed me the youthful face of the custodian, Grant Labruzzo.

The woman I followed rushed off behind a counter that

blocked most of the room. Three teen girls looking downcast sat near me. Pictures of past presidents hung on walls, along with school pennants. The counter held trophies and wire trays with tossed-in papers. The protected side of this room sported a few open doors. People in that area worked behind computers near a copy machine.

One man and a woman whom I supposed were teachers bustled past me. The man with shaggy hair, a bulldog expression, and wearing P.E. shorts yanked up a desk phone and barked at whoever was on the line. The woman, tiny with enormous black hair, complained to a calm man with skin so tan it looked roasted. No one paid attention to me.

"Excuse me. Um, excuse me," I said louder.

A woman leaned out from behind her monitor. "Yes?"

I threw back my shoulders. "I need some information."

She glanced to her side at others involved with their tasks. Appearing harried, she shoved up from her chair and came near.

I put out my hand. "I'm Cealie Gunther."

Gingerly, she accepted my handshake. "I'm Cynthia Petre, a secretary." She wore slicked-back hair, her only makeup coral lipstick that surrounded teeth bound in shiny braces. Her crimson blouse clashed with her orange skirt and reminded me of Thanksgiving dinners. "May I help you?"

"Hi, Miss Petre. I'm interested in doing some substitute teaching," I said, aware that my voice gave away my lack of conviction. I wanted to teach the kids I'd seen in the hall about as much as I wanted to smash my fingers with a hammer.

Her face brightened. "You are?"

I forced a nod. "Uh-huh."

An ill-sounding horn blasted, and I jumped. From the hall, voices lifted even higher than before. A large well-dressed woman walked out of a room near the secretary, who told her,

"Oh, Mrs. Little, come here. I want you to meet this lady."

"I'm in a rush." Through slender frameless eyeglasses, Mrs. Little gave me a once-over that said my face didn't register. She wore a peach-colored tailored suit. Gold hoop earrings that I could have swung on shook beneath her highlighted hair.

"This lady wants to sub," Cynthia Petre said.

Mrs. Little's arm extended over the counter, her hand pumping mine. "You do?" A massive smile replaced her pinched expression.

I cringed inwardly. "I went to the school board, and they're running a check on me to make sure I'm not an escaped criminal." I gave her my best grandmotherly smile. "I have a degree in education from Northwestern and did some post-graduate work while I taught near Evanston. It was a small private school with top-notch students. Of course that was long ago, and I don't even know if it still exists. I only taught a little while because I got married and moved, and my husband and I decided to go into business." I noticed her eyes had glossed over. Behind her, everyone looked so busy.

"Anyway," I said, "I wanted to come over and introduce myself and show this letter from the school board that says I'm otherwise qualified. So if you ever have a need, I'm available."

"Ever have a need?" Mrs. Little's face skewered as though I'd asked the dumbest question. She barely glanced at my letter. "I always have a need, and teachers have been calling in sick like crazy. We have to hire a sub for every absent teacher, and lately that's been as easy as plucking your eyebrows with pliers."

The image made the skin above my eyes ache.

"I'm Anne Little, one of the vice-principals," she said. "But lately it seems my main job is taking care of hiring subs."

"Well, if you need me, especially within the next week or so."

She tightened a viselike grip on my hand. "I need you now."

"Now?" The word squeezed up my throat.

"Not this minute, but tomorrow. Can you come?"

I reminded her about the board running a background check on me.

"The larger districts are pickier about waiting for those results to come in, but I'm desperate, and you've taught before." She skimmed my high-cut dress and the wrinkles my liquid makeup failed to hide. "I don't think you killed anyone. Other than that, we'll take you."

Suppose I had killed someone, I wanted to suggest. Or maybe before tomorrow, I could smash my fingers. No such luck. Hammers were another of the many things I had shed myself of. "Tomorrow," I said, no conviction in my tone.

"Yes." The thin scar in the center of her chin almost hit her top button with her nod. "We're going to have teachers out for meetings, and there's this virus going around."

Maybe I could quickly catch it. "So tomorrow," I said, thinking maybe she would amend that decision.

"Great!" Anne Little rushed off. She stopped when a man and a woman wearing mournful expressions walked in from a rear hall. "Tom, Hannah, how was the funeral?"

I paused, pretending to dig for keys from my purse.

"Horrible. I felt so sorry his family." My peripheral vision located the speaker, Hannah. She was about five foot seven and probably nearing fifty, nicely built with high breasts jutting beneath a cerise suit. She shook her head, making her bobbed hair sway.

"He was a nice person," Anne Little said. "What a shame."

"Yeah, a pity." Tom, a rail-thin man pulling off his brown suit jacket, made the comment. He peeled off his tie and popped open the top button of his shirt. The area below his neck looked concave.

"It seemed strange not having you around here," Anne Little told him, "even if it was just for a couple of hours. You're always the first person to check in."

I lifted my key as though I'd just found it. Cynthia Petre spoke in a loud whisper. "Hannah, you started your period." Hannah straightened from her bent position above an open drawer and twisted to see a dark spot near her right hip. "That happened to me last month," Petre said, twisting her head to check her own rear.

The kids seated behind me snickered. I swerved my eyes aside and headed for the door. I had been through that embarrassment before, way before.

"Let's go to my office," Tom said to the girls seated behind me.

"Damn Tom Reynolds," one of them muttered before they rose and followed him.

The office held too much unpleasant commotion for me. The hall outside it appeared friendlier. Brick walls the same chilly oyster gray as the school's exterior weren't intimidating. The floor must have been waxed at one time, for patches of its glitter ran the length of the hall's outer area. The walls were long and flush. Didn't they make lockers anymore?

I strolled outside to my car thinking maybe teaching wouldn't be so bad. I'd get to know some students and possibly help them. I knew lots of things. I'd taught, been a parent, and survived having teens around. Really, how bad could one day be here?

In the parking lot, I needed to get my bearings. Way out past the jumble of student cars, I'd find my Lexus. Some vehicles had vacated parking spaces. Maybe students like the thug who shoved me had gotten off early. They could be seniors, taking half-day courses and then leaving for jobs or college courses. Probably I'd misjudged them.

That concept came to me right before I spotted the Lexus.

Someone had sliced the polished champagne finish across the trunk.

I cursed, not caring if any teens were around to hear. One of them had keyed my car. I took deep breaths and pressed the remote to unlock doors. Going to open mine, I found a dent the size of a huge shoe along its bottom.

Creative curses left my mouth. I threw myself into the Lexus, cranked the motor, and hightailed it from students' vehicles as though their very existence could contaminate mine. For tomorrow, I'd have to prepare. Maybe I could purchase a billy club.

No, I didn't want my purse to get that heavy.

I wanted to give up, to stay the hell away from that school and let others take care of their problems, but giving up was not an option. Instead I'd come up with another way to meet life, including those vicious teens, in the morning.

CHAPTER 4

The Lexus needed to go to a repair shop, but I couldn't take it to Roger's place. He didn't need extra worries about me going to Kat's school. And since Gil had suggested that I not get involved, I didn't plan to tell him I'd gone to Sidmore High.

I uttered more ugly words about teenagers. Paying for damages to my car wasn't the problem. My problem was what I'd do without wheels for the time it would take for repairs.

Driving through a business section, I read Johnny's Auto Repairs on the front of a metal building with no apparent rust spots. The man working outside appeared decent. Straight black hair, clean face. His jumpsuit told me he was Johnny. "Sure, I can fix this," he said. "The dent and stripped paint will be invisible when I finish. I'll have her ready by Sunday. We'll be open all day."

I had spied a car dealership two blocks away and walked back there. A spindly salesman scooted over to me, his firm handshake saying I was the most important person in his life. "Do you have any rentals?" I asked.

"Just about anything you could want. And if you like what you try, you could own it. What were you looking for?" He guided me around showcase autos, some vintage, and everything in-between. What would teenagers not go for? I wanted to ask but decided not to. Newness of the Lexus had probably attracted them. I lolled through the lot, watching the sales guy's fake smile. He slowed near the new cars that would earn him a

44

nice commission.

"That one," I said, turning.

"That one?" His smile inverted. "Are you sure?"

"That one's me."

"I'll have to try and find the keys. Are you sure you want that one?"

He watched my foot tap and eventually slunk toward the sales building.

"Perfect," I complimented myself while I headed toward the condo. The vehicle I drove had a silver metal interior and its steering wheel on the right-hand side. It wasn't equipped with air conditioning, but an oscillating fan perched on its dash. This boxy baby wouldn't attract teens' keys or feet. Large side mirrors stuck out everywhere, and the huge empty space in back would hold lots of items Kat and I could purchase. The gears had been stripped but repaired, the salesman told me before I left. And the owner had purposely repainted it this color. The Lexus would be repaired soon, and I'd be subbing at school just one day. I needed a day at Sidmore High to get everything straightened out with Kat. Then the Lexus would give the exact feel I wanted for attending her graduation.

"You're driving a what?" Kat asked once I returned to the condo and phoned her.

I grinned. "A mail truck."

"One of those little white trucks that the mail carriers use?"

"Yes, but this one's green. Avocado."

She gave the neatest chuckle I'd heard from her in some time, which confirmed my selection of vehicles.

"You have to see it," I said. "I'll take you for a ride." I clunked through the kitchen with the phone, glancing again at the answering machine, wishing I'd missed something. Gil knew where I was staying. He could have found me. Maybe I hadn't looked hard enough. Maybe the red light blinked when my eye did, and I'd missed it.

I hadn't. I shrugged off disappointment and thrust a dish into the microwave.

"What are you doing?" Kat asked.

I made my moves quieter. "Fixing dinner."

"So early? What're you having?"

The microwave screamed, and I yanked out my meal. "A corn dog. Want one?"

"No thanks. I have fettuccini if you'd like some."

Moisture flooded the floor of my mouth. But Roger would stare at my hair. Even if he didn't speak, I'd know what he was thinking. *Natural burnt sienna, right.* After my experiences at school, I didn't need more rejection. And I was in no mood to attempt to make him cheerful. "Next time. Maybe save me a little?"

"I sure will."

I had briefly entertained thoughts of dinner at Gil's place tonight. I'd eat his great food. Sit beside him, smell his singular smell, feel his hand on mine and tell him, "I'm too old for this struggling with teenage students." No, I thought. I wasn't too old for anything. Whenever anyone asked my age, I said I had a son in his thirties, but I'd given birth when I was four. Okay, ten. Actually, I had decided that I would be whatever age I felt, and I had been feeling just fine.

My real problem today was the way one of those big punks had looked at me. The Lexus. Apparent riot. And I was going back there? The trouble wasn't that I was too old. I just normally used better judgment. But I had decided. I was returning. No matter how big those teenagers were or how rude, I'd be at Sidmore High in the morning. And I hoped neither I nor anyone else would get hurt.

"So what did you do today without going to school?" I asked Kat cheerily. "Did you cook and clean house for your dad? Your place never has time to get dirty, you know. The way you keep everything scrubbed, you could serve your meals right off the floor."

"I went to the funeral."

"Oh." I had no other stupid response to give. When Kat didn't say more, I asked, "Did other people from school attend the service?"

"I saw three or four students. The boy I broke up with, John Winston, was there. Couple of administrators. A custodian." A hitch altered Kat's tone.

I didn't ask whether her Spanish teacher had gone. But dating a boy at school would be great for her. "Is there a chance you and John might make up?"

"No. He wants to get serious. I don't."

I understood. "Baby, I really need you to do something for me."

"Sure. What?"

I glanced at my wilted corn dog. "Come to school tomorrow."

"Come . . ."

"I think I got myself in real trouble. Nothing new, but this time it's something you could help with."

"What do you mean, come to school?"

I hadn't planned to tell her I'd gone there. "I'm going to be a substitute teacher, and I need you around. I need support, Kat."

Absolute quiet came from her end of the line.

"You, teaching? Why, Gram?"

"I wanted something to do." *Get you back to classes. Taking exams. Crossing a stage.*

"You don't need the money, do you?" She sounded concerned.

"Oh no. The problem is . . . I really needed things to do with

47

my time." I pinched my right palm. Told God I was only playing.

Extended silence said Kat didn't believe me. God probably didn't either.

"You always find tons of things to do, Gram. Fun things."

Okay, so I'd out and out lie. I set my corndog down and crossed my fingers. I'd tell her better later. "I wanted to be around people. Young people."

Kat snickered. "Now that, I believe." Good. She was so gullible. "Knowing you," she said, "I bet you'll be running the school by tomorrow afternoon."

"I might." Concerns from the day made me famished. I nibbled on the corn dog, pretending it was fettuccini, while Kat made up her mind.

"But do you know what today's teens are like?" Her warning came a few hours too late for the Lexus.

"Not so different from when I was growing up or teaching." Kat either giggled or choked, and I added, "I know some things changed, but I have dealt with teens before."

"It's been a while."

I set my food down. "C'mon, kid, support me. I was hired."

"Oh, Gram."

"Just a day, baby. They really needed subs." I was getting no response so I pushed harder. "Kat, I went there. It's a scary place."

She inhaled sharply. "Do you know whose place you'll be taking?"

"No. But that shouldn't make a difference, should it?"

Kat sighed. "Just one day?"

"That's all I'm giving the place. A big guy ran into me today. His attitude stunk."

"And you think the other kids' attitudes will be better?"

"Can't get much worse."

She coughed, and I whined, "Will you come? Be my protection for the day?"

Her exhale sounded like resignation. "Going there will be hard for me."

I wanted to hug Kat and say everything would be peachy. But I couldn't. I had no idea how keen the experience would be for me, much less for her. Could her beloved adviser be a killer? With my inquisitive self, I'd find out what the trouble was, and I'd serve my major purpose. I'd have Kat returning to classes. "I know it won't be easy," I said. "But I'll be there for you, and you will be near for me."

"Supporters of each other."

I smiled. "You got it."

"See you there around seven," Kat said, and then she hung up.

Seven? Was that an hour in the morning?

"Who wakes up before seven o'clock?" I asked Minnie cactus after I got off the phone. "Surely kids don't crawl out of bed, eat breakfast, and get to school fully dressed by that hour. We used to start classes much later."

Minnie kept her pink head steady while I finished gobbling my corn dog. I laid out my clothes and dove into bed by 8:30. At 5:32 a.m. my alarm shrilled. I slapped it and drifted back into dream world.

A half hour later I sprang up, stared aghast at the glowing clock face, and scrambled. I showered, holding my head back to keep my hair out of water, since I wouldn't have time to dry and fix it. Damp hair ends stuck to my neck while I dressed. I folded a slice of bread and ate it, tossed back some orange juice, and dashed out the door.

The green truck appeared uglier with the sun's first rays glistening off its side, its putrid hue making the juice sour in my stomach. No one had told the mail truck this was supposed to be an important morning. It kicked and balked. I cranked the key, stomped the foot petal, and called the truck nasty names. Eventually it decided to cooperate. After all, today I was a teacher.

I reached the school and parked in a different spot. Sliding down from the truck's seat, I stood a moment and straightened my spine, proud of my new status. Big kids were tumbling out of cars and trucks with tremendous tires. Rap music blared through open windows, the deep *boom boom-boom, boom boom-boom* from its bass seeming to pound inside my head.

A sudden urge to dance struck. It always did when I heard the lively strain of "The Mexican Hat Dance" coming from my shoulder bag. I reached inside it and took out my cell phone. Few people had its number. The readout showed the call coming from my Austin office. "Good morning!" I answered.

"Mrs. Gunther?"

"Yep, it's me." I leaned back against the mail truck.

"This is Brianna Thompson."

"I recognized your voice."

My newest hire as manager, the young woman with minuscule thighs and a penchant for details. She was quiet a moment, faked a cough, and then asked, "Shouldn't a predicate nominative come after a linking verb?"

"Absolutely." I watched more vehicles pulling into the lot. Most of their rear bumpers held a Sidmore High School parking sticker.

"Well, when you answered . . ." Ah, Brianna was correcting me. "Shouldn't you say 'It's I'?" she asked.

"Do you know how dumb that sounds?"

Silence. "Yes."

"Brianna, whenever you're thinking, do you think *I shall do that?* Or *this is I?*"

"No ma'am."

"Whenever our agency creates promotional literature or edits for businesses or individuals who want proper grammar used, we make certain it is. But if we went around speaking properly all the time, we'd sound like we were trying to be high-falutin.' You wouldn't want that, would you?"

"No ma'am."

"Neither me. Now don't correct me. And I've told you, call me Cealie."

"Yes ma—Okay, Cealie."

"Great. So did you call because you wanted to hear my pretty voice?"

She finally laughed. "I was wondering if you'd be coming around here soon."

More vehicles with loud music pulled into the parking lot, making it difficult for me to hear her. "Did you need me?" I asked.

"Not really. I just wondered."

"My plans aren't definite now. Unless you need me there for something, I'll see you whenever I see you, okay?"

"Sure. Are you having a nice time?"

I peered at the school building looming ahead, at the muscular almost-adult males giving me unhappy stares. "It's unusual."

"Just like you. Nice talking to you, Cealie."

"You too, Brianna. And please don't go in to the office so early."

She laughed, and we clicked off. Teenagers leaving their vehicles stared at my mail truck. Some of them yelled. "Yo, mamma, what a beauty." "Neat wheels." "I'd like to go riding in that thing!"

I gave them a big nod. They appreciated distinction. I did have a unique means of transportation. Bouncy steps took me toward my new job. A boy even held the door open for me. His eyes were a brilliant shade of aqua, highlighted by his smartly cut sandy blond hair. "Thanks," I said. "I'm Mrs. Gunther. I'm teaching here today."

"And I'm a student here, but only for a few more days. I'm John Winston."

Kat's former boyfriend. I skimmed him again. Clothes neat, a nice-looking boy. And polite. Too bad she didn't find him right for her.

Teens coagulated in the cavernous hall. Today they looked calm. None smelled of wet doggie. "Good morning," I bid the students I passed, but they all seemed asleep behind half-open eyelids. I empathized. I scanned the corridor for Kat.

Bodies unidentifiable as to sex slumped on benches and against walls. None was my grandchild. At the moment, it didn't matter. I'd see her sometime during the day.

My steps slowed. Suppose Kat didn't show up? Then I'd be here all alone?

I scanned zombie-like bodies dotting the hall. Yesterday I saw what they looked like when they came to life.

Fear crawled through my stomach. I breathed, coating my mind with my mantra: *I am woman! I can do anything—alone.* My final stomp on anxiety came from envisioning Kat in a cap and gown. Hiking my chin up, I pushed into the office.

Life bustled. Unlike those dulled children outside, people darted through this space. A few adults greeted each other, some ducked into inner doors, others grabbed papers or dropped some, cursed, and made off for the holding area, where I saw more glum teens gathering in chairs.

I stood on the guest side of the room, assembling my senses. My senses said to scoot. Rush back out the door. But I recalled my mission. Get Kat here.

"Oh, Mrs. Gunther," vice-principal Anne Little said. She

wore a slimming plum-colored dress and appeared glad to see me. "I have your assignment. Come on back here."

On my side of the counter, more angry students sat. With them, miserable-looking adults, probably parents. I sprang across to Anne Little's side of the room like I'd been offered the key to the city.

A teacher scuttled past, rushing to get what she needed. She seemed to need discipline forms to write up students. And classes hadn't even begun.

Tom Reynolds came through the office area. He took papers from a secretary's desk and noticed me, a smile replacing his scowl. I smiled back, and he turned away. The woman he'd accompanied to yesterday's funeral approached. "This is our principal, Hannah Hendrick," Anne Little told me. Hannah wore a peacock blue pantsuit with a navy collar. Not one wrinkle in her fabric. Anne Little told her, "This is Cealie Gunther. She'll be taking Jack Burdell's place today."

Hannah Hendrick clasped my hands. "I love you," she said.

"Thanks. And we just met." Was it me making them so happy? Or did these women's pleasure stem from having someone replace that teacher, Jack Burdell?

"You have no idea how hard it's been lately to find enough subs," Hannah said.

"Glad to help." I almost meant it now with such warm greetings.

A teacher's complaint called Hannah away, and Anne Little handed me keys. "I'm also keeper of the school keys. This one is for the classroom. Lock it whenever you leave the room. And this one's for the desk. The biggest one is for the ladies' restroom."

"You have to lock classrooms and restrooms?" I asked, and she nodded and rushed off. *Why lock those rooms?* I wondered.

Cynthia Petre sat behind her monitor. Her mousy brown hair

was clamped back, and she wore a purple blouse with an emerald green skirt. I told her hello. "Good morning," she said without looking at me.

"But I didn't do it, Coach!" A lanky boy stormed in from the hall behind the bulldog-faced man in coaching clothes. The tiny woman with big black hair who'd been with Coach yesterday came in too, looking like she could spit fire. Everyone in the area appeared angry now, as though ready to kill. With so many, how could police sort out just one who might actually do it? Were the police still here?

A hand tightened on my arm. "You might want to get to your room," Anne Little said. "It's almost time for the bell."

"Ah, the bell." Pleasant memories returned.

"You go down that hall," Anne Little said, indicating the outer hallway, "then turn left, and when you get to a corridor, turn left again. Room 111. You can't miss it."

I opened my hand. Stared at the keys.

"That one." She pointed. Her mouth did a little twitch, and her squinty-eyed gaze told me she wondered if I could handle subject matter if I couldn't even remember what key to use. "A substitute folder should be on Jack's desk. It'll tell you everything you need to know."

Okay, I told myself, I could handle this. Someone died here this week, but being around this school wouldn't pose a real problem. I just needed to go to a classroom, do whatever the absent teacher instructed in his folder, and after a few hours, I'd leave.

I headed out the office and passed a scrawny woman with skin so pale it appeared translucent. She hustled inside to Anne Little. "Did you hear about Jayne Ackers?"

"What about her?" Little said.

"Shot last night. She died."

The entire staff stopped what they were doing. Faces whipped toward this woman as though a puppeteer had jerked a string joining them. Everyone uttered astonishment.

I turned to the pale person with news. "Who's Jayne Ackers?"

She frowned as if I had no business asking. Still, human nature surely made her reply. "Jayne was one of our substitute teachers. Not too popular with the kids."

My heart thudded. Wide-eyed, I walked through the doorway to become a sub myself, and glanced back at vice-principal Anne Little. "Miss Ackers only subbed for us a few times," she said, as though that would give me some comfort.

CHAPTER 5

"Do the cops know who killed her?" someone asked, and the pale news-bearer shook her head.

"She was shot near her home," she said.

I crept out the door, questions flooding my mind and breeding fear. Why had someone murdered Jayne Ackers? There was absolutely no connection between me and that substitute lady—was there? And was I supposed to be content because she hadn't subbed here often? Certainly, I wouldn't become popular with the kids in one day.

The hallway had come to life. Large kids shouted and shoved. But this time adult guards who must be teachers stood in their midst. They stood rigid, their gazes skimming the loudest teens. None of the sentries appeared worried that an emergency situation might be occurring. Hope filled me. Maybe they were plain-clothes detectives. Maybe today they'd discover what really happened to the custodian, while also keeping me safe.

I nudged through throngs, searching for Kat, and noting how the students dressed. Lots of the skirts barely skimmed girls' underpants, making me recall Legs from Gil's restaurant. I frowned, pushing that image aside. Twisted green spikes of hair stood on a boy's head. Other males I elbowed past wore bicycle chains around their necks, while still others wore thick gold necklaces that revealed their names.

The eyes of many young adults shifted down toward me. I wondered how they had all grown so tall. A glimpse at the shoes most girls wore revealed platforms of three inches or more. Some of the teens stopped in mid-sentence, their chins jutting toward me. Their peers turned to stare.

"Excuse me," I said, nudging through thick groups and locating a corridor to the left. *Good job, Cealie,* I thought, mentally patting my shoulder. I had a positive beginning to this day. I'd located the first hall.

The next passage was easier, sprinkled with fewer students. They seemed polite. "Good morning," some responded to my greeting. A tiny girl smiled at me. She wore an ironed blouse and nice slacks, conservative, like my Katherine.

To this one I said, "Sweetie, could you tell me where to find room 111?"

A horn blasted, and I jumped, squeezing my eyes shut. The girl giggled. "That's the bell. One-eleven's right down there."

The teens had begun moving. My students were coming! And I hadn't even gotten in the room yet, much less learned what I would be teaching.

I saw 111 above a door and drew out my keys. Tried one, failed. I tried another, while shoes clomped nearer. The key fit.

I entered the classroom, ready to become a public high school teacher.

The odor of stale chips mingled with perspiration and created a gagging instinct in my throat. I bit back the urge to vomit and scanned the room. Dust particles drifted through the sunlit air. Grime coated the windows. Mismatched desks coated with graffiti needed straightening. Scribbled across pale gold walls were kids' names, people they loved, and who was a bitch. Posters hung askew, displaying large drills. Others showed the cutaway view of walls with wires and plumbing. Chalk smeared a faded green board. Big people began to plod in.

I scurried to the long main desk and searched through scattered papers for what I'd be teaching. Behind me, shoes shuffled and clacked. "Aw damn, who's that?" a boy said. "Where's Mr. Burdell?" Desks squeaked while teens splayed themselves into them. Desk legs scraped the floor while I flipped through desktop papers, trying to discern my subject matter. Beneath sheaves of test papers, the corner of a manila folder stuck out. I grabbed the folder, satisfied to see that a red marker had printed on it *Substitute Teacher.*

"Would everyone please stand for the Pledge?" a woman's familiar voice called through a wall speaker.

I straightened, ready to look over my students. I knew things. I was intelligent enough. I could teach.

The teenagers rose. Kat wasn't among them. Three males and two females still sat with smug expressions, leaning back in their seats. I was anguished to find any youths so unpatriotic and signaled for them to stand. They peered at each other. Glanced at me. Took their time and finally stood slouching.

I pledged allegiance and then put on my bifocals. My heart fluttered while I yanked open the manila folder that would give instructions for whatever I would momentarily teach.

The folder held nothing.

I flipped the Substitute Teacher folder around but found no hidden slits in the rear. No hint to suggest what I'd be doing. My right hand was still pressed against my chest, feeling my heart's rapid thump-thumps, when a guttural voice said, "The Pledge is over, Grandma."

Students snickered and dropped to their seats. A motley crew. Half of them seemed to be trying to get back into sleeping position. Some girls wore tight sweaters across bulging breasts. One girl's cleavage hung out like ripe cabbage. I had hoped Kat might be in this class but now felt relieved that she wasn't.

But that nice girl from the hall was. She sat in front of me. I smiled at her, but this time she didn't smile back. Most of the males were wearing black or gray T-shirts with various messages. I noticed a sneer. My gaze found the cruel lips that had called me grandma and traveled up to the mean eyes. They belonged to the thug who hadn't been sorry when he ran into me yesterday. And now he was smirking.

I gave him a bigger smirk. "Be polite, big boy. I'm in charge in here."

Many of the teens grinned. The voice I now recognized as Hannah Hendrick's made announcements through the speaker, and I took the opportunity to ferret for material. No textbook. I shuffled through papers, grabbed one and stared at its heading. *Construction.*

Construction? That was one class I'd missed. What the hell would you teach?

"This concludes the announcements," the principal said, and I silently cursed her. Why couldn't she have spoken longer? At least given me a chance to discover something about my subject matter. What could I discuss in a construction class?

Deep voices grumbled while I glanced at the wall posters. Maybe I could speak about how to build things. But I had absolutely no idea how to do that. Deliberate coughs and laughs came from the class, making me realize how ridiculous I must look, panic-stricken, again flipping through everything on the desktop.

"Just how old are you, Grandma?" The thug cocked back, his shoulders draping across the rear of his chair, his arms stretching to the floor. The boys who had accompanied him when he ran into me sat on either side of him. My attacker wore bottle-streaked shaggy hair that dripped to a wide face, its lower half coated with stubble. His heavy jacket showed that he'd lettered in football. He rolled dark eyes at his buddies, who both smirked. The thug's lips curled up high at the edges.

Most of the students appeared to be holding their breaths, waiting for my response to him.

59

I placed my hands on the desk and leaned forward. "I'm old enough to have told your parents not to even *think* about having you." Laughter erupted. I gave it a minute to quiet and then told my opponent, "But I'm not too old to allow you to run this class, if that's what you're planning."

His lips flattened into a grim line. Color rose to his cheeks, his glare telling me it came from fury. *You haven't won yet,* his stare said.

For the moment, I had. And if I'd worn my sluttish outfit, he probably wouldn't have called me Grandma. With momentary respite, I again fingered the papers. I tried opening drawers, fear building when I found three of them locked.

The sweet girl leaned and whispered, "We're taking a test today."

"Where is it?"

"He takes them out of the bottom drawer."

I yanked on that drawer, relieved when it opened. Stacked papers were labeled Test Eleven. "You'll be taking this test today," I said, my head and voice rising. "And I am Mrs. Gunther. I'm taking your teacher's place today."

I asked for someone to hand out the tests and saw gazes divert. A thin African American girl jumped up. "I'll do it." She bounced around, passing them out, and then a hush blanketed the room. Faces dropped toward the papers. Pencils and pens swiveled. I waited. No one made more rude comments, and thank goodness, nobody asked questions. The teens seemed to forget I was there. I sank to Mr. Burdell's chair, found a leg of it unstable, and scanned the class.

Quiet, the teens appeared much less hostile. I watched them scribbling and saw only the tops of their heads. These children seemed normal. Maybe I'd made too quick a judgment. Not worried about them anymore, I mulled over Kat's situation. So far, I hadn't learned anything about the dead man. Didn't even know whether Kat had come to school.

I moved toward the students' desks. The sweet girl seemed to be determining a building's dimensions. I touched her shoulder. "Do you know Katherine Gunther?"

"Uh-huh."

"Great. Did you see her today?"

"Uh-uh."

A boy wearing dreadlocks sat behind her. I went to him. "Hi. Would you know Katherine Gunther?"

"No."

Other eyes had lifted toward me. Instead of tending to their task, most students were watching. I returned to my chair. The teens waited. When I did nothing but watch them back, they rolled eyes back down to their tests. I tapped my toes and gazed at students, my thoughts far from this room.

The girl who'd handed out papers wagged a finger, and I went to her. She said, "I saw Kat today."

Happy scenes swelled in my mind. I had accomplished my mission. Kat was back at school. She'd take exams, graduate, and all would be fine.

"Thank you," I told the girl. Returning to Mr. Burdell's desk, I peered at my shut door. What had happened at this school? A custodian died. A woman who'd subbed here had been shot. A chill slithered along my spine. I looked at the young adults in desks. A gangly boy leaned over another guy's shoulder, looking at his test. I coughed, and he sank back. Big thug stared at me, his harsh gaze unmoving. So was mine.

His eyes lowered. He took up his pen but didn't write. If a killer was in this room, I could point out exactly who it was. The thug flung a glare at me that lasted only a moment but warned: *I'll get you.*

Anxiety struck my belly. I calmed it with the knowledge that I had only a few minutes left to be near this young man. And I wasn't his mamma.

A blessed bell sounded, ending class. I wished the students a good day, hid my crossed fingers, and said it had been nice being with them. The thug tossed his paper on Mr. Burdell's desk and stalked out past me, bumping my arm. "Watch that," I said.

His buddy with a square build nodded toward me and spoke, his voice loud. "I guess she doesn't know what happened to that janitor who messed with you, huh, Sledge?"

Trembles replaced my earlier jitters. Behind me, a new group of teens headed in. A girl wearing a silver nose ring came close. "Who're you?" she said.

"Mrs. Gunther." I looked into the hall for Kat. And to make sure Sledge wasn't lurking. I didn't see him or my grandchild. I backed in to meet the class. "I'm taking your teacher's place, and I'll be giving you your test." How confident I felt, now knowing what I would do.

The teenagers groaned. The girl with a nose clamp said, "That's not fair. I didn't think we'd have it today since he wasn't gonna be here. I didn't study."

"That's your problem," a boy told her. He turned to me. "Are you gonna call roll?"

I skimmed the desktop. No roll book. "Not today."

With little ado, everyone started the test. I wanted to find out more about Jayne Ackers but didn't think it appropriate to question students about the murdered woman. Did any of them know something about Sledge and the dead man? Probably not wise to ask that either. I walked beside desks and stood watching a seemingly intelligent young man fill in numbers. He turned his face up to mine. Nice-looking youth. Annoyed face. "Sorry," I said, vacating his space.

Class ended without incident, and before I walked to the door, more teens came in. This group sat in silence. I gave my spiel, and they took tests, making no comments. Maybe today's students weren't too bad, I considered. Except for Sledge and his entourage. What had his buddy meant about the janitor? Was he saying Sledge killed the man?

I needed to pass on what I'd heard, just as soon as I could get back to the office. In the meantime, I had to watch these kids. I scanned them. Most appeared clean-cut with decent hair. Boys wore light-colored shirts, and girls had their bodies covered, no boobs or bottoms showing.

Legs, I jotted on a scrap of paper. Then I wrote *Gil.* Mmmm. I was only thinking of his restaurant and getting hungry, I told myself. I stood up and strolled between desks. Returning to my chair, I waited. Did people really get paid to do this? Other names came—Kat, Grant Labruzzo, Jayne Ackers, Sledge. I needed to go to the restroom. That last name made me know it for sure. Where was the ladies' room, and when did we go? Surely I couldn't leave students alone while they took tests. I crossed my legs and swung them. Staring at the large wall clock, I tried to rush it and pondered.

Could a teenager have murdered the custodian? Of course some kids killed others, but what motive would a student have for killing a man who cleaned the school? After I gave an administrator my information about Sledge, Kat's favorite teacher would be cleared. Then Kat would have no problem finishing her last semester. I mentally patted my shoulder for solving her troubling situation.

A bell rang, and students waited until I dismissed them. "Have a nice afternoon," I said, my bladder ready to burst. Kids vacated the room. I waited. Peered down the short hall and saw no one. I stepped across the hall to another classroom, where a woman possibly a few years younger than I sat at a desk, scribbling. She glanced up, reddish-black bangs shielding the top portion of her eyes. "Hi, I'm Cealie Gunther," I said, "and I'm subbing for Mr. Burdell. Nobody's coming now?" I scanned her room, void of students but filled with brand new desks. Lagoon blue curtains hung on her shiny windows.

"It's lunchtime," she said.

"Wonderful. And after lunch, what do we have? Another class or two?"

She held up four fingers.

"Four more classes!" I couldn't fathom having so many personalities to contend with.

"Well you have three classes like me and then seventh period off for parent conferences and planning. I'm Abby Jeansonne. I teach physics."

"You have my utmost admiration. The sciences weren't my best subjects."

"They aren't for many people." Abby's face pinched up. "Jack Burdell's shop is outside. It's being worked on, so they put him and his goons in this hall. I can't wait until they're outside again." Abby sprang up and neared me, her loose dress sweeping the floor. "You heard what happened here?"

"What happened?"

"To the janitor."

"I heard he died. That was terrible." But now someone was about to talk to me about the incident.

Abby's mouth puckered so much I was afraid she would kiss me. "Not just died. He was murdered!"

My head jerked back. "Are you sure?"

Flamingo-colored fingernails shielded her face from eavesdroppers who may've hidden behind walls. "The police are sure—You know," she said secretively.

I nodded. "Murder."

Her bangs shifted, and I saw one brown eye. The eye winked. "Somebody shoved him off that balcony in the auditorium."

I shuddered, imagining anyone even being up there. My twelve-year-old cousin Eddie had tried to shove me off our movie theater's balcony when I was seven. I arrived home afterward still whimpering, and Eddie told our parents he'd only been playing. Maybe so, but my child's mind had panicked, and the apprehension never totally let go of me. Another of the reasons I sometimes tried to avoid relatives.

Abby drew back her shoulders. She wore a shapeless denim dress, the red schoolhouse embroidered on its bosom looking elementary for this setting and for someone her age. I fought the pain in my bladder and spoke as though we were colleagues. "Are police still around?"

She did the flapping-bangs nod. "Two detectives. Plain-clothes."

Ah. I'd figured. "Do you have any idea who would have killed the man?"

Abby jabbed a finger toward the hall. "Talk to Anne Little. She's one of those."

"One of those?" I said.

Abby nodded, and before I could ask one of those *what*, she'd walked me out and withdrawn to her classroom. She shut her door.

Contemplating her words, I strode to the main corridor. The inmates were in tumult again, but a scan through the area let me locate a well-dressed man. He was darkly tanned and wasn't yelling for help. He wielded a weapon for crowd control, so I felt safe walking through. "Smart idea," I said, indicating the long stick in his hand. It was wrapped in blue and yellow school colors, the stick I'd seen leaning inside the office window.

"Our spirit stick," he said. "Different grades win it when they yell the loudest at pep rallies. And sometimes we carry it to show the kids our school spirit." He smirked.

I took the stick, surprised by its weight. "This is heavy." I swung it and watched its long blue fringes shake. Giving the stick back, I introduced myself and said, "I saw you in the office. You looked like the only calm person there."

"I'm a guidance counselor," he said as though that title explained his unruffled demeanor. "Harry Wren." Harry turned to the students, his gaze daring them to act up.

The groups seemed friendlier, probably because they were feeding themselves. I enjoyed whiffs of their nachos and pizza and chocolates. Many students held throwaway plates and guzzled food as quickly as my car with the biggest tank had sucked up gas. Fewer people were out than before, and I could walk through the hall without having an elbow strike my head. I could also look for Kat. First I needed to find the right facilities.

I saw a girl who'd been quiet in my class and asked directions to a restroom. Her face withdrew inside her Buster Brown haircut. She pointed toward what I supposed was a door hidden behind a clump of teens.

"No," a girl near her said. "That one's for us. She needs the teachers' one."

"Thanks," I said, "but it really doesn't matter. This one should do fine."

The room smelled of hair spray and smoke that created a misty dome. Squeals of alarm sounded, and someone announced, "A lady's in here."

Four toilets flushed at one time. Tendrils of smoke drifted above closed stalls. Since no one was smoking in front of me, I felt duty-free of taking charge of this conduct, which must freely occur. I entered a stall, found the lock broken, and read who loved whom and who was a whore, a word all of the writers had misspelled.

Emerging from the cubicle, I considered that I might begin my afternoon classes with a brief spelling lesson: "*Ho* is something Sir Lancelot might have yelled, like 'Onward, ho!' The word is not a noun."

I saw Kat. She came through the door behind three other girls. Excited, I called, "Hi, Kat."

She ducked her head, made an about-face, and rushed out.

CHAPTER 6

The girls that Kat had followed into the restroom stopped and stared at me. "Hello," I said, my granddaughter's behavior making me troubled. I needed her friends here to explain. They all spun and went back out without doing whatever it was they'd intended.

I left the restroom and scanned the wide hall. Some teens lounged against walls and talked softly. Others hustled along and yelled. No sign of Kat. Had she come into the restroom to smoke? Or worse, had my presence embarrassed her?

I wandered around, looking for my grandchild. Some halls I found were labeled Mathematics, Science, English, Business, Computers, and Swimming Pool. Other pathways weren't named. The scent of fast foods reached my nostrils, my stomach responding with a twitch. It was late morning, much earlier than I normally ate lunch, but my slice of bread had evaporated eons ago. I'd have to feed the gnawing in my belly before worrying more about Kat or getting my information about Sledge to Anne Little. And Abby Jeansonne had said I should question Mrs. Little about the murder.

"Which way is the cafeteria?" I asked a hefty guy cramming a whole folded slice of pepperoni pizza into his mouth. He gurgled, and I followed to where he pointed, until my nose began leading the way. The aroma of fried chicken and homemade rolls didn't escape me. A bell clanged, and I wondered what it meant now. Why were some kids withdrawing?

The cafeteria hall had almost emptied, and I was happy to easily make my way through. A young woman who came through an exterior door was so tall she could have eaten her lunch on top of my head. I realized she was the same person with the quiet voice who had initially guided me to the office. "Hi," I said. "Thanks for helping me out yesterday. Today I'm subbing. I'm Cealie Gunther."

"Hello." She patted down her fluffy blond waves. "It's so windy out there. Now I've got duty hair."

"Duty hair?" I grinned, and so did she.

"This is what hair looks like after you've had duty outdoors on a windy day. We had an accident a few days ago, and since then, all teachers have to pull duty. We're monitoring all activities here more closely." Her shoulder-length hair set off a flawless complexion and eyes the color of copper. She was slender, and the bodice of her knit top lay almost flat, yet little nubs poked up. She wasn't wearing a bra.

A woman who chose not to put on underwear for work? I admired her for making that choice. "I'm Marisa Hernandez," she said.

Kat's mentor! I reached out and pumped her hand. "So nice to meet you," I said, needing to talk with her about Kat.

"Whose place are you taking? If you're coming this way, I'll walk with you."

"I'm subbing for Jack Burdell, but I'm not sure which direction the room is now."

"Oh, then we won't be heading the same way. You'll go down that corridor to the right, turn right again and then left."

"Thanks. I'm going to eat first. How about joining me?"

"That bell meant our final lunch period was over. The cafeteria's closed." Marisa Hernandez sauntered off, and facts clicked in my mind. She was Kat's beloved teacher. And a murder suspect. The hem of her skirt swept muscular calves, her arms swung loosely, and I wondered. Could those dangling arms and long hands have shoved a man off a balcony?

And what did she mean—lunch was over?

Students had disappeared from my hall. I shoved the cafeteria door open, and the fried-chicken smell greeted me. Scores of round tables sat empty. I spied covered food bins but no ladies with hairnets in the area. I could grab a drumstick and gobble it while making my way back to class. But then I'd be greasy and need a drink. It might not be prudent to watch a class taking a test while I gnawed on a leg bone.

I turned, feeling my belly button striving to reach my backbone. Immediately across the hall I faced double doors, the word above them capturing my attention—*Auditorium.* That was where the custodian died.

I scooted to the doors and grabbed a handle. Pulling slowly, I found the first door locked. The second door sucked open.

Darkness and even blacker shadows stretched inside. The room's absolute quiet engulfed me like a shroud. The balcony was somewhere above. And below it, the space where Grant Labruzzo had lain lifeless.

An icy chill made my arms tremble. I let the door go and scooted away. I needed to release the tension in my jaw and teach a class. Digging orange Tic Tacs out of my purse, I chewed them. Two men stood ahead, both wearing suits and dress shirts without ties. Their commanding stance and take-everything-in demeanor made me decide they were detectives. The tall one looked older. He was hairless, with black-rimmed eyeglasses and a thick waistline. The younger one was brown-skinned. His shoulders were wide, his hair short, his waist trim. I could tell them what Sledge's buddy mentioned about Sledge and the dead man.

I started toward them, but the older cop stopped me with his stare, his gaze nailing me as though I had done something wrong. Maybe I shouldn't have opened that auditorium door. Police might still be checking out that room. Or classes might have started. Since I wasn't in my room yet, my students could be rioting.

What happened when a teacher or sub didn't show up for class? Imagining the damage my worst students could inflict on a room or other students, I took off at a trot. My gaze skimmed halls, my breath catching in my throat. Suppose I couldn't find room 111 from this direction? I angled down another hall, where Abby Jeansonne's voice greeted me. She stood outside her door, angrily eyeing her room and mine. "I was afraid you had run out on us and were going to leave the afternoon groups all alone," she said.

A backward sweep of my hand dismissed the idea. "No way." *Not unless I could get away with it.* Then I could pursue Kat. What was happening with her?

I couldn't just sneak away. I'd have to come back around these people for graduation. I hoped.

Both of our classrooms were quiet. I glanced in Abby's room. Colorful physics posters and framed pictures hung on her walls. Sunlight slanted across her quietly seated students. Slits of light fell on Sledge, his mean-eyed gaze freezing against mine.

My returned stare told him "I know what you're thinking." At that moment, I really did believe he could kill someone. Me.

"We can get to work now, class," Abby said, her voice breaking the spell between Sledge and me. I rushed inside my room.

Students looked like they'd been hit with a stun gun. What I surmised were three males and one female had cheeks down on their desks. "Wake up. Wake up," I said, strolling down rows and tapping my fingers on desktops. A boy with a small mustache drew his head up and fixed his glassy eyes on me.

Then like some great magnet pulled it, his head fell. He was snoring by the time I handed out papers.

All but the sleeping boy started their tests. These students must be working on credits for graduation, but if naptime was more important to that fellow, so be it. He was old enough to make his own decisions about his final average.

Just like Kat?

I hated to think she might make an unwise choice now that she was so close to the end. But Kat had agreed to come to school today, and she was attending classes, preparing for finals. Surely she'd decide to take them to keep her grades up. I had planned on checking into what happened to that custodian, but now I didn't have to. The police would determine what took place. And if Kat's friend Miss Hernandez was involved, Kat would have to learn to live with that fact.

I headed for the teacher's chair when a girl waved to call me. I went to her, hoping she wouldn't ask about building things. A glance at her paper told me her name was Roxy. She'd written no last name. The smell of stale smoke clung to Roxy's stringy hair. "You called Kat," she said, and I recognized her as one of girls who'd gone in and out of the restroom.

"Yes," I said, excited, hoping I'd found an ally, "she's my grandchild."

"Your grandchild? Damn, how old are you anyway?"

Faces throughout the room turned up. The sleeping boy let out a snort.

If I'd been a person to get embarrassed, I would have now. A smart retort blasted to mind, but I stuffed it. I was too mature, but not too old, to trade quips with a student. *Age doesn't matter! Just don't ask what mine is, or you'll make me a liar,* I might tell her. And almost as much as I hated depression, I abhorred telling untruths. But sometimes I needed to resort to telling them—with crossed fingers. "Young lady," I said, ignoring other stares, "I won't humor you with an answer. But I will tell you it's not proper to address a person that way, especially an adult."

Roxy's cheek tightened, pulling up an edge of her lip. Pencil-thin plucked eyebrows formed teepees above her eyes that appeared navy blue. An offset edge near one iris revealed that she wore colored contacts.

I shared stares with Roxy, my peripheral vision seeing smirks of the teens anticipating the fun of our encounter escalating. How often did teachers today have to go through this?

Roxy opened thin lips that she'd painted brown. She inhaled, and I knew smart words were about to come out. Her lips formed the letter *F.*

"Don't," I warned.

She took deep breaths, her expression saying she was trying to decide whether to continue this contest. Her hands spread on her desk, and her palms pressed on its grainy wood. She looked ready to shove herself up.

And then what?

I walked away. If Roxy was going to fight me, she'd have to come over to the next row. But I could certainly imagine her throwing down desks to reach me. "All right, class," I said, brazenly turning my back to her, "get busy with your tests. You don't have much time left."

Gazes swerved from me to Roxy and then me again. Some teenagers looked disappointed, some reassured. The sleeping boy sat up, appearing wide awake.

"Ugh," Roxy sighed. Her elbows crooked out, and her cheek struck her desk. Roxy's arm shoved her test to the floor. She readjusted her head against her bent arms.

This was school? Where was the anticipation of learning? Where was school spirit? What in the hell had happened to kids? Of course someone in this school could badly harm another person. The anger broiling inside me let me know I could smack someone's hind side for sure.

I turned away from Roxy, reeled in animosity and decided to look for pleasant youths. I meandered around desks, pausing near some and drawing stares. I offered smiles and was warmed at receiving a few. Every test except one had been turned in when the bell rang. "Hey Roxy," a boy called, slapping her back on his way out, "class is over."

Roxy's arm whipped around to punch whoever hit her. She saw the room vacated except for me and uttered, "Shit."

I decided now wasn't the time to teach her alternate terms. As she stood, I said, "Don't forget your test." Roxy stared at me, and my gaze shifted to the floor, to that piece of paper, which was about to earn her an F. She muttered a word starting with the same letter and grabbed the test. Flinging it on Mr. Burdell's desk, she stormed out.

The release of my breath felt extra peaceful. But Kat was friends with that girl? I yearned to curl up in a bed. I'd lose myself in a novel, one that would make me smile, for this day seemed barren of humor. In a classroom was not where I wanted to remain. How could today's teachers cope with these potentially violent kids day after day? These teenagers were certainly not, as I'd hoped, vacuums waiting to be filled with knowledge.

One recollection made me grateful. I wasn't expected to fill their hungry minds with how to use hammers and drills. Mr. Burdell had done that. Bless Mr. Burdell. The next class came, and without incident, took their tests. They left, and I awaited my final group of students.

"Hey," a big fellow shifting into the room said, "aren't you the woman who came here in that old mail truck?"

I stood straight, awaiting his jeer. "I am."

While other teens hustled in behind, the fellow raised his massive hand. It went for mine. "Neat wheels!" He slapped my palm. With a broad grin, he announced, "Hey everybody, this lady's cool. She's got that goofy green mail truck."

Teens commented with smiles. I smiled in return, getting ready to end the day on a positive note. This was a great group. They knew distinction when they saw it. I introduced myself and gave out papers. Sledge was coming in the door. I blocked him and said, "You were already in here today."

He shoved his hands deeper into his jacket pocket, and my heart skipped a beat. Would he pull out a weapon? He lifted thick shoulders and dropped them. "Stupid teacher kicked me out of class. She told me to come sit in old man Burdell's room." Sledge nudged past me and slunk to a desk in the rear.

My comfort had left. I dropped in the teacher's chair. I wanted out of here. If I ever considered being in a classroom again, I would kick myself silly. I'd never even drive near a school.

But then there was Kat. She was here. And although I hadn't really spoken to her—because she avoided me, which especially hurt—she was attending classes. Her grades should improve. But she had come into that restroom with Roxy.

My fingers tap-danced on the desk. Two people involved with this school had died this week. Could the deaths be connected? If the custodian was murdered, I could already give a list of suspects. Sledge, now giving me dark-eyed stares, topped my list. Roxy could hurt someone. That ferocious-looking coach and his tiny sidekick in the office always looked like they might kill. But who had a motive? Or an opportunity?

Did anyone here know a man died? Did anybody care?

Kat did. The death occurred after school, she'd told me. I kept a watchful eye on Sledge and wondered who else might have been here at that time. The police were still questioning people. They'd find out. Same for the substitute lady, who'd been shot near her home.

I pulled out keys for the classroom, restroom, and whatever the third was for. I would be ready to leave.

My eyes swerved back to the keys I held. Would the school have been locked when the custodian died? If so, then who else had access to this building? Some of the people in charge. The principal. Vice-principal Anne Little, whose mouth had done that nervous twitch; anyone whose main duty entailed hiring people to sub with these students must have a violent streak. Band directors usually had keys to get in buildings. So did coaches. Probably other teachers.

I peered at my three keys, each a different size and shape. I hadn't been given a key for the main building, but what about regular teachers? Other custodians? Anything was possible, I determined, glad I didn't have to prove who, if anyone, had done the killing.

I closed my hand around the keys and stared at Sledge, who watched me. Papers rustled, and erasures sounded. My belly rumbled, needing food. I could call Cajun Delights and ask if they'd bring me some.

No, then Gil would know I'd come and stuck my nose in police business.

Maybe a pizza place? I studied the poster of a large saw and worked hard to avoid thinking of eating. I tapped my foot, running my gaze over students who were writing. Only a few minutes left. I grinned, realizing I never had to do this again. The room was silent when "The Mexican Hat Dance" played.

Students jumped. "What's that?" "Who's got the phone on?" they asked. Heads swiveled. "Somebody's mamma's calling." "A drug deal," they blurted.

"It's just my . . . go back to what you were doing," I told them. Grabbing my purse, I scooted out the door. "Yes?" I whispered into my handset, poking my head in the room so the students could see I was still watching.

"Hello, Cealie." Gil's baritone voice warmed me to my toes.

CHAPTER 7

Hearing Gil on my phone made me move away from the classroom door.

I glanced back through it and spied a girl with wavy auburn hair already sliding a notebook out from her desk. She saw me and shoved her notebook back.

"I thought you might give me a call," Gil said.

I smiled. Normality. "How'd you reach me?" I turned away from students. Who cared what they were doing? This was my life.

"You kept the same number, didn't you?" Sex appeal reverberated in his tone.

I was beginning to feel things I didn't deem appropriate while I was filling the role as a teacher. I glanced in the room. Eyes shifted away from others' test papers. With regret, I told Gil, "I can't talk now."

"Oh, caught you at a bad time."

"You might say that." I moved inside the room, my stare daring anyone to cheat.

"Then I'll let you go." Gil sounded disappointed. I liked that. What I really wanted was to sit back and chat with him until the last bell rang, the final student left, and I could sip a tall strawberry daiquiri. Two or three would be even better.

Inquisitive teen faces turned to mine. "This really isn't a good time," I told Gil.

"Call if you get a free minute? I'll be at the restaurant."

Yum, Gil *and* food.

I smiled the rest of the period, which passed quickly. If Sledge stared at me, I missed it. I gazed at the wall and my inner eye showed me Gil. I was hungry. Gil was sturdy. Still well-muscled. He was at his restaurant, awaiting my call. The dismissal bell rang, and with smugness, I told the class 'bye. Once they'd gone out, I straightened all the desks, picked wadded paper off the floor, and found a cheat sheet. Some desks held candy wrappers. Wads of gum clung beneath desktops. I hauled a small trash can around the room, tossing in all the rubbish, but not the used gum. The room still didn't look appealing when I left it.

"How'd you make out?" Abby Jeansonne asked, as we met coming out of our classrooms.

"It wasn't too bad." I rolled my eyes to let her know I was kidding.

She picked one key from her ring filled with oodles of them, locked her room, and went off. I was forgetting that classrooms now needed locking; for what, I couldn't earlier imagine. Now I knew. It was to keep out cheaters, thieves, and maybe killers. I locked Jack Burdell's door. I needed to return my keys to the office and pass on what Sledge's friend had said about him and the dead man. Better yet, I'd see the detectives again and tell them.

The central corridor was empty, except for cans and containers on the floor. A girl emerged from the restroom, and I went in it to see if by chance I'd find Kat. I didn't. I did find the office. Glancing at the custodian's obituary, I shuddered. Grant Labruzzo had been nice looking. But his expressive eyes were now shut and would never open again.

I passed beside annoyed students to get behind the counter. Coach was back, again ranting on a phone. "Those damn kids!" he snapped, hanging up. I somehow knew the small red-faced woman with huge black hair would emerge. She did, and I nudged close to a girl standing near me and asked the woman's name.

"Miss Gird," the girl snarled.

Coach and Miss Gird looked like they could've ripped off a person's head. Could either, while angry, shove a small man over a balcony railing? Easily. Their killer vibes permeated this area.

The bell rang to end seventh period. Hannah Hendrick passed through the office, heading toward a rear hall. She saw me and her tense face brightened. "Mrs. Gunther," she said, coming over, "how was today for you?"

I considered telling the principal a lie. "It went," I said with a grin.

Hannah's bemused expression told me she understood. I spied some staff members, but not Anne Little. I'd have to tell the principal what Sledge's buddy said. I handed Hannah my three keys. She thanked me, and before I could say more, students roared in through the door. A sour-faced boy yelled to Cynthia Petre that they all needed to use the phone. Their bus had taken off and left them behind. I didn't blame the driver. An unhappy adult accompanied a male student through the door. Hannah touched my arm and said, "May I speak with you a minute?"

"Of course."

She gave the angry people another once-over. While I followed where Hannah led, she told me a vice-principal would handle the situation with those students. The boss-lady escorted me through a narrow rear corridor past open doors. Inside small rooms, men and women looked overworked. Some pondered over papers, some spoke to students. The custodian's obituary was taped near a room labeled Vice-Principal Tom Reynolds. Reynolds, the thin man who'd accompanied Hannah to the funeral, sat inside this room. He listened to a long-haired boy complaining, and the boss pointed to the next door. "My office," she said.

Ah, headquarters. I felt special. I half expected to see push-button controls. Panels that would cordon off scary areas. Weapons for crowd control.

Hannah's spacious office held flowers, portraits, cougar pictures. "Please sit down." She waved a hand to a dainty chair and dropped into a nicer one, but not the leather chair behind her desk. "I asked you to come in here because it was getting so loud out there."

"It does get rowdy."

"And would you believe, it's sometimes quiet?"

I merely grinned. Hey, I could be happy. I wouldn't have to return here. And Gil was out there, awaiting my call. My stomach made a noise sounding like a cheer.

Anne Little swooped into the room. "I gave Ms. Hendrick the keys," I said, expecting that Anne had come after me. "And I need to tell you both something."

Anne nodded absently. She was carrying the spirit stick. "Hannah," she said, "could you come out here a minute? Trouble with a parent."

"I'll be right back," Hannah told me. She left with Anne, and I checked out her office.

Silk flowers in yellow and lagoon blue stood in a vase on a side table. I recognized the real flowers on her desk as tulips. Frames on her walls held pictures of cougars: some fierce, some whimsical. Photos showed Hannah with students: her arm around a homecoming queen, she handed trophies to other teens.

Nostalgia swept through me. As a child, I'd often wondered what mysterious items the principal and teachers kept away from our eyes. In high school my teachers and principal had me file papers. I then saw all their photos, spindly plants, and messy papers, destroying all my exotic imaginings. Just like the tragic events from this week had surely destroyed Kat's. But she had been here already, with some knowledge of the nasty creatures in this place. How sad. My schools had contained more innocence. So had the private school where I'd taught.

When Hannah returned, I was eyeing a picture of her standing beside a boy in a track uniform. He looked familiar. He'd come into my morning class and fallen asleep. "Your son?" I asked.

"My cousin."

"He looks fairly young for that." I slapped my hand over my mouth. "Not that you're old."

"Actually, my cousin's son." She seemed to disregard my blunder and returned to her chair.

"I have cousins, too." I grinned and then frowned, remembering the one who'd sent e-mail. Why had Stevie wanted me?

Hannah's tulips drooped a little, making me think of Minnie on my kitchen counter. "Did you grow those flowers?" I asked, ready to glean knowledge about raising plants.

"I bought them." She looked ready to say something else.

Anne Little interrupted. Walking in, she pointed the spirit stick at me. "Mrs. Gunther, you wanted to tell us something?"

"There's this big guy," I said, gazing from one woman to the other, "they call him Sledge." Both of them nodded, so I went on. "He and I exchanged words, and then a friend of his said I mustn't know what happened between Sledge and the janitor."

The administrators peered at each other. I glanced at both of them and said, "Do you know anything that transpired between Sledge and the man who died here?"

Anne Little's eyes swerved aside. Hannah leaned forward, clasping her hands on her lap. "Our custodian caught Sledge doing something inappropriate behind the main building."

"Inappropriate?"

"He was kissing a girl and, well, fondling her."

"She was fondling him back," Anne Little blurted.

Hannah made a polite smile. "Anne gave them both after-school detention."

"That doesn't sound like a terrible punishment," I said.

Anne took a deep breath. "But the detention made Sledge miss football practice, so Coach wouldn't let him play in the last district game."

"Was that a major problem?" I asked.

Hannah spread her hands. "Sledge thinks that was why he didn't get an offer to play college football."

I sat back. "Oh, a major overhaul of his future plans. Is Sledge that good an athlete?"

Hannah shrugged. "He and Coach Millet think so."

"Coach Millet," I said. "An older guy, wears a bulldog expression?"

The women grinned at each other. "I'll get your information to the detectives," Anne Little told me. "They stay around, investigating."

She walked out, and then I remembered Abby Jeansonne's comment. This time I excused myself from Hannah for a moment, entered the hall and said, "Mrs. Little, the custodian who died. He wasn't murdered, was he?"

Her eyes widened with her startled expression. "Grant's death was unfortunate. Certainly an accident." She exhaled, tightening her grip on the spirit stick. "The police haven't ruled out foul play yet. But they will."

"That's a comfort."

"Yes. Well . . ." She spun and scurried toward the main office area.

I stood in place, wondering. Why had Abby Jeansonne told me to talk to Mrs. Little about the man's death? What had this vice-principal told me that I hadn't already surmised or could have easily learned? I needed to consider more but had to return to Hannah's office.

Hannah smiled when I entered and sat. "Mrs. Gunther, I wanted to talk to you because I know about the classes you had today."

"You do?"

"I know Jack Burdell and . . . well let's say he doesn't have the choicest students. And he isn't our top disciplinarian."

"That explains some things." I waited. I was famished. I wouldn't tell Hannah I couldn't find food in time. Was she going to offer me a bonus for spending an entire day with Jack Burdell's students?

"But," she said, "other classes aren't the same."

"No?" What good news.

"Well, a few are. But lots of them aren't. The point I'm trying to make, Mrs. Gunther—"

"Call me Cealie."

"Cealie." She smiled broadly. "And you call me Hannah. But what I wanted to ask is . . ." Again that hesitation. Did she want me to guard the entire school? "Quite a few teachers will be out tomorrow."

Uh-oh.

Hannah's hazel eyes narrowed. "We've had so many problems lately trying to get substitutes. If you could only—"

My mind cut off her plea. I didn't want to hear it. I was woman—not a teacher. I was no longer required to guard anyone. And what about Anne Little, whose main purpose now, she'd told me, was locating teacher replacements? Had she backed out of that chore, instead finding the handling of furious parents more appealing? My head swiveled while Hannah spoke. *No way.*

Her hand clasped mine. "I know Kat is your grandchild. She

would be so pleased to see you here again."

Kat. The magic word. "How do you know about her?" I asked.

"We get to know most of our students, especially the troublemakers and the honor students. You can be proud of that young woman."

"Kat's a sweetie." My smile came and faded. "But that custodian's death really got to her."

"Tragic. It's affected us all."

I hadn't noticed anyone who appeared especially bothered by the man dying. And I didn't want to come back here. I had learned to say no and prided myself on that major achievement.

"Cealie, Kat has an extremely high average. But some of her teachers mentioned that she missed their classes this week. That's so unlike Kat. And if she doesn't attend every class and get the rest of teachers' instructions for finals. . . ."

Her other words washed over me. I finally left Hannah's office, surprised to see some faculty members still in the hall. Coach Millet and Miss Gird looked different merely standing still. They peered solemnly at the obituary posted outside Tom Reynolds's office. I paused near them, wanting to get their reactions. "Such a pity, that young man dying," I said.

Coach stuck his thick finger on Grant Labruzzo's picture. "Called himself a janitor. He didn't even empty our trash cans."

"Hmp," Miss Gird said, nodding toward the vice-principal's office, "and Tom got the man hired. So how does that look on him?" She and Coach stomped away.

I shivered, watching the full-bodied man and the small woman both pumping their arms with their strides. Together, that pair could easily shove someone off a balcony.

The detectives stood on opposite sides of the main corridor. They were speaking to adults I didn't know while writing on pads. The administrators would tell them what I'd heard about Sledge. I hoped the police were learning what they needed. I hoped the man's death was accidental. It was dreadful, the loss of any life was, but I prayed that no one here, especially Kat's mentor, had caused his fall.

The skin between my eyes tightened. Why had Kat eluded me in the girls' restroom? Soon I'd have to find out.

Students bustled out the school. A few sat on benches, talking and flirting. Two custodians, a thick-shouldered male and a squat female, swept floors. Teachers appeared exhausted, lugging sacks of papers. From what I'd experienced, I would forever appreciate today's educators.

My avocado mail truck stood out in the nearly emptied parking lot. I wished I'd learned more, but Sidmore High had given me a quick education. With trying to keep order in classes and worrying about finding the restroom and food, I had done all I was capable of achieving in one day.

I drew closer to the mail truck, anxiety building inside my chest. Had anyone messed with my vehicle?

Teenagers were touching various parts of my truck. A gangly fellow had the driver's door open. All of the kids turned when I neared. I rushed forward, expecting them to run off. "We're scoping it out," a girl with an earring clamped to her eyebrow said to me.

A boy of Asian descent smiled. "This is one cool set of wheels."

I could see no scratches, no dents. "Thanks."

The teens moseyed away, nodding and glancing back at the mail truck. *Hey, I'm cool,* I told myself, climbing inside. The threesome hopped into a Jeep and tooted when I drove past. I turned on my oscillating fan, returned the kids' waves, and considered buying the vehicle I drove. An unusual truck with a unique color. I could have it shipped wherever I went.

A light drizzle began and smeared my windshield. I drove into a gray sheet that separated the sunshine from rain. Wanting to return Gil's call, I pulled my phone from my purse. I set it on my lap, found the windshield wiper knob and turned it.

No wipers came up. Rivulets twisted down the glass in front of me, but I could still see. Until thunder crashed. It ushered in a downpour. Waves smeared across the windshield, and water gushed in my door's big square window. I gripped the knob and turned it like a churn.

Sadly I discovered why this creation hadn't sold. My door had no window.

I squinted to see while my truck rumbled down the road. I wanted Gil's balmy shelter. His terrific meals and his comfy body.

My side was soaked and the right side of my hair was all stringy by the time I drove out of rain. My muscles all felt stressed to the max. I should go home, fix my hair and change clothes. But the flip-flopping in my tummy won out. I headed my truck for Cajun Delights.

Who cared what I looked like when Gil saw me? He had vacated my life and had Legs now. Food was the only thing I was after.

CHAPTER 8

"I couldn't find the cafeteria in time for lunch," I told Gil when I strolled into the restaurant and found him standing near the checkout counter.

Gil's head leaned back with his hearty laugh. Then it bent toward me. I was tempted to kiss his lips and cling, knowing they'd make me warm. So would his body. Especially his body.

I spied Legs. Her pretty heart-shaped face glanced out from behind the buffet.

I tilted my head to indicate her and asked Gil, "That wouldn't happen to be a daughter or niece of yours that you didn't tell me about, would it?"

He looked at her. When he turned back, I hated the smirk he gave me. Gil shook his head, and my earlier enthusiasm vanished. "You couldn't find a cafeteria?" he said.

"It's been one of those days I'll have to write about in my memoirs." The less I thought about the day, the better, especially considering what Hannah just asked me. And I didn't want to tell Gil I'd shoved into Kat's school. "But now," I said, "I need food. You have some?"

"Anything you could yearn for."

I could yearn for other things, especially with him so close. But I was weak from hunger, and his girlfriend was here. Maybe she was co-owner now, sharing his responsibilities. And his bed?

My mind answered that question affirmatively and caused my throat to make a deep growl. She might come over and sit with us. I dreaded meeting the cute young thing, but worse things could happen. I had seen that at Sidmore High.

Most tables were empty since it was mid-afternoon. I joined Gil at the place where he'd sat before, and he ordered for me. For himself, he asked for a light whiskey sour. Then he turned to me. "I was wondering whether Kat made a decision about school."

I shrugged. "Wish I knew for sure."

"In a couple of weeks I'll be leaving to start up a restaurant in Tennessee. I wanted to make sure I'd still be around if she graduates."

Gil would soon leave. I would, too. But knowing he'd depart brought about a strange tugging in my chest. "Where in Tennessee?" I asked, voice pitched too high.

"Gatlinburg."

I nodded. "It's a lovely town."

He scooted his chair close. "Well now you have to tell me what my friend Cealie has been doing since she left me."

His friend? And *I* left?

Yes, I did, I recalled. I'd lost Cealie sometime during my long marriage and was now discovering her again. I liked that. I could smell Gil's skin. Distinctive. Manly. I controlled my voice. "I've traveled, seen some exotic places that I hadn't been to before." I smiled as though I'd enjoyed every minute.

"That's what you wanted." He leaned back hard in his chair.

Not long before we'd separated, Gil had appeared sad but said he wouldn't become baggage that I'd have to lug around in my freedom. *I have to tell you, Cealie, I'll live by your decision. But parting from you isn't my choice.*

It was my choice. Then why did the back of my eyes burn and their fronts feel all misty? I swiped a hand across them and scanned the buffet. Didn't see his new woman. It sure hadn't taken him long to get over our separation. Why was his girlfriend just lurking while I was sitting here with him? Probably he'd told her I was an old friend. Well, ancient compared to her. "I like your restaurant," I said, shunting the conversation to a new direction because if he asked more about my adventures, then he'd tell me about his. With that woman? No way.

Gil's dark eyebrows crimped. He didn't like a chilled, indirect conversation. He knew that I didn't either, but if I'd shifted our talk another way . . . He peered across his establishment. "I'm pleased with it, too."

A waiter brought drinks and my salad, and I dug in. Gil lounged back and watched. His gaze made my face heat up, its warmth spreading down my body. I avoided looking at him. I ate my cup of chicken and andouille sausage gumbo, my belly quieting with the comfort food, and then my entrée arrived. The Seafood Sprinkler held bite-sized fried catfish tidbits and jumbo shrimp stuffed with crabmeat. The soft-shell crab was to die for. I eventually shoved my plate aside. "Why don't you have some?"

A great smile lit Gil's face. "I've eaten. You go on, do it some real damage."

I finished damaging his food and my diet. "I can't eat another bite," I announced. Spying an oyster hidden beneath fries, I grabbed it.

The smile lines near Gil's eyes deepened. He sipped his drink, and our talk after the meal remained guarded. We were no longer lovers. We both tried to present ourselves to each other and the world as almost strangers. We succeeded fairly well.

He walked me to the door, and I shifted my feet while he remained still. Inches apart, we gazed at each other. Gil leaned down and said my name from that spot deep in his throat. I rose on tiptoe, my lips nearing his.

Legs leaned out from behind a wall.

I dropped flat on my feet. My hand shot out. "Thanks for

everything," I said to Gil, grabbing his hand and shaking it.

"Any time." He spoke with lackluster eyes. "I'll walk you to your car."

"No, it might still be drizzling."

"I'll get you an umbrella."

"Thanks, no." If I used one, I'd have to return it. And coming back around Gil and leaving him again wasn't an experience I cherished. When I did that before, a void opened in my heart. It remained unfilled.

And now he had someone new. She'd probably ask him if I always looked so disheveled. Gil hadn't mentioned my drenching. He's surely noticed, but was too much a gentleman to say anything.

The sky had cleared to a baby blue, I saw when I went outside. I wiped the wet seat of the mail truck and drove to my condo, emotions swirling with my thoughts. Faces of people—possible murderers—a student or teacher. Kat. Legs and Gil. Being near him had felt disturbing. Wonderful.

No. You know what you want, I reminded myself. I wanted freedom, no more major responsibility. No more waiting for plumbers or worrying about children, like I was doing right now, worrying about the child of my son. Of course I cherished Roger and Kat, and I'd stay near and take care of them, but they'd let me know I wasn't wanted for that task any longer. Domesticity was no longer in my life's blueprints. And that included romantic entanglement. I'd never make love with Gil again.

I stomped the foot pedal. Passing a stretch limo, I tried to peek into a shaded window. Nothing was visible, but the image made me mentally concoct the long svelte legs poured into Gil's partner's black stockings. *Ugggh.*

By the time I reached the condo, I had pushed Gil and his

woman from my mind. Trying to make sense of the day, I paced. "Why would any person with a grain of sense want to become a teacher today? Those students are really something," I said to my cactus Minnie in the kitchen. "And I used to think teachers were intelligent people."

The pink puffs on Minnie's head appeared to be spreading. She didn't look quite as healthy as when I'd bought her. A bath would probably jolt her ailing system back to heath. I dumped water on her and said, "I hate teaching!"

Anger curled through my stomach. Hannah Hendrick had asked, using Kat as enticement. Pounding inside my chest told me I had done something stupid. Dread of the unknown, and especially the known, made my arms quiver. I had given in. Tomorrow I would again be a teacher.

"But Ms. Hendrick spoke about Kat's problem," I explained to Minnie, trying to placate me. I walked a small circle in the kitchen. "I need to go back to Sidmore High to make sure Kat keeps going." Minnie appeared stronger with water droplets holding to her head. Talking to plants was good, I'd once heard. I touched her soft prickers while students' reactions ran through my head. Kat had avoided me in the restroom. Some kids had slept. Sledge had seemed threatening, and then there was Roxy. "When kids turn thirteen, they should be put to sleep until they're twenty," I suggested to my friend Minnie.

Her stem slanted. Maybe hearing too many problems would upset her. With plants, who knew? How much study had been done on plant feedback? I left the kitchen. I wasn't ready to talk to Kat yet. Still too much turmoil inside me from her behavior and from being around Gil. Sprawling on the sofa, I checked the day's top news stories on my cell phone. The temperature in San Francisco was fifty-six. I touched the memory button for my office there, but stopped when a rock-hard knot formed in my throat. Freddy and I had moved there and started that business in our home, editing papers for college students and brochures for local companies. I smiled, recalling the rickety typewriters we'd used. How much time it had taken to determine the space we'd need to leave at the bottom of pages for term paper footnotes.

I rubbed my eyes, not surprised to find them damp. I loved Freddy. Still did. But he'd left. I understood Roger's plight. Of course he wanted Nancy to still be with him. But she couldn't. And Kat needed her dad. I needed to make certain I'd get her to school tomorrow before I could focus on how to help him.

I connected with my Deluxe Copyediting office in San Francisco, and my manager Betty Allen picked up. "Hi, Cealie," she said brightly. To my inquiry, she said they weren't having any problems. "Only the usual, the client who likes everything on his brochure we created—except for the headline and the visuals. The graphic designer I worked with sure got a laugh about that." Betty Allen and I both chuckled. "And we just got a call from the marketing director of Mega Hotels, Inc. He wants their work completed yesterday—because he procrastinated in getting the mock-up to us." Betty Allen snickered. "I just hope our days keep getting warmer."

"And how are your sweet husband and new grandson?" I asked.

"Fantastic."

"Wonderful. Give them a bunch of kisses for me." She agreed to do it, and then we hung up. I phoned Orlando and afterward, Cape Cod. Warm in Florida, still too chilly way up north. Other than that, my managers all said business remained steady. I decided not to call the other cities. People who ran my agency's offices did their jobs exceptionally well. Conglomerates now mainly used our services, and most of the work was completed online. The agency could be operating with only one or two large offices, but I wanted to keep the individual touch available. There were still so many people without much computer knowledge who started small businesses, and they seemed pleased that we had an office they could drive to, where a person would help them create a brochure. And often still, women retired and decided to write memoirs. They needed help reworking and editing their creations. And most wanted a person they could sit and chat with, especially since many of them didn't even know how to send attachments. I could easily relate. In many ways, I was still a techno-dummy. But the majority of people I hired weren't.

How nice to own a business. How great to work with sensitive, proficient people. The livid faces of teachers at Sidmore High came to mind. The scowling teens, most appearing as motivated as slugs. And tomorrow I'd subject myself to them again?

No way, I decided. When I'd received my degree in education, children knew about manners and values. In just one more day at Sidmore High, I wouldn't be able to instill those things in all those teenagers.

Happy that I'd learned I couldn't change the world, I phoned Information. "Please connect me to the office at Sidmore High School," I said to the information lady who answered.

Instead of me returning to school, I'd somehow bribe Kat to keep attending.

Satisfaction soothed my tensed muscles. "Sorry, I was in my stupid state when I told you yes," I'd tell Hannah. "But tomorrow I absolutely will *not* cross your school's doorstep." I smirked, waiting for someone to pick up the ringing telephone. Surely people were still in that office. I had seen many staff members roaming through that area. Custodians must still be cleaning. I'd tell anyone. *Let an administrator know I won't be there.*

Hours seemed to pass while I waited. I closed the phone,

cursing everyone who worked at Sidmore High. No one could have murdered Grant Labruzzo after school hours. Nobody stayed at school that long.

I calmed my breathing and created new plans. All I really had to do was make certain Kat continued to attend. It was time to talk to her.

I climbed into my mail truck, wondering why I needed to determine how a stranger died. I wasn't a detective. I hadn't needed to sort out such things last month, when I trekked through jungles with men who wore skins and spoke Swahili. The only death I worried about then was mine, if those lions we'd viewed from afar decided to visit while we slept in hot tents.

Parking in front of Roger's house, I recalled the last time I saw Kat, when she ran out on me from the restroom. I climbed the steps, rang the bell, and she opened the door.

Kat's cheeks colored. Her gaze swung away from my eyes. She was expecting chastisement.

"Hi sweetie," I said, kissing her cheek and trotting in without invitation. I faced her in the dark living room. "Come riding with me, Kat."

"Where would we go?"

Wherever it takes to get you to talk. "I need your help with shopping."

Her lips formed a half grin. "What do you need to get?"

"School clothes. Maybe a denim dress with a little school-house."

Kat made a real smile. "I can't imagine you wearing anything like that, Gram. And why would you want a dress that resembles school?"

Thickness formed in my throat. "Tomorrow I'm going back to Sidmore High," I said with a shudder, hating to urge Kat to return. Some people in that place gave off horrible vibes.

She said, "Oh," and a quiet moment passed. "I heard that more teachers would be out. They often are, on a Friday or Monday."

"Why Fridays and Mondays?"

"Listen, Gram, I've—"

"You ignored me today. I didn't like that."

She fell silent. What was it about teens? Did you have to tug every response out of some and stare down others to make them shut up? When God decided to create teenagers, He'd surely grinned, presenting us adults with major puzzles. I had to figure out this one.

"Kat, I met Miss Hernandez."

Her shoulders drooped. "That's why I didn't talk to you in the bathroom. You would have asked me about her. And I probably would've cried."

I wrapped my arms around Kat, and she held on, her back trembling. Pain for her squeezed through my heart. Too much distress inside this young person. I yearned to pull it all out and toss it away. Why would a question have caused her such pain? Had she become too sensitive, or too attached to that teacher? We let each other go, and I sat beside Kat on the sofa, with Nancy's face surrounding us. "Did something happen between you and Miss Hernandez today?" I asked.

Distress remained in Kat's face. "I didn't see her, but I couldn't concentrate in my classes. Somebody passed me a note. It said the police were arresting her."

I clutched Kat's hand. "Was it true?"

"I don't know."

"I met Miss Hernandez right after noon recess. When did you get the note?"

"During the period after that. Later on, I asked some friends, but none of them had an afternoon class in her hall. Nobody saw her."

I grabbed my cell phone, called Information, and connected with the police station. "Can you tell me if Marisa Hernandez was arrested today?" I asked the friendly-sounding man who answered.

"Sorry, I can't give out that information."

"But it's important. My granddaughter's her best friend."

Kat made a weak grin, and the man repeated that he couldn't help me. I hung up, told Kat what he said, and watched her grin wilt. "Is there anybody else I could call?" I asked. "An administrator? Another teacher?"

"No. If it's not true, I don't want to start another rumor."

"But who'd start a rumor like that?"

She folded her hands on her lap. "The boy I broke up with was in that class."

"John Winston? I met him."

"You meet everybody, Gram." She almost smiled.

"Would John make up a lie just to taunt you?"

"He wasn't very happy when I quit dating him."

"Can't blame him for that," I said, tweaking Kat's nose. "So we probably won't know the truth about Miss Hernandez until tomorrow. I'll be at school to find out if she shows up. Will you?"

Kat stood. "Let's get something to drink."

We walked to the kitchen, and I said, "Your dad's late. Any chance he went out with the guys after work?"

Kat smirked. She poured glasses of iced tea and we sat sipping our beverages, staring out the bay window, watching evening descend on Roger's flowers.

"Do you know a boy called Sledge?" I said. "He and I butted heads today."

"I'm not surprised."

"And I spoke to Roxy. She seems dangerous." I looked at Kat. "Are you smoking?"

She grinned and shook her head. "Why would you think that?"

"You came into the girls' restroom with Roxy. She only came in there to smoke."

"I was just walking behind her. But you're right. Roxy could be dangerous."

I mentally patted my back. I knew killers when I saw them. I'd seen many on television.

"Roxy hasn't been at our school long," Kat said. "I don't remember where she came from. But the first time I saw her, I walked in the bathroom and it was really crowded. Somebody shoved me in a corner. It was Roxy, drawing a knife on me."

My heart jumped to my throat. "A knife?"

"Just a tiny pocketknife."

"A knife is a knife, no matter how big. Knives cut. They can kill."

"I know. When Roxy did that, I tried to shove my spine into the wall."

"And then what happened?" I asked, pulse racing.

Kat sipped her tea. "Nothing. Roxy closed the knife, put out her hand, and introduced herself. I shook her hand and she left. Ever since then, we've been cool."

I was cool. Students said it. But my relationship with people didn't involve knives. "How cool are you with her now?"

"We're not close friends, not enemies. We usually grin at each other."

Having Roxy grin at Kat didn't console me much. Another fearful thought came. "You wouldn't have a class with Miss Gird? A tiny woman, follows a coach, face gets all red when she's mad."

"Yes, I know. And I do."

Uh-oh. "Did you ever see her hurt anyone?"

Kat laughed. "Only a boy that she heard yelling filthy stuff in the hall one day. Miss Gird slammed him against a locker."

I knew it. More ideas popped up. "Kat, why does it seem that so few people at the school miss Grant Labruzzo?"

She shrugged. "He hadn't worked there long, so most people probably didn't even know him."

I mulled on these new insights. Another previous worry returned. "Did you know a substitute teacher named Jayne Ackers?"

Kat moved off to the refrigerator. "She's tall and blond, looks kind of like Miss Hernandez. Gram, I have to fix dinner. You can stay, but please let's quit talking about school."

Obviously she didn't know Jayne Ackers had been shot. And since Kat had enough concerns, I chose not to tell her now. "I ate."

"Already? Where?"

"At Cajun Delights."

Kat's face brightened. "Oh, with Mr. Gil."

"The food was good."

Kat eyed me, her grin suggesting she didn't believe I'd only enjoyed the meal. I quickly changed topics. "I'll really need somebody to pick out things that I could give a special young lady as a graduation gift."

"Gram . . ."

"And then I could hide them. The graduate could pretend to be surprised at what's inside all the gift wrap."

"Graduation gifts are for people who graduate."

"Yes."

Kat narrowed her eyes. "Don't push me."

I wanted to push. I wanted life normal and this child happily finishing high school. She and I exchanged a brief kiss at the front door. I drove away wanting to dash back in there and pin Kat down. Would she come back to Sidmore High? If I had to be there, then she should be. She was the reason I'd be putting myself in that position, even knowing what I currently knew about students.

A picture flashed into mind. I was holding Nancy's cool hand, giving the assurance that I'd take her place. All of the worry wrinkles on Nancy's forehead smoothed out.

Deathbed promises. Were they all so difficult to keep?

In the condo I kicked off my pumps and listened to my feet plat-platting across the floor. I strode through rooms, reminding myself of a caged tiger I'd once watched in a zoo. The majestic creature's space was so small that I wanted to set him free. Not a good idea with a ferocious animal, I'd determined. I left his area when golden fur from his shoulder rubbed off against the bars.

I was starting to feel as he must have. Too many concerns. Too little space in which to take care of them. And alone, just like that tiger? I didn't have to be. My decision.

To remind myself of choices, I walked to the stove, grabbed a towel and buffed. "There," I said to nearby Minnie but really to me. "I can still cook on one of these. Or not." In the den I ran the towel across an end table. "And I can keep dusting furniture like I used to." I crumpled the towel. "Or let someone else earn a living doing it." I draped back across the leather recliner's arms and stared at the chandelier, its teardrops glistening. Kat could probably be salutatorian of her class if she tried. And she might get offered a nice scholarship to a major university. But her bright future and her worries tugged at each other. On which side would she fall?

Kat's future could include her becoming a top graduate. Or she could avoid school and fail exams, which would make her grades drop. She could choose not to attend her high school graduation. But Nancy had lived her whole life with a sense of failure, only because she hadn't pressed on to receive that one piece of paper—a diploma—in her hand.

I slammed down my fists and drew myself up. Kat would *not* fail!

I envisioned all those mean students from Sidmore High School and knew—tomorrow I'd be the teacher from hell.

CHAPTER 9

I strutted through my den feeling newly empowered. I knew what to expect from high school students now. And I knew what I'd do with them.

I needed to calm down. The clock rang early on school days. By now the police had my information about Sledge and were probably discovering what happened between him and the dead man. Maybe the brute was already behind bars. Then Marisa Hernandez would no longer be suspect. Kat could resume life as before, attending final classes, confiding in her mentor.

I relaxed. I wanted to read something that would put me to sleep, which excluded my latest Kinsey newsletter. In the kitchen I told Minnie hi and opened the dishwasher. The bottom shelf, holding my multicolored cookbooks, rolled out. Since I never planned to bother these appliances with lots of soiled dishes, I'd found the dishwasher a perfect place for storing my books. And a kitchen pantry shelf, without tons of food and often located near the back door, usually became a great space on which to place boxes of my shoes.

I fingered the orange cookbook from Georgia, the tan one from Toledo, the white one from Denver. I selected *The Best Dishes of Montana*. Whatever people ate in Montana might not let me stay awake long.

Lying in bed, I read their recipes for hors d'oeuvres. The first six doused me with sleep.

Morning brought me into my closet, where I picked through

widely spaced items. A few women teachers at Sidmore High had worn knitted droopy pants and matching tops with pictures. I didn't want to wear that and had nothing resembling it anyway. Pushing aside my already wrinkled pantsuit, I bypassed my slut clothes and considered an ecru linen jacket with off-white slacks and a silk blouse. My mind's eye embroidered the outfit Marisa Hernandez wore, the classic knit dress with no bra. I envisioned the tailored suits worn by Hannah Hendrick and Anne Little and then decided on a compromise.

After a brisk shower I blew my hair dry, noting its roots wanting of more natural burnt sienna. Today I didn't have time to find a hairdresser. I brushed my waves and strode through the condo, sans clothing. Gil had taught me to feel comfortable in the skin God gave me, even if much of it now pimpled with cellulite and other parts sagged toward my waist.

Yesterday's dinner at Gil's restaurant had been early, my growling belly reminded me. I swallowed cranberry juice and spied Minnie's head drooping. If this juice drenched humans with vitamins, how much better must it be for plants? Pleased with my inventiveness, I coated Minnie's soil with the wine-colored liquid. "You should feel perkier within minutes," I said and tossed my cup in the trash, smiling as I considered what the cafeteria might serve. Today I could find it. And today I knew how little time there would be for eating. I'd get to those pans of food in time for my noon feeding.

My outfit consisted of a suit. Navy, a no-nonsense, power color. Pads built up my shoulders. Epaulettes with gold buttons gave me the air of belonging to the military. I straightened, enjoying the authority I saw in the mirror.

Since I also liked Marisa Hernandez's idea of having no underwear even when standing before those bloodthirsty people, I wore no panties. Instead I drew on sheer pantyhose. Beneath them I normally wore briefs. Not today. "You have a great day,"

I told Minnie, " 'cause I will. I'll make those teens sorry they ever messed with me." Minnie didn't look stronger, but maybe that would take a few hours. I grabbed my navy pumps from the pantry and slipped them on. I was ready.

A thought made a jolt of concern strike my stomach. Had Kat avoided school because she was scared to attend? After all, a man had died there. Sidmore High must have been a frightening place even before his death. Someone had keyed my Lexus the first time I went, when nobody there even knew me. Now Sledge and a few others must hate me. And some, like Roxy, knew Kat was my grandchild. I needed to make certain Miss Hernandez was at school. But suppose she had spent the night and morning in jail?

My head spun with dilemmas when I slipped my shoulder bag up above my arm. The phone inside it played *da-dunt da-dunt da-dunt*. I kicked my feet to the cheery tune, and expecting Kat, I answered, "Hi, sweetie."

"Hello, sweetheart."

My belly balled up. "Gil? You're up early."

"So are you. I wanted to ask you something this morning."

Anticipation bit in my chest. He'd question why I was going out at this hour. I wouldn't tell him about my subbing brainstorm.

He said, "How can you tell if a person is a Cajun?"

I smiled. This had to be from the restaurant's joke contest. "I guess by the person's name. Or maybe by the accent." I crossed to the door and paused, spending a moment to feel close contact with Gil.

"Wrong answer."

"Okay, tell me."

"A Cajun is someone who lets his black coffee cool off and then discovers that it's jelled." Gil made a hefty laugh.

"Cute," I said.

"And did you hear about the fire that broke out at Bou-dreaux's place?"

My absolute favorite. A Boudreaux and Thibodaux joke. "No, what happened?"

"Boudreaux's buddy Thibodaux phoned the fire station and said they needed the firemen to come out. The fireman asked for the best way to reach his house. Thibodaux thought a minute and said, 'Don't y'all still have those big red fire trucks?' "

How good it felt to be laughing in the morning.

"They came from the contest last night," Gil said. "If you'd stayed longer, you would have heard them."

A cold rag could have been slapped down between us. Both our voices changed, no smiles left in them. "I'm sure it was nice," I said. Of course Legs had remained. "Thanks for sharing the jokes with me."

"Any time."

"I'm sorry, but I really have to run." *No, don't say run.* "There's something I'm doing." He'd probably think I was ready to take a shower.

"I'll let you go. But we didn't get to talk much yesterday. Would you like to have lunch?"

"Lunch?" Oh goodness, getting to sit in the cafeteria would take almost too long for the little break allowed for the meal. Surely there wasn't time to drive to the restaurant, eat and return for afternoon classes. "Sorry again, I can't make it."

"Well maybe some other time."

"Maybe. Thanks for the invitation." We said goodbye and clicked off. Damn, I'd have to eat cafeteria food, and if memory served, those meals weren't anything to anticipate. And I'd have delightful company: the students. I snarled and then went out the door.

Driving up to the school, I parked my avocado mail truck without worrying. I swung my epaulette-clad shoulders through the humid air and walked inside the building. Someone had removed Grant Labruzzo's picture from the office window. Nobody seemed to have mourned him for long.

In the office I boldly projected myself into that sacred space, behind the counter. Staff members lolled about, yawning and gathering coffee in mugs with written sentiments. I didn't see Marisa Hernandez, but I had arrived early. Anne Little bent over and searched in a file drawer. Again she wore a suit, carnation pink silk, and almost dead center on its skirt rear was what appeared to be an ink stain. Schools did that to you, I surmised, recalling the purple stains on my teachers' blouses and hands after they ran off our papers. I had enjoyed the smell of those tests taken right off the old ditto machines. But that ink might ruin Anne Little's lovely suit.

Secretary Cynthia Petre was wearing her hair down. Today it looked rich and full. She appeared more attractive than she had before, except for her brown top with a maroon skirt. A mid-sized calendar stood on her desk. Days had been crossed off with huge red X's, the countdown to summer vacation. I noticed that today was May third. Ever since I'd begun creating my new life, I seldom paid attention to calendars. Such a great feeling, freeing myself from most time constraints.

"Good morning!" I announced.

Two women groaned, and Anne Little glanced up but gave no response. Cynthia Petre waved to call me. "I have your keys," she said, her braces flashing.

I knew what keys. Did they pass from hand to hand, not returning to the person who had told me she was in charge of them and hiring us subs?

Cynthia Petre handed me a key. "For the classroom. It's number 115 down the science hall." Great, I could find that. "And this one's for the bathroom," she said, giving me another.

Anne Little frowned as she approached me. "Mrs. Gunther,

yesterday I saw you going in the girls' restroom. The faculty ladies' room is down the cafeteria hall. Do you know where that is?"

"Absolutely."

"Or if you're around here, you can use the one for the office." She pointed to a door directly to the rear. Ah, I'd moved up. I was privy to the administrative toilet.

Hannah passed through that rear hall, and Mrs. Little trotted off after her, saying, "Can you believe it? Tom Reynolds just called in sick."

"I don't give a damn what you were doing!" a man shouted behind me. "You shouldn't have been around there." Coach Millet clenched a tall boy's arm, almost dragging him, and flung a furious gaze across the secretaries. "Where's Anne Little?"

"Back there." Cynthia Petre nodded toward the rear hall, and Coach tugged the boy toward where the administrators had disappeared.

Chills scooted across my back. A killer at this school? One might be out in the hall and peering in here. Or one could be right in this private area. Was Kat here today? I wanted her to be, yet felt a strange fear for her if she was. Hurry up, end of school.

Cynthia Petre obviously read questions in my face. "That kid might have been smoking weed," she said, explaining Coach's behavior. "Probably out in back of the stadium. That's where a lot of them go."

"Oh." The calendar beside her regained my attention. May third. Why was that date important? Gil's birthday! Scenes scattered through my brain. Experiences we'd shared, the joy, the intimate moments. The hot sex. Imaginings made me smile. Then I recalled things were different now. I needed a gift, but one that wasn't remotely romantic. I borrowed Petre's phone book, looked up a number and called.

Waiting for an answer, I spied the older detective I'd seen yesterday coming in from the corridor. He guided Marisa Hernandez through the office. She kept her gaze down toward her denim jacket, not making eye contact with anyone, and went with him into an inner office. The door shut.

A recording responded to my call. "Sorry we're closed. Your business is important to us, so please leave a message."

"I'd like to rent someone," I said, giving all the information. I left my phone number in case they'd have questions and hung up wondering about Hernandez.

Anne Little returned from the rear hall and came to me. "Did I remember to tell you that today you have duty?"

"Duty?"

She nodded, and her gold hoop earrings danced. "Lately we've had teachers pulling duty. But yours is duty five, so it's not until your hall's lunch break. And then after school with the buses." She stretched a long finger to the left. "At noon you go out the door down that hall. And after school, you go out there." While she turned, I saw her skirt's ink stain. I smiled, not about to tell her she had it. How dare she give me duty! "Just see that nothing looks suspicious and nobody gets in trouble," she said. "Make sure nobody drinks liquor or smokes, especially weed. And after school, don't let any kids get in anybody else's car."

"Is that all?"

"And if a fight starts, break it up."

Being here to make Kat graduate suddenly seemed much less appealing. But maybe while I stood on duty, I'd have an opportunity to speak with Kat. She could keep me company. Maybe she'd know who belonged in which vehicle and who might try to puff weed. And maybe Marisa Hernandez would be out there on duty again. Then all three of us could chat. I could help clear up any misunderstanding they might share. Ah, this duty thing was sounding better.

I returned the phone book to Cynthia Petre's desk and accidentally knocked over her calendar. Replacing it, I noticed a framed picture, which had stood beside it. Kat's ex-boyfriend. "John Winston," I said.

Petre's smile showed me the rubber bands that stretched across her braces. "John's my nephew. We're so proud of him."

I made no comment and started out the door. Hannah Hendrick came from behind. "Oh, Mrs. Gunther, today you'll be taking Miss Fleet's place. She said she would leave a sub folder." *With something written in it?* "It will tell you everything you have to do."

Administrators here seemed to know little about what transpired in teachers' classrooms.

A perspiration odor oozed through corridors, especially from large boys showing off too-heavy jackets with letters from sports. A clump of long-haired males gave off an unusual tangy smell that might have been marijuana. I glanced back, making certain they weren't smoking. I saw some teens who'd been in class with me. Others I wasn't certain about, for the sleepers had kept their heads down. A few kids looked me over. I answered their stares with my teacher-from-hell glare.

"Yeah, they're asking her about that janitor," a female voice said. I turned and saw that Roxy was the speaker. Spying me, she made angry eyes and spun away. Had she been talking about Miss Hernandez? Surely the girl would not tell me more. But I hoped someone would.

Abby Jeansonne's door was open when I found the hall I'd been in yesterday. "Hello," I said, poking my head in her room. She was scribbling on papers, the red-black bangs draped over her eyes.

She flung her hair aside to see me. "Back again?"

"Yes, today I'm Miss Fleet."

"Oh, chemistry."

"Chemistry!" I recalled little of science, and my knowledge of chemistry could fit into my smallest finger. "I never took that subject," I said, willing myself not to panic.

She shoved the reddish mane off her neck. "Chemistry's not too difficult. It'll come to you."

That was easy for a science major to say. But I bolstered myself, recalling my mission. I needed to discover some things if I was going to get Kat to remain here these next few days. What was being said about her favorite teacher, and why had that cop taken her into the office? A less-than-direct approach seemed most appropriate. I said, "Oh, yesterday I met Marisa Hernandez. She seems like a nice person."

Abby wrinkled her nose. "The Spanish lady."

"Is she from Spain?"

"No way, born and raised a few streets over, around Grant Labruzzo's house."

"Really? What kind of teacher is she?"

Abby gave me a one-eyed stare. "She's another one of those."

"Ah." I inclined my head. "One of those . . . ?"

"Yes." Abby returned her attention to her papers.

I was no farther along than before. But my students would come to class soon, and I would have to teach chemistry. I unlocked Miss Fleet's door, dreading what I'd find.

CHAPTER 10

My apprehension level soared as I stared into the chemistry lab. I felt less prepared to go into that room than any I'd ever entered.

A sulfurous odor seemed imbedded in its pale green walls. Stained glass beakers clustered on shelves, alongside liquid-filled jars holding small items that might have been unborn things. A skeleton hung in a far corner near a sink. Posters with S's and P's and other letters teased me in formulas. For all I knew, they'd been written in Swahili. Framed black and white pictures of old men hung on the wall, and Einstein's was the only face I recognized. The room might have been in order, yet to me it appeared chaotic.

I plunked my purse down on Miss Fleet's worn desk that held only one folder. Fine print labeled it *Substitute Teacher.* I dropped to Fleet's chair, held my breath and flipped the folder open.

Seating Charts headed the pages that were paper-clipped together. These pages were covered with squares, and each square named a student. Handwriting that slanted to the left gave instructions. *Please give out these worksheets. Students will know what to do with them.*

I exhaled. Material on the attached worksheets looked abstract. How nice that the teens would know what to do with them. I certainly didn't. Miss Fleet also wrote *If any student gives you trouble, just pull the string attached to the wall speaker, and someone will come from the office.* I glanced up behind her desk and located the speaker with a clean white string dangling. I was ready. Armed with the worksheets and a string.

The bell rang, and I sprang to my feet. Outside the door I stood erect, confident. I was their leader. Teacher from Hades.

Students swarmed toward my room. Ruffians who had been in class with me yesterday came, but to my relief, they turned toward other doorways. A girl with a springy step neared. "Hi!" she said, looking me straight in the eye. How different. Few teens from the construction class had made eye contact.

"Hello," I said, a smile rising to my face. I shoved it away. *Teachers shouldn't smile until Christmas,* I'd once heard a teacher friend say. Christmas had long gone, but I thought I'd pay heed to that warning. Today I was the gruff sergeant. I plastered on a frown and merely nodded to the kids who entered. John Winston came through the doorway and gave me a big smile. He and the others all sat. These youths appeared clean-cut. Pleasant expressions. Where were all my bad guys? The loudspeaker crackled, and everyone rose. They slapped right hands on their hearts, and every one of them recited the Pledge.

A conspiracy. They were waiting until announcements were over. And then—

"Some students haven't picked up spring pictures yet," Anne Little said through the speaker. She then reminded seniors to mail their graduation announcements.

Was Kat in a classroom, hearing those instructions? I wouldn't wait for her to mail my announcement; I'd take mine in hand. A sudden thought made me grin. I had a mail truck. Wouldn't it be fun if I delivered mail for a day? But I didn't know most streets in this area, I realized, letting the idea fade. *Streets.* Miss Hernandez lived near the man who died. Could their locations be important?

I didn't know that or whether Kat showed up today, but

students were smiling at me. Mrs. Little quit talking. Now class should start. I stared at young adults—they at me. One young man wore facial hair cut in the slimmest beard that circled his chin and ran up to his earlobes. A hand shot up. "Yes?" I said.

An adorable boy spoke. "Miss Fleet said to tell you her roll book is in that top drawer."

"Thank you, Mr. . . ."

"Cody Steward. Our names are on those seating charts."

Oh, the charts. I opened the sub folder to first period. "I'm Mrs. Gunther, and I'll be taking your teacher's place today. Would you please answer the roll? Cindy Adams," I called.

"Here." A girl lifted her hand and lowered it.

"Cathy Adler," I said.

"Present." Cathy's fingers slid up and down.

"Chad . . . Cherish . . . Charity." I was reciting a litany of C's. "Rodney," I said, grinning. "Ah, Rodney."

"Right here." A dark-skinned boy with a friendly smile raised his hand. I nodded, realizing I also smiled. I couldn't help it, but wasn't worried. If a killer was at this school, he or she wasn't in this classroom. "Would you like me to pass out the worksheets?" Rodney asked.

He did, and with little noise, students began working. John Winston took out an ink pen. He'd worn his hair longer in the picture on Cynthia Petre's desk. Halfway during the period, all heads were still upright. No one snored. These kids didn't even look tired. Most took their time, pondering the worksheet questions. John Winston's eyes scanned words quickly before he penned answers. He looked like the all-American boy, much too pleasant to have made up that lie about Miss Hernandez to worry Kat.

So Marisa Hernandez had not been arrested yesterday. She was here today. But she was with the police. Of course they'd been questioning lots of people.

I wandered down aisles and stopped beside John. He glanced up, and I pointed to his answers. "Those look good."

"Thanks. Do you know how to work these problems?"

"Sorry, I didn't take chemistry."

"Lucky you." He waited until I moved on before he wrote more.

Students set their completed worksheets in a tray on an old credenza. They returned to their desks and read. No one seemed worried about my age or their naptime, and I adjusted to the sulfur smell. Wondered why a detective had Miss Hernandez. Why someone had told Kat that she'd been arrested. I trotted back to John Winston's desk. Leaning close, I spoke softly. "Kat's my grandchild." He didn't look surprised, so I continued. "Yesterday Kat received a note in a class about Miss Hernandez."

John made no change of expression. "So?" he said in a quiet voice.

"You were in that room. Did you happen to send her the note?"

John's demeanor altered. His aqua-blue eyes narrowed. "I don't pass notes in classes!" His voice carried enough to make nearby kids stare at him and me. "Did Kat tell you I sent her one?" John asked.

I shook my head. "She doesn't know who wrote the note."

"It sure wasn't me."

During the rest of the period, John's shoulders kept a rigid set. He didn't write on his worksheet. Irritation built on his face. Class ended with a bell, and teens waited to be dismissed. They left in orderly fashion. Most told me goodbye, they hoped I'd come back. John stared straight ahead and said nothing. Tension in my neck told me that maybe I shouldn't have said anything to him about Kat.

Rowdy kids roared toward me, not giving me time to

contemplate. I stood firm, getting ready for them. They turned into other doorways, and smiling youths approached mine. Where were my hoodlums?

I spied Sledge. He stopped, dead center in the hall, and nailed me with his glare. I planted my feet on the floor and my fists on my hips. Sledge growled a low mutter. He shifted into another room.

The fear that had sprung to my chest fluttered away, and I found my second class well behaved. So were those in the next period, which zoomed by. All of the teens seemed normal, like Kat. "What happened?" I asked after another bell, when I stepped across to Abby's room. "Did somebody ship off the students I had yesterday and ship in a new friendlier batch?"

She didn't look up from the papers on her desk. "Today you have mainly honor students. Most of them are in the band."

I immediately liked the band. And looked forward to my next classes. Kat had never played anything but her stereo, but she was taking honors classes. I couldn't recall whether she'd scheduled chemistry. Returning to my room, I sat. Abby's voice came from the corridor. "Thank goodness for lunch break."

"Lunch break. When is that?"

"Now."

I sprinted through the hall past Abby. "Where's duty five?" I asked over my shoulder.

"Down the main corridor and out the front door."

I smelled pizza. "One more thing. When do teachers on duty eat lunch?"

"We bring a sandwich. You have to eat while you're out there."

My stomach grumbled almost as much as the students who began filling the halls. I went past them into the yard, and wind pressed my skirt into a mold of my lower body. I tugged the fabric loose. Breezes had swept off the earlier humidity and left behind sweet cool air. No students were out yet. They'd gone for lunch, I decided, dropping to a bench and wishing they would bring me some.

I was pleased to see tiny red flowers growing in a small rectangle of grass, contrasting with the surrounding concrete slabs. Students might find slivers of nature here if they looked hard enough, and the unhappy teenagers might calm down. The sidewalk before me seemed to lead to outdoor classrooms. Parked in front of them were sedans, newer model trucks, and SUVs, surely belonging to teachers. I moved closer and saw doors numbered 1, 2, 3. The *3* stopped me from looking at more. Today was the third, Gil's birthday.

Musing made me smile. We'd held hands often, and each of us touched the other's back when we walked by. We'd made love and then fed each other Gil's fresh-baked cookies, the chocolate chips melting on our fingers. One time Gil smeared the moist chocolate down my breasts. We laughed afterward because he couldn't let all that good chocolate go to waste.

I scowled, thrusting away those mental pictures. They had come from the past. They made me lonely. And hungry. Gil's smile jumped back into view. How would he like receiving my gift today?

Male students with deep voices came out the front doors, followed by girls with giddy laughter, and I was glad they'd stopped my unproductive thoughts. Until I saw Roxy. She was describing someone, loudly using creative expletives. I stopped her by saying, "Hello, Roxy."

A girl near her muttered a curse. The girl scurried back inside, shoving something into her purse. She probably wanted to smoke, but because I stood guard here, she might now try it in the girls' restroom.

Roxy did an about-face and reached for the door handle. "Have you seen Kat today?" I asked before she vanished. Roxy shook her head and yanked on the door. I touched her shoulder.

"Do you have any classes with her?"

"I don't talk about nerds," she spat.

"Oh." I slipped my hand off her arm. "I didn't know Kat was a . . . well, I should have figured."

Roxy let the door go. She turned to me, her navy eyes not quite so harsh. "Kat's not that bad. I mean, she is a nerd and all. But she's not like the rest of them."

I smiled. Here was a kid with edges. Roxy seemed hard to the core, but she probably wasn't. "You seem to like her."

"Kat's all right. Yeah, she's okay." Roxy appeared to have forgotten her mission, probably of smoking. Maybe pot. Blankly, she stared out at the red flowers.

"Aren't they pretty?" I asked.

She didn't reward me with another response. Roxy gazed at the parking lot, the wind blowing her stringy hair, revealing a thick brown scar along her neckline. From a recent knife fight? I shuddered, thinking of what this child could have done to Kat.

A crinkling sounded as Roxy drew a bag of Cheetos out of a small purse. She yanked the bag open, tossed golden puffs into her mouth and crunched, making my mouth water. "Want some?" she said.

"Just a couple." I grabbed four.

"Catch a few more." Roxy widened the bag and made my belly very happy. She sent the empty bag flying to a plastic barrel, brushed crumbs off her fingers and grabbed the door handle. "You don't know much about schools, do you?" she asked.

"It's been awhile."

She grinned. "You're short, you know that?"

"Vertically challenged," I said.

Roxy laughed. She spun around to face me. "You're pretty cool, just like Kat."

Again I was cool. So was my grandchild. "Roxy, is Kat here today?"

"Don't know. I didn't see her."

Disappointment dropped in. But since I was cool, maybe Roxy would tell me other things. "I heard you talking about the custodian this morning," I said.

"Yeah, the dead guy."

"I saw policemen here. They're still checking out the accident?"

"Accident, ha! Somebody killed the dude."

I moved closer. Her harsh eyes stopped me, and I took a step back. "Who would have done such a thing?"

She gave me an incredulous stare. "Haven't you seen all the punks around here?"

"You think a student could have murdered someone?"

"Just like that." Roxy snapped blunt fingers. "Or a teacher."

My chest sank. Yesterday I'd told myself someone here could have killed, but I hadn't really believed it. Not here. Not a student or teacher near my precious Katherine.

"The cops keep on asking us, 'Who'd you see? Where were you when it happened? Right before that? Then afterward?' " Roxy stared at me. "Man, you'd think this was the great inquisition."

I was pleased that she knew such a word. "They're asking all the students?"

"Some of us, some people in the office. Teachers." With a grim face, she peered at the flowers as though needing something positive to hold onto. "I gotta go."

"Roxy, are there any teachers that you believe could have done it?"

I watched the rear of her head, mentally begging her not to say Miss Hernandez.

"Have you checked out Ms. Jeansonne?"

"Abby Jeansonne?"

"And while you're at it, we have a really mean coach." Roxy vacuumed herself through the door with a grim warning, "I didn't say nothing."

The flowers faded as I stared out at them. Maybe my mind was painting a less-than-lovely scene. Abby, my friendly neighbor with bangs. Did she keep them long to hide her eyes so they wouldn't reveal a deadly nature? She'd wanted to make certain I knew about a murder here. I knew some killers wanted lots of recognition. And a school this size must have many coaches. But the one who appeared ready to thrash people stood out in my mind. Of the faculty members Roxy mentioned, I'd give my vote to Coach Millet.

A few students milled outside. I wandered around them, hoping to hear snatches of conversation. If Roxy knew something, surely other kids did, too. I peered at flowers the wind shook and pretended to ignore students, my hearing cranked to high gear. I glanced at the door in case Kat came out. The teens all drifted back inside, and I was left alone. Disappointed not to learn anything new, I was pleased a moment later when the bell rang.

I scuttled inside the building. Some students rushed, while others lounged around, stalling. Most moved to other halls so that the central corridor became maneuverable. An extra-tall, slender woman with blond hair and a shapely denim dress walked a distance ahead of me. "Hi, Miss Hernandez," I called, trotting to catch up. She didn't glance back, so I yelled, "Miss Hernandez. Marisa."

Neither name brought a response. I paused to ask a nearby student, "That is Miss Hernandez, isn't it?" I pointed ahead and saw the woman turn. I had never seen her before.

The boy that I'd asked continued to stare at his arm, where I had just tapped. His face rose toward mine. *Sledge.* Total hatred formed his grimace. "Don't touch me," he snarled.

My eyes widened. "Did that hurt you?" I tapped him again.

Sledge smoldered. He hissed, and his big shoulders spread even wider. In that moment, I knew. This boy-man could knock me to the ground and pummel me until I was dead.

My mouth zapped dry. I took steps away, praying Sledge wouldn't follow. He might be carrying a weapon, and I was certain he could use it. I turned the corner and reached a corridor filled with people. At least if Sledge stalked me here, I might find help.

My glance at surrounding students revealed many that I'd had in yesterday's classes. I doubted whether any of them would come to my aid. A detective emerged from a room, and I breathed easier. The unhappy youth with him was Sledge's buddy who had said I mustn't have heard about what happened between Sledge and the dead man. The young muscular cop scanned the hall. His gaze stopped at Sledge, now leaning against a wall near me, his mean gaze fixing on the cop. The detective wagged a finger to call Sledge, who unglued his back from the wall and followed.

I surmised that they had probably called Sledge's friend in for questioning because of what I'd told the administrators. And now they would question Sledge. Great. Teenagers closed in around Sledge's friend, and I slowed down to listen.

"Those damn cops," the boy said. "We all know who's got keys to get back in this place."

My steps faltered. The sole of my shoe squeaked, and the teens all rolled their heads toward me. They muttered and scattered. I strode to the science hall, considering what I'd gathered thus far today. Anne Little had dubbed herself keeper of the school keys, but today Cynthia Petre gave me my keys. John Winston said he didn't start the rumor that worried Kat, but had he lied? Now that I'd witnessed his anger, I could more easily imagine him as someone who would. The idea of Sledge shoving a person over a balcony rail became conceivable. He would be strong enough. And he could've been here after school hours, almost anyone could have stayed and hidden, it seemed to me, without other persons knowing.

I spied a woman coming to the science hall and wondered where she was heading because I couldn't imagine anyone going to teach looking like that. She was a runt of a person with orange-red hair teased up like an Afro, although she was Caucasian. Her hairdo, even back in the seventies, would've been too extreme. Her face appeared flushed, as though she'd just run a marathon. A suspicious-looking creature if I ever saw one.

I had to stare. Anyone who looked like that wouldn't get embarrassed—she flaunted her differences. I peered directly at her face. She had unashamed big brown eyes and an attractive slender nose. She wore a navy blue suit and on her shoulders, gold buttons. "Oh, damn," I shouted. "I have duty hair!"

Someone snickered. A girl was the last straggler except me. She looked away and went into a classroom, and I returned my attention to the mirror. It was long and wavy like those I used to see in fairs. This one was tinted pink, with a computer-generated sign above: Let Science Straighten You Out.

Okay, so much for my complexion. But the hair—that bush had to go. I ironed my hair down with my hands, straightened and entered my room.

Every youth was seated. Flustered as I was from seeing myself, I attempted a smile. No use. I called roll and handed out worksheets. Teens went right to work. My stomach gurgled. I pressed a hand on it, urging quiet, and recalled Gil's invitation to lunch. His cooks' tasty food. His firm body. I grabbed my handset out of my purse and stepped toward the hall. "How about dinner?" I'd ask him. I'd suggest mid-afternoon.

I tossed my phone back in. Gil would have plans for this special day, with his evening mapped out. Legs was surely included, probably until morning. Or they might be living together. A freckled boy's hand shot up, and I snapped, "Yes?"

"Are you coming back again?"

"No!"

I thought he'd say great, but his eyes saddened. His lips formed a pout. Giving him a thankful smile, I touched his paper, asking what had baffled me all day. "Why is everyone so intent on doing this? Nobody's complaining, and everybody is taking this work seriously."

"We're seniors, and this is practice for our exam next week. We want to graduate, you know."

"I'm sure you do."

"And Miss Fleet told us a sub was coming. She said if we want to pass her exam, we'd better practice. This is tough."

I glanced at his worksheet with letters of the alphabet in various assemblages. "I couldn't do that," I admitted, to which he grinned. "Tell me something," I said, "do you have class with Ms. Jeansonne?" He shook his head, and I asked, "How about Coach Millet?"

"I don't have him either. Why?" He stared at me with innocent baby blues.

"Just wondering if you knew them well." I patted his shoulder and left him to practice. What could I have told him? That Roxy suggested one of those teachers might be connected to a killing? Would I ask if he'd seen them do anything vicious?

I returned to Miss Fleet's chair. This babysitting with honor students wasn't a chore. If I had known how different they were from so many of the horrible kids I'd had yesterday, I would have brought something to read. A novel. Maybe cookbooks. But they would put me to sleep.

Scanning the group, I wished Kat were here. I still had no

idea whether she was at school today. The only sounds in the room were an occasional cough, one sneeze—to which three people muttered "Bless you"—and erasures. I didn't want to interrupt their intent study with more questions. The quiet lulled me into wishing I could nap. I stood, stretched, and rearranged pages of the seating charts. I fingered the roll book. Yanking it open, I skimmed names from the upcoming group.

Gunther, Katherine.

Kat would be in my next class!

CHAPTER 11

I was so excited to find my granddaughter's name on the roster that I almost shouted, until I looked at my hushed students. I closed the roll book. "Yes, ma'am?" a tiny girl said, peering up from a front desk.

Obviously I'd made a little squeal. "Nothing," I said. "Go on, good luck. I can't help, you know. Miss Fleet . . ." She gave a nod. Of course if she believed her teacher had told me not to assist her, I couldn't help that. Not really.

Kat had escaped my notice all day, but I'd been on duty. She would really laugh when I told her about my duty hair. My mirth fled. Miss Hernandez had called her own coiffeur that yesterday. Had Kat been around her today? That's all Kat really needed, for her guru to notice her again. When Kat came in next hour, I'd be able to tell by her demeanor whether she had spoken with Miss Hernandez.

I clutched the roll book. I could check out Kat's grades. The blush I felt rising came from guilt. I shouldn't be doing this but flipped the pages to the next period.

"Where do we put our papers when we finish?" a boy asked.

I shut the roll book and told him. I meandered down rows, smiling. Kat was coming soon.

Class ended, and I stood at the door, bidding students goodbye. I awaited the next group when a reddish mop of hair flipped out from a doorway. Abby Jeansonne stalked out of her room, half-smiling, and came toward me. I shuddered, recalling what

Roxy suggested. "How's it going?" Abby asked.

"Oh, fine." My voice had pitched high. I forced it low, shifting to get more space between us. "How about you?"

"Anything's good on a Friday."

"Fridays are nice," I said, not sharing that I'd long ago decided God was surely a woman, and She had done well to include many Fridays in a year. I watched for Kat, eyeing students heading for my room, and found myself trying to withdraw from Abby. I forced my body to stand still. She wouldn't harm me. She did have an odor, like something scientific that might have come out of a stained lab tube.

"Did you get your absentee list today?" Abby asked.

"I don't think so."

She glanced behind my open door. "Nope, you didn't get one either." Nonchalantly, she sauntered away, and I told myself Roxy was wrong. This woman couldn't physically hurt anyone. My gosh, she was a teacher.

Abby passed up her room, which I noticed no students had entered. Some were coming in mine, so I knew this wasn't a lunch break. Thank goodness. Then I might have duty again. And more duty hair. Abby's mass of hair suddenly whipped to one side as if someone had grasped it and tossed it over. Her head swerved back one hundred eighty degrees. Both of her eyes were uncovered by bangs. Those eyes narrowed, hard and threatening, exactly like those of a vicious cougar on Hannah's office wall. Abby could have also had a long tail to swing at me.

My knees wobbled.

"Hey, teach," a girl said. I glanced down and found someone even shorter than I. She was cute, cocoa-colored, confident. I told her hello, and while other teens filed in, she remained close. "I had to run back for my P.E. clothes after lunch, and I saw you staring in that mirror. You looked funny."

I didn't feel funny at the moment. I swallowed, glancing

toward Abby Jeansonne. The rear of her skirt whipped around the corner.

"The mirror's convex," the girl said. "There's another one that's all squiggly."

"Glad I didn't see that one," I said, and she giggled. I scanned the empty corridor. "Do you know Kat Gunther? Did you see her?"

The self-assured girl strolled into my room, saying, "Kat's not here today."

My voice dulled when I called roll. I wrote *absent* behind Kat's name and when my stomach grumbled, ordered it to shut up. I was here again, but Kat wasn't. All of my efforts at keeping her at school had failed. Minutes into class, I thought of grades. I felt like a criminal but didn't care now. I reopened the roll book.

All of Kat's test grades were A, except for the last one. She'd made a C. Was that after Marisa Hernandez became a suspect? A quick addition and division told me Kat had an A average. In chemistry, wow! I put the roll book away and went to the desk of the nice girl. "If students here miss final exams, what happens to their grades?" I asked.

"Without a medical excuse, we'd make F. Exams count for one-third of our grades."

So if Kat didn't take her chemistry exam, her A average would drop to B, or possibly lower. Her averages in every other class would fall, too. A 3.0 average wouldn't be bad, but wouldn't earn any of the scholarships her parents had hoped she'd receive. Kat's concerns about Miss Hernandez would soon end, but suppose Kat waited until it was too late? What if, during these last few days of her senior year, she ruined all of the grades she had worked for twelve long years to earn? Why did she pick as a mother-image a woman who'd become suspect in a man's death?

Why hadn't she turned to me?

My spirit dulled even more. If I hadn't been so caught up in my own business and life, Kat's problem might not exist. She might be another carefree senior, excitedly looking forward to graduation. I plopped back on the teacher's chair, struggling with grandmother guilt. Was I responsible for Kat's situation? The first time I'd met John Winston, he looked proud to be a senior. Had I overstepped my boundaries by questioning him?

My thoughts were shut down by an emergency system's wail. The continuous high-pitched alarm shot me to my feet. I jumped about, looking for an invader I'd have to protect these children from. They bustled out the door, leaving open books on their desks, most of the students laughing. "What's going on?" I asked a boy walking past.

"Just the fire alarm. Some kid's always pulling it."

I swooped out of the room with him. Throngs of people headed for exit doors. Adults directed traffic in the main corridor. "Should I stay here?" I called to a gaunt woman. "I'm subbing."

"Where's your class?" she shouted. "You have to stay with them."

My class? I peered at the multitude. No students looked familiar. Where the hell was my class?

I sank into the tidal wave of kids shoving out through the doors. On the landing, Hannah Hendrick was speaking to the two policemen I'd seen around. She looked flustered, and I didn't blame her. I'd be furious if some prankster was always disrupting the whole school like this. "It didn't come from the office?" the older detective asked her.

Anne Little and Coach Millet stopped to listen, and Hannah shook her head. She scanned those of us leaving. I hoped she wouldn't notice that I wasn't following people who looked like my students. Where were they? I scanned a sea of people hustling down the steps and gathering around cars on the parking lot. One clump of teens resembled those who'd last been with me. I headed toward them when I caught another part of the conversation. ". . . so we'll dust, but whoever did it probably wrapped his hand with a coat or something."

"Don't they always?" Anne Little asked the detective, and Coach Millet made a grumpy sound.

I paused on a stair, pointing to direct traffic. Big teens who poured past ignored me. A snippet of the detective's words let me know firemen and more police officers were on their way, but they probably wouldn't find whoever pulled the alarm. "So we'll be leaving," he said. "We finished questioning students and teachers."

"And your findings?" Hannah said.

The detective shook his head, and Anne Little told him, "We know you can't tell us everything yet."

A shift of my bent head let me peer beneath the arm I was raising slightly. Anyone might think I was inspecting for deodorant. The officer made a barely perceptible nod exactly like Roger's. What would my son think if he knew I was teaching here? And snooping? I already knew what Gil thought.

Since everyone else had vacated the stairs, I needed to move down. A cluster of teachers, Marisa Hernandez among them, urged students to get farther from the building. Most kids looked glad to obey. Boys were dashing toward what resembled a field house. Coach Millet yelled and turned them away.

I neared Marisa and told her hello. Her copper-brown eyes scanned me, her expression changing to one of recognition. "Oh, hi." She lowered her face toward mine. "Not a nice way for you to spend the afternoon, is it?"

I peered up. Clear pure blue sky. "At least it's not raining," I said, pleased that the mail truck wouldn't be leaking again.

"It's really not fun being stuck out here in the middle of a downpour."

I couldn't fathom that. If a child pulled a fire alarm during a thunderstorm, I would find that kid and—

"It's a shame we can't find out who does it," Marisa said.

"They never know?" I asked. She shook her head, and I noticed that in the wind Marisa's tresses, like mine, once more began to resemble "duty hair." Except her hair was blond. Mine was—whatever color I chose to make it. That thought made me cheerful. This had been my first day to experience duty, and also to participate in what I'd thought might be a fire drill here but wasn't. Pranksters. I'd never have to be caught in the midst of them again.

And some people here, I thought, skimming a plethora of faces, could be much more. I spied John Winston in one group, Sledge with his buddies in another. Some of these youths and teachers might be thieves. Or killers. We were down on the grass, but I felt the wide-open space surrounding me close in. My gaze ran up. The woman whose arm brushed on mine might have committed a fresh murder.

"Are you cold?" Marisa asked.

"No." I forced my voice bigger. "Why?"

She smiled, her hair whipping about her denim-clad shoulders. "You have goose skin." Marisa touched my forearm. New bumps sprouted, and she grinned. I didn't think it was so funny.

Rhomp, rhomp, rhomp sounded from the building. The hair on my neck sprang out. A new emergency?

"That was the all-clear horn," Marisa said. "We need to go back inside."

Youths whooped while returning up the stairs. Some jeered, saying whoever pulled the alarm needed to do it again so they could stay outside longer. "We need a bomb threat," a girl said.

I spun around. Roxy had spoken. To my stunned expression,

she lifted a shoulder and said, "Hey, we get those all the time."

By the time I reached my room, Anne Little's voice came through the speaker. "Everybody return to class. Get your books, then report to your next period."

The students returning to my room griped. The interruption had disrupted their work, and they hadn't had time to complete their practice worksheets.

"Take them home," I said, happy to see them concerned. "I'll leave Miss Fleet a note about the fire alarm. Good luck on your finals."

The seniors thanked me, took their papers and went out. I propped against the doorjamb for support. What new person or event would come to greet me now? What purpose would it serve a student who'd set off that fire alarm? And why, I wondered, watching Abby taking a stance outside her classroom, would sane adults want to do this?

I speculated about those who pursued the teaching profession today. If they knew what they were getting into, what was in their personalities that made them want to suffer? *Did you actually think you could do some good?* my thoughts asked Abby and all the teachers that I couldn't see who were probably standing outside their doors. *Are you a martyr? Or insane?*

I peered at students shuffling into Abby's room. Some shrieked with laughter, and big guys shoved each other's shoulders. Only two or three of the young adults wore serious faces. *So this is our future,* I thought, my spirits further draining. I needed to bolster them.

Searching for positives, I recalled all that Kat had achieved during her school years. And I thought of those pleasant kids who'd come into this classroom today. My new ardor surprised me. There *were* some good teens. Many came seeking learning. Even those like Roxy showed up at school for something. Most of these youths were old enough to drop out if they chose to,

but they stayed. Maybe those who behaved so badly were only experiencing a temporary period of instability.

Abby swooped into her room behind her final student. Her door slammed.

No one had come to my room. I took a breath, walked over to Abby's door and rapped on it. She shoved it open, and I said, "I don't have any students."

"You're off now."

"Off?" My enthusiasm soared. "I can leave?"

"Of course you can't leave. It's Fleet's conference period. She'd meet with parents or plan lessons or grade papers."

I was off! Parents? I'd like to meet some. I'd suggest what they could do with their kids. But some parents might not own chains.

I returned to my classroom, shut the door, peered across empty desks and science equipment, and welcomed the silence. Whoever created conference periods in the midst of teachers' hectic days had done a wonderful job. Sitting on Miss Fleet's chair, I folded my arms on her desk and dropped my head. I closed my eyes, trying to form absolute quiet in my brain. I needed to sort through what was happening. There was no Kat, my main problem. Why wasn't she here?

I envisioned Marisa, apparently friendly and so tall. She might prove to have murdered the custodian, but Sledge's murder-filled countenance entered my mind. Other faces crowded in. Coach Millet, always looking on the verge of killing someone. And Roxy cast a doubt about him and Abby, maybe connecting them? But Roxy also pulled a knife on Kat. Roxy and Anne Little both had scars. Miss Gird normally followed Coach. Did she teach with him, or maybe have a crush on him? Were they having an affair?

Someone I didn't know could have done the killing. Or maybe Grant Labruzzo just leaned too far over the balcony rail and fell. The police seemed to believe that. Jayne Ackers, a sub, had been shot near her home. Coincidence?

My fingers rubbed circles on my forehead, and I squeezed my eyes tighter. I envisioned Gil. How I wished I could discuss all of this with him. Today was May third, and one thing was certain. I'd try to see him within a couple of hours. Heat spread through my body. I stopped it, reminding myself that he might not be there. Gil and the young woman with long legs surely had other plans.

I sighed, my knuckles massaging my warm eye sockets, and replaced Gil's image with Roger's. Such a sad picture. How excruciating to watch my son becoming a shell of a man without Nancy. I groaned, and tears soaked my fingers. We all loved Nancy, and I wished I could get her back, but couldn't . . . Roger kept refusing counseling—but *I* could get some. Sure, I could go to a therapist and learn how to help him. I'd find one with really good credentials. Maybe I'd fly out and locate Dr. Phil.

Just one thing seemed absolute. Kat had to attend graduation, even if she missed exams and her average dropped to the bottom half of her class. She needed to walk across a stage for a piece of paper. For Nancy, for Roger, for herself.

Reputed experts, I knew, usually assured people that meditation was good for the soul, but my soul was aching, along with my head. It felt too heavy to lift.

A slight sound came from the door. Creaks told me it was opening. Chilly air in the room warmed. I anticipated a student saying she had forgotten something.

I wanted to look up, but a vague intuition told me to wait, listen. After all, there was some mystery to be solved here. And this moment felt mysterious.

The door rubbed against the floor's vinyl. I could take only so much pondering. I lifted my head.

Change in air pressure came with the door's slam. I jumped up and headed for the door. Behind me, glass shattered.

A picture had fallen, knocking a beaker off a shelf. Liquid pooled on the floor. Noxious fumes rose.

I grabbed the doorknob and found it slick, impossible to turn. Somebody had locked my door.

The spilled chemical on the floor clogged my nostrils, its vapor shooting a flood of tears to my eyes. I grabbed the doorknob with both hands and twisted. My palms burned, vision blurred. "Help! Help me!" I screamed, pounding on the door, an irritant raging in my lung and not letting me breathe.

The string. That dangling string. I rushed behind the teacher's desk and pulled. "Somebody's trying to kill me!" I yelled at the wall speaker. "Can anybody hear? Help!"

CHAPTER 12

Without pause, my door opened. I darted out the room, my arms flailing. I bent over and gasped, inhaling the hall's nontoxic air.

John Winston stood holding my doorknob and grinning. Teenagers and teachers filled the narrow hall. A few people looked frightened for me, but most of the kids were laughing. Abby came, a big key ring in her hand. "What's the problem here?"

"They tried to murder me! Somebody locked me in and tried to get me with poisonous fumes."

She turned to John Winston. "How did you get her door open?"

He shrugged. "I just turned the knob."

Abby swept in past me, ignoring my warning: "Don't go in there. That room's deadly!" She snatched up a shard of beaker glass. On part of its wet label I read *sulfide*.

"This isn't toxic," Abby said, her lower lip folding down, telling me maybe she'd have liked it to be. She ordered her students back to class and sent John to get a janitor with a mop bucket. "The smell won't kill you," Abby said, bangs flinging away with her head turn. I saw both of her eyes and they said *You're so stupid.*

"They put that stuff in fart rocks," a grinning boy said to me.

"Fart rocks?" I asked.

Abby ignored the teens' snickers. "They're little rocks that some kids throw down in the halls, and they smell like—" She scrunched up her nose.

Teachers beyond the laughing kids grumbled about me interrupting their reviews for final exams. "Some kid pulls the fire alarm and now this," a well-dressed man griped. I spread my arms and opened my palms. Well what did I know?

A lot, I remembered. I knew much about human nature. Maybe I lacked knowledge about chemicals, but not about people. Someone had opened my door, peered in at me, and then slammed the door hard enough to knock down a picture and the beaker. Who did that? And why?

My grandma used to talk about her step-ins. I paid particular heed to mine now, then recalled I wasn't wearing any. I was pleased to determine that no dribble ran down my pantyhose.

Harry Wren came shouldering through the crowd. He stopped and calmly appraised me. "You had an emergency?"

I shook my head. "Not really." He'd obviously come because I pulled that string and shouted at the office. He glanced at students standing around, and they started back toward their classrooms. An idea came. I said, "You're a guidance counselor, Mr. Wren. Do you usually handle problems in the classrooms?"

His eyes looked like pinpricks in his tanned skin. "Tom Reynolds ordinarily takes care of—situations. But he didn't come to school today." People returned to classes, and Harry Wren left.

On instinct I questioned a student who was heading toward Abby's room. "I imagine that I stopped Ms. Jeansonne from teaching your class some important material?"

"When you started yelling, she wasn't even in the room. But she has a key that opens all the doors in this hall. She would've let you out—if you really would've been locked in." The girl gave me a cocky smirk.

I could have given her fat cheek some firm pats. The child was intelligent enough to go away.

What do you do when you believe someone's just tried to kill you? I considered, standing alone, my arms stopping their quiver and my pulse slowing.

I decided. *Eat lunch.* My belly made little squeals, and I headed for the cafeteria. Food from Cajun Delights could later become a mid-afternoon snack.

The halls no longer seemed a maze. I knew exactly where to locate the room emitting pepperoni smells. I could eat a good pizza. Would they have mushrooms and black olives?

A sign taped to the door said *Closed.* I hit the door and tried to shove it open. I'd rustle up at least one slice of pizza, even if it was only plain. But the cafeteria was locked down. I yanked my cell phone from my purse. I'd have a pizza delivered. Lots of black olives. Pile on the mushrooms.

I pressed zero for Information, reconsidered, and clicked off. The school day would soon be over. I'd wait. Then I could go ahead with my plans to eat at Gil's place. It seemed that I was supposed to do something else right after school, but I couldn't recall what. I tossed Tic Tacs in my mouth and turned away from the cafeteria.

The auditorium doors stood in front of me. Tension squeezed through my upper abdomen. I didn't want to look in that room. Grant Labruzzo died in there.

Nobody else was in this hall.

I stepped across, fighting the sudden urge to go to the restroom. I clasped a door handle and yanked. The door opened.

Total darkness swelled. I tiptoed inside, keeping a hand on the door to keep it from closing all the way. I couldn't see a light switch. It was probably hidden so that students wouldn't flick the lights off and on. A hollowed quiet reverberated. I could make out a short flight of stairs leading to a landing. A wall flanked an open door there and probably beyond that was a huge space that held many seats. A podium in front. And up above me, a balcony. I could go all the way in and try to determine where Grant Labruzzo fell.

I needed to go to the restroom. There was no way I was going up near a balcony. And in the dark? Two scares today had been enough for me. I backed out the room, went to the restroom and took care of my bladder.

Cynthia Petre was the sole person in the office's outer area when I reached it. She sat at her desk and muttered, staring at her monitor and punching computer keys. Miss Gird hurled herself in from the corridor and ranted to Petre. I passed them and entered the rear administrative hall. A clipping of the death notice was still posted near a door. I stopped to read.

Grant Labruzzo, originally of Coral Gables, Florida, had been only thirty-seven when he died. How horrible to lose someone so young. He was survived by two brothers but neither parent. Gosh, they'd died young, too. Labruzzo's wake had been brief, from eight until ten in the morning at All Believers' Church, followed by the service.

He'd lived near Marisa Hernandez, Abby told me. Maybe this evening I could ride by their houses and discern some connection.

I returned to the outer office. Miss Gird was gone, but other secretaries had returned to their computers past Cynthia Petre's. They carried scents of roasted chicken, which I imagined they'd just eaten. My stomach growled. Petre glanced at it.

"May I use your phone book?" I asked.

I reached for it, but she lifted the book and handed it to me. "Here."

I turned so no one could see where I looked and searched for a listing for Grant Labruzzo. Bunches of L's. Not even one Labruzzo. Most staff members here probably had unlisted numbers, and I didn't blame them. I wouldn't want some of the students I'd met knowing where I lived.

Cynthia Petre stared at me, her wire-bound teeth not showing. She held out a hand.

"Thanks," I said, shutting the phone book. She snatched it from me and carefully set it down behind the frame holding John Winston's photo.

I returned to the rear hall and skimmed words on the obituary, then stared at the picture. Such a handsome young man. Sincere eyes and a trace of what his full smile must have looked like. A head of thick dark hair. A lost future.

Cynthia Petre bumped into me. She'd come from the office. "Oh, you backed up when I was passing." She turned toward where I'd been staring and peered at Grant's picture. Strangely, moisture coated her eyes.

"Did you know him well?" I asked.

She glanced at me. "Grant was a friend." She started away, and I walked with her.

"That's a nice shade on you," I said, nodding toward her brown blouse. "It highlights your rosy complexion." Her lips had been tight, but they drew apart, her smile revealing the braces. I returned the keys she had given me. "I won't need these anymore."

She slid them into her skirt pocket and brushed at a blue smudge near her waistline. "Somebody left an open pen on the edge of my desk, and I rubbed against it."

"School must be the place to get lots of smudges," I said with a grin.

Petre looked at me with no expression. She turned and entered the administrative restroom. Tiny Miss Gird came out.

"My granddaughter is in your class," I said.

"What's her name?"

My chest swelled. "Katherine Gunther."

Miss Gird's eyes seemed to lose their vision while she apparently did a mental roll call. "Oh yes. Second period, third row."

She strode away.

"Kat's been a great student," I told her skinny backside.

"All of my students are."

Not according to your fury, I wanted to tell her. But I didn't need to get any of Kat's teachers angry with her now. What I really wanted was to hear bragging about Kat. I needed to know what would keep her in school these final days. Continuing down the hall, I glanced in Hannah's office. She was holding a phone, waiting for someone. I poked my head in. "Do you get to see Kat often?"

"Every once in a while."

"She is a good student, isn't she?"

"All teachers wish they had classes full of students like Kat."

I stood, letting pride fill me. Hannah replied to someone on the phone, and I ambled down the hall, glancing in rooms with open doors. Adults worked their computers, with papers and files spilling across their desks. A few unhappy teens filled their extra chairs.

All these inner workings appeared foreign, yet similar to my recollections that these rooms evoked. Ceilings had been higher when I was a child, with dark wooden desks and doors and wall panels. The changing times had brought new schools, modern equipment, and maybe more knowledge. One thing I definitely would've wanted to see retained was the respect that all kids showed when I was a student.

"Minnie!" I cried, spying my cactus in an office.

The light was on, the door open, room vacant. I walked in.

"May I help you?" The man who entered behind me wore a suit. He appraised me when I turned and then said, "Oh, you again."

"I'm Cealie Gunther. Yes, Mr. Wren, you came to my class when I pulled the string. And we met yesterday when you were on duty in the hall."

"Guidance counselors don't pull duty," he said as though I'd insulted him. "I was just coming from lunch and stopped to talk to the students."

Or scare them? He'd been carrying that heavy spirit stick.

"I thought this cactus was mine." I touched the plant with a pink head that sat on a wall shelf lit by spotlights. The cactus stood amid a grouping of others. Clay pots held individual cacti. Bowls held assortments. Some spindly cacti had ridges, short scaly ones had minute flowers, and some plants with circular leaves bore spears.

Harry Wren admired this assemblage.

"But this plant's not exactly like Minnie," I said. "I see it has three of these pink poufs around its head. Minnie has five."

"They might have any number of these tufts." Wren placed a hand gently on the plant.

"Those things make me think of sponge hair rollers," I said.

He didn't seem to hear my words. Harry Wren stroked his cacti, one after the other, almost like a parent might do with a newborn. But he had bunches of them.

"These plants are easy to grow," I mentioned.

"Yes, but they need the right conditions. The proper soil. Container. Nourishment."

"But if one of them is already in a pot from the nursery, all you have to do is dump water on it sometimes, right?"

"Oh no! You need the right proportions of everything. And never just dump water. And not often. Too much would kill it."

Uh-oh. I wouldn't dare ask what ailment cranberry juice might create.

"And that man killed my perfect Cero," he said, his tone solemn.

I touched his shoulder and said, "I am so sorry." I had no idea what he was talking about, but his face had creased with wretchedness.

Wren shook his head. "He knocked her down."

"Couldn't you have just put her back up?"

His face snapped toward me.

"Mr. Wren?" A weepy-eyed teenage girl stood at the door. "Can I talk to you?"

He nodded and gave a final glance to his cactus garden.

"Nice plants. You know a lot," I said, ready to walk away but deciding to touch what looked like hard stickers on some wide leaves. They pricked my finger. I drew my hand away.

Harry Wren stopped walking toward the distraught girl. He stared at me, looking haughty. "I have been an active member of the Cactus-Growers Society for many years. I study the on-line malls, view all the galleries."

"Wow," was all I could say as I strolled out. The girl sulked in, and his door shut.

Since Mr. Wren was a counselor, maybe I should ask him for suggestions about keeping Kat in classes. Possibly after he spoke to that troubled student. And after he got over his misery about somebody killing his plant. I ambled away, wondering whether Minnie got lonesome while she was alone at the condo. Lots of pets became lonely. Did plants?

Harry Wren had made me feel guilty, acutely aware that I needed to learn more about my sidekick, Minnie, if she was going to accompany me on my current journey toward locating myself. Minnie was my acquiescence to keeping loved ones with me. Of course I'd only bought her a few days ago, so we hadn't yet totally connected. But that was coming. Minnie and I were friends, I mentally asserted, striding to the end of the rear office hall. She listened as well as my dearest neighbor I'd left behind. If I pampered her enough, maybe one day she'd learn to love me as much as Gil had and all the members of my family.

I stopped, overcome by a tremendous sense of loss.

What price was I paying for my newfound freedom? Was it

worth what I gained?

"Yes," I said, nudging aside the self-doubts. I couldn't remain around my family members, hoping I could solve each of their troubles, which in turn would make my life feel more meaningful. I had finally begun to discover what made me unique and why Cealie mattered. I'd shrugged off that image of myself as a wounded half of what had once been a happily married couple. Then Gil had added to my joy. But Gil knew exactly what he wanted from his life. I wasn't certain about mine yet, but I kept learning. If I gave up my independence to stay with him, I'd never get to totally know me.

A burnt-coffee odor inundated my space. *Clack-clack-clack* came from a room across the way. I headed for it, remembering that my final teaching day was almost over. The last bell would soon ring. I passed four students with a teacher. Even the grimaces they all wore couldn't stop my smile from appearing. TEACHERS' LOUNGE said bold letters above the door up ahead. My own instructors used to disappear into mysterious rooms labeled with those words. Clearly, students were never allowed entrance.

I'd always wondered what was in such forbidden rooms and what our adored teachers did inside. Did they plan all the marvelous lessons they'd teach us? My child-mind had imagined them sharing stories of all our splendid deeds. When I taught, we did speak kindly about our students while we took breaks in the lounge that was nicely decorated with pictures of landscapes and new comfortable furnishings. Now as I opened the door and entered this teachers' private space, I hoped to find adults who might lead me to understand more about Kat's behavior and any connection to the dead man.

A slim woman in a long purple dress hunched over a noisy copy machine, running off papers. Her snarled hair needed washing. Another woman with a double chin and a black lightweight jacket sat at a round table, using a red pen to grade papers. Her opposite hand held a sandwich. She absently ate and purposefully graded.

The coffee stench came from an empty carafe sitting on a burner, the red light still on. Another copy machine stood near the one being used. Two long tables resembled dumping grounds for unwanted cups and magazines. Mail cubbyholes flanked a far wall. A bulletin board posted notices from earlier in the year. Mismatched stuffed chairs and a pair of old sofas cluttered the room. A hand reached up from the sofa I stood behind. The hairy-knuckled hand waved back at me.

I rounded the sofa and found a large man with sparse graying hair stretched across it. "You're new," he said. I introduced myself, and he scooted over, flinging a hand out to shake mine. "Brad McClellen." His twang said he wasn't from around this area. "That's Millie at the machine and Deidre at the table."

The ladies gave me an unenthusiastic hi, barely missing a beat with their papers.

"Everybody always seems so busy here," I said, settling down beside Brad. At the machine Millie nodded, her moving lips indicating she was counting pages. "Have you been at Sidmore High long?" I asked Brad.

"Much too long, mainly teaching some math classes."

"Do you happen to know my granddaughter, Katherine Gunther?"

"Absolutely. But never had the pleasure of teaching her."

"I did." At the table, Deidre smiled. "I had Kat for American history. Wonderful girl."

Millie's mouth recited silent numbers. Apparently the counter was broken.

"Did Kat get close to any of the staff?" I asked, hoping to bait anyone who might give me more information than I'd been able to glean thus far.

Millie glanced toward me, her pale eyes widening. I looked at Brad. He was giving away nothing. "Marisa," Deidre said, her lips tightening.

"Marisa Hernandez," I said. "Yes, I met her. She seems like a pleasant person."

The women's heads swiveled toward each other. The copier stopped. It started clicking again. Deidre's red pen made angry marks. Brad McClellen smoothed his thin hair and looked at me. "Have the police talked to you?"

"Should they?"

His noncommittal gaze held on me. "Brad," Millie called. "This damn thing is stuck again."

"Patience, Millie." Brad sauntered to her silent machine and opened a side panel. "Just another paper jam."

"That's all we do around here," Millie snapped, "try to be patient. With the office. With the kids and the cops—" She noticed me staring and then hurled around to her papers. Muttering curses, she dared the machine not to work again.

"Some people get frustrated," Brad said, joining me on the sofa. He repositioned himself, spreading his arms and legs.

"But you don't," I observed.

"No use. Nobody'd listen anyway."

"You can say that again," Deidre uttered. Millie's harrumph, I figured, was a ditto.

"What can the administrators do?" I asked. "Do they have enough clout to make much difference?"

Brad shook his head. "Not much they can change."

"Not much," Deidre commented, red ink smearing those papers.

"And the police," I said, determined to turn this talk back around. "About the dead man."

"Aw, him." Brad shifted on the sofa. "That was bad."

"But that was one guy who couldn't even empty a trash can," Millie said.

"Oh now, Millie." Brad's drawl made this almost one word.

"It's true, Grant did a crappy job of cleaning up around here." Millie turned from the machine. "He left spitballs between desks and paper on the floor. And all he had to do was push a dust mop."

"And empty our trash cans," Deidre said. "And half the time, he missed that."

Millie stomped over to Brad McClellen. "You tell me, did he always get your can empty?"

"Maybe he missed it a time or two, but we all forget some things."

"Right," Millie said, "nobody's perfect. But that man missed his profession. It certainly wasn't being a janitor." She returned to the machine, slapped a button, and pages spit from the copier. Some flew to the floor. "Damn machine," Millie sputtered. She must've had on one of those shove-up bras because when she leaned forward, her cleavage shoved up to her throat.

"That fellow hadn't been around here long," Brad said to me. "He was friendly, a nice-looking youngster."

Millie scooped up her papers. "But all those people from that warehouse church are crazy."

I wondered what she meant and surmised something else. "Grant Labruzzo must have been the person who knocked down Harry Wren's plant," I said.

"Harry Wren. The man's nuts about his stupid cactuses," Deidre said.

A fighting instinct surprised me. How dare she call cactuses stupid? I forced myself to calm and addressed Brad. "Do you know why the plant died?"

"Yeah, everybody heard about it. We were out for spring break. Grant passed his mop in Harry's office, and the handle knocked that thing over. Grant scooped up the dirt and the plant, and he threw 'em away. The damned thing just looked like a bunch of vines anyway."

Deidre snorted. "It was the one time Grant really cleaned."

"How could anyone just throw away a cactus?" I said, considering Minnie.

Brad peered at me as though I were weird. He faced the women. "Wonder why Tom's not here today. He's never absent."

Neither woman responded, and I recalled the curious reaction I'd seen moments ago in the rear hall. "Brad," I said, "was Cynthia Petre a close friend of Grant Labruzzo's?"

Millie snickered. "Didn't she wish?"

The bell rang, and Millie cursed in response. Deidre muttered oaths of her own. She dumped papers into her book sack. I said, "We're done now?"

Brad shoved himself up. "One class left to go."

"Dammit, another class," I said without thinking. I calmed myself. I had one other question to ask. "Do the doors to any of your classrooms ever get stuck?"

"Nope," Brad said. The women only scowled while dealing with their papers.

I walked out. Pausing to glance back, I sadly realized that disillusionment had replaced my earlier nostalgia. It seemed that as teens had changed, so had teachers. Surely some, like Brad McClellen, would still say positive things about their students. And maybe their co-workers would, too, when they weren't harried like those I saw. But everyone in this place constantly seemed to be going at a hectic pace, all except McClellen. Maybe Harry Wren.

I made my way back through halls, my belly making little yowls. I sucked on a peppermint and stood outside my classroom, noticing Abby's door was shut, the slit beneath it dark. Annoying questions filled my mind. Where had Abby been when someone opened my door, peered in on me, and slammed my door hard enough to make a vial break? Had that person known it would happen? Was my room safe now?

Gingerly, I opened my door.

Fresh air rushed in behind flapping mini-blinds. A wide area of floor in front of the room looked damp. The glass shards were gone. Einstein's picture that had fallen again hung on the wall. No foul odors remained. No poisons to choke students. No signs of what had transpired.

Apprehension registered in my brain. I couldn't hear any students or their noises approaching.

Surely I wasn't lucky enough to have *two* conference periods. Where were all of the students and other teachers?

Loud voices resounded from a distance. I rushed down the hall toward them and careened around a corner to the main corridor, running smack into a mob. I shrank back. Riot?

"Get back!" a man yelled. The thick wall of students didn't budge. Teens crowded together, facing a room that stank. I tried nudging through the young adults, and the voices surrounding me swelled. Between people's heads, I could make out emergency workers backing from a small room.

"Everybody get to class!" Hannah called.

Anne Little motioned with her arms. "Back up! Give them room!"

Students shifted when someone forced a path to let the others get through. I'd been on tiptoe but began making small jumps so I could see above shoulders of those who'd abruptly grown quiet. Policemen and women forced spectators further away. People in uniform moved into the room that was emitting chemical smells. A strong odor of bleach filled my nostrils. "Let her through," a cop hollered.

"Clear this hall!" others ordered, moving the crowd. I was pulled away with the wall of kids. Tears stung my eyes, and my nose ran. I was reacting to foul smells the room gave off.

"Will she be all right?" a whimpering girl asked.

I spied the stretcher. What my limited view let me see made my whole body tremble. A blanket partially covered a woman who wasn't moving. Her blond hair reached denim-clad shoulder.

Marisa Hernandez!

CHAPTER 13

Emergency workers rushed her past me. I had a clearer view of the woman, and although oxygen tubes stuck out of her nostrils and blocked part of her face, I was certain of one thing: she wasn't Marisa Hernandez. She was the person I'd seen earlier whom I had thought was Marisa. Both of them had pale blond hair and wore denim today.

"Who is that?" I asked any of the numerous students surrounding me.

Teens jabbered to each other. "Man, she might be dead."

"Yeah, maybe."

"No, they'd cover her face if she died."

I stared directly into a girl's wide brown eyes. "Who was that?"

She sniffled. "Mrs. Peekers."

Police blocked off the fetid room down the hall and the area outside it with yellow tape. Others joined teachers to shoo away students. In a reassuring tone, Anne Little told the teens backing up that they would learn about what had occurred, and the kids quieted to hear. "We don't know what happened yet," she said. There would be an investigation. Then everyone would be told. "In the meantime, you have one more class. And remember, seniors, exams start Monday."

Groans echoed off the walls. Students moved off, wondering aloud what happened to this teacher. Hannah told a group she'd be coming to Mrs. Peekers's room. A few teens and teachers stood talking, but most moseyed toward classrooms. I glanced at the school's front doors, where the last white outfits turned and rolled Mrs. Peekers down a ramp.

Sirens wailed, and big girls near me cried. From the end of the corridor, I watched a man snapping pictures of what appeared to be a custodians' supply room. Outside the room, a liquid wet the floor. Custodians thrust huge fans into the area and turned them on. Beside the room stood cardboard boxes, the flaps on two of them open.

A policeman ordered the rest of us back to classes. I hurried to my room. Students spoke loudly while they neared. I saw the girl that I'd spoken to outside Abby's room and asked her about Mrs. Peekers.

"She teaches English. She went in the janitors' room to get an eraser and somebody locked the door."

Goose bumps sprouted on my arms. "Locked in—just like me."

The child frowned. "You just didn't turn the knob all the way."

"Yes, I did." My statement made the girl look annoyed. "But why was Mrs. Peekers on a stretcher?" I asked.

Another girl turned and said, "Some kind of cleaning stuff spilled under the door."

"What cleaning stuff?"

"I don't know, but I'll bet whoever left those boxes there is gonna be in real trouble."

My animated students had become too riled. I made them sit, assured them Mrs. Peekers would be all right, and gave out worksheets. It took a while for everyone to calm and get to work. Then I stared over their heads, my thoughts reeling. Was what happened to Mrs. Peekers and Grant Labruzzo related? And someone *had* locked me in this room. The purpose?

I envisioned the woman I'd first thought was Marisa Hernandez, lying motionless on that stretcher. Spasms jerked through my stomach. What the hell was I doing in this place? I felt weak, with a headache looming. Hunger? Or fumes from out there and earlier inside this room? I wanted Kat away from this school!

The final bell rang. The kids went out, and I scribbled a note for Miss Fleet. *Nice students. Completed worksheets are on the side table. I let one class take theirs home to complete because a fire alarm shortened their period. A beaker accidentally broke in here.* I signed the sheet, left it on her desk and scanned the room. How different without students. With a skeleton, formulas, and scientific posters, the classroom appeared a center of learning. I noted the quiet. And then the door, making certain it had remained open.

I went out and shut it. I'd already returned the keys.

In a hall, girls wearing shorts practiced cheers. Boys wore baseball uniforms and lugged smelly canvas bags, following a coach. Teachers flocked, peering at the now cordoned-off hall area. I waved to the male and the female custodian pushing wide dust mops. Two men I didn't recognize sauntered ahead of me. Marisa Hernandez fell into step at my side. "How did it go today?" she asked, glancing at my face and my hair.

I remembered the duty hair and swept my hand across it, feeling one section patch up. "Routine, I imagine." We exchanged small laughs that said we both knew what my day had been like. "I hope Mrs. Peekers will be all right," I said, eyeing Marisa for her reaction.

She stared at me, making a grim nod. Her eyes showed compassion. I wasn't afraid of this person. She touched my hand. "I've been so fortunate to have gotten to know Kat."

I really liked Marisa.

She gave my hand a squeeze. "I know Kat's worried about me." A flicker of concern reached her eyes. Something captured her attention, and her hand slipped off mine. Three uniformed police officers were striding toward the office. Marisa looked at me. "Please tell her I'll be all right."

"Couldn't you tell her yourself? Kat really misses getting to talk to you."

Marisa's gaze flitted toward the officers. "I'll try. I'm glad I met you, Mrs. Gunther."

"I'm glad, too." We exchanged smiles with closed lips. She took off toward an exit, its doors propped wide open. I liked the way some teens yelled, "Bye, Miss Hernandez," and she called back to them. I truly loved the way she'd helped my granddaughter. And I hoped like hell she wasn't a killer.

Turning away, I almost rammed into Abby Jeansonne.

"One of those," she said, eyeing Marisa. To Abby's silly expression, I merely grinned and walked past. "Just like Kat," she said.

I spun around. "What do you mean, just like Kat?"

"She's one of those, too."

"One of those *what?*"

Abby shoved her bangs aside. "Females that Grant liked."

"Grant—Labruzzo?"

Abby's nod flipped the bangs over her eyes. She started away, but I caught up and grabbed her hand. "What do you mean, he *liked* them? Not Kat?"

"She and John Winston broke up, didn't they?" Abby yanked her hand away from mine and stormed off.

Implications of her statements froze me in place. I needed to talk to Kat.

"Damn kids can't even drink their crap or throw their papers in here!" a lanky man holding a dust mop complained to a male teacher. The custodian indicated empty chip bags lying around a trash barrel. Dark liquid spilled from dumped cola cans.

Little gratification must come from his job. And he and a couple of others had to clean this entire school. I couldn't imagine. "Now I'm going to have to mop all this," the custodian said, although the other man had walked off. "Aw, crap, I can't go in there." He'd turned toward the room holding his supplies, the entire hall blocked off with police tape. Numerous fans blew toward an exit.

On a whim I spoke. "Are custodial supplies kept anywhere else in this school?"

He peered at me, his face clouded. Was I some foreign creature? He stared as though I were and then jerked around, dragging his mop to some other place.

Could Mrs. Peekers have gone somewhere else to find clean erasers? And would the same thing have happened in that room if someone besides her had been inside?

Grant Labruzzo liked Kat? And he liked Marisa, Abby said. Earlier, she'd mentioned Anne Little as "One of those."

I opened my cell phone. Kat answered on the third ring. "You weren't at school," I said, experiencing mixed feelings about that fact.

"No," she said, unapologetically, "I wasn't."

I waited until a young couple holding hands walked past me. "Kat, was Grant Labruzzo interested in you?"

"What do you mean?"

"Did he ever flirt with you?"

"No. Where'd you get that idea?"

"I just thought . . ."

"Gram, I really need to go."

I reminded Kat that I loved her and let her click off. I wanted to sit in a corner and dwell on all I had learned. More students and teachers moved past, glancing back at me. I was standing in the hall, staring at my phone. I put it away and headed for the office.

Had someone tried to kill that teacher? A chemical could have accidentally fallen over, but she'd been locked in that room, just like I'd been in mine. Hair on my arms sprang up. Were our locked doors connected to the custodian's death?

Kat would surely tell me the truth about him showing her any interest.

A group of students hustled out an exit door, and others scrambled in. New voices came from girls carrying tennis rackets. They headed toward another exit. Today so many people were scurrying about after school hours. How could anyone have found Grant Labruzzo alone and killed him?

My mind whirled around questions and the day's unsettling events as I reached the office and barreled past the counter. Only Anne Little was left, except for a few students waiting for a phone. I stared at them, and Anne told me they needed rides home. She blew her nose and sounded hoarse.

"Today was kind of nice," I told her. "Except for the emergencies."

She shook her head, making the gold hoops on her ears swing. "Kids will be kids. They aren't happy unless somebody's pulling a fire alarm or dumping things. And now my sinuses are driving me crazy."

The teens near the phone frowned at her.

"I hope that teacher will be okay," I said.

"Me, too. What a stupid accident."

I watched the students, their changed expressions suggesting they didn't believe the latest incident was accidental. They saw me watching and took on stony expressions. Hannah's voice emerged, along with a man's. Policemen came with her from the rear hall. They were speaking about Mrs. Peekers. The oldest cop noted people out here and changed topics. "We'll see about who pulled that fire alarm," he said. His gaze skimmed the waiting students as if searching for information.

I headed out. Exiting propped-open doors, I inhaled. Fresh air expanded through my lungs.

"Thank God duty's over," one woman told another. Beyond her, the last students climbed into a bus that squealed and rumbled off.

Duty. Duty hair. My lunchtime duty and—I'd missed afternoon bus duty!

I rushed toward the students' parking lot. Only about two dozen vehicles remained. No smashed bodies on the ground. *Excellent.* I took bouncing steps toward my mail truck. I was glad I hadn't taken that final duty. I'd done enough. I was famished.

Gil would be especially cheerful on his birthday. That would make me happy, at least for a short time, even if he was going off with Legs. I needed to call Chicken Boy to finalize my gift.

Bliss filled me while I neared the mail truck. "Yes!" I shouted, throwing my arms up. I was free to leave and never had to return to a school.

My vehicle sat like a big chartreuse box as I walked closer, drawing out the key.

A red marker had scrawled across my door LEAVE OR DIE BITCH.

Seeing the stark crimson letters bleeding across my mail truck's ugly green, I cursed and spun around, searching for anyone who could have written this.

In a field near the parking lot, boys practiced baseball. I couldn't see anyone around the school's extension that housed the swimming pool. Across a narrow road, girls slammed tennis balls across nets. Hard to imagine any of them writing this graffiti. Easy to envision Sledge, with a stolen red marker, penning these mean words on my vehicle. *My* vehicle? I already had one car in a shop for repairs.

I slung myself into the mail truck and slammed the door so hard that anybody around would know I was furious. I cranked the engine and sped out of the lot. Whatever the school board paid substitute teachers wouldn't be nearly enough to cover my repair bills. What had I done to warrant all this vandalism?

The Lexus wouldn't be ready yet, and I couldn't bring this truck to the same repair shop. Explaining the damage to both was beyond what I wanted.

I drove around until I found a decent-looking repair center. I told the man with a broken front tooth that some kid who thought he was clever wrote this. "How long till you can repaint it?" I asked.

He rolled his eyes up as though the answer were inside his eyelid. "Couple a days, if I can match this color. You got insurance?"

I said I'd pay cash and left my phone number and address. Then I strode across a boulevard and walked the long block to Sanders Auto Sales and Rentals. Along the way, I phoned Chicken Boy. We made final arrangements while my belly did flip-flops and yodeled. I reached the dealership and went straight to a rental lot that was filled with numerous makes and models. I didn't want a truck and I wouldn't have to worry about kids at school anymore. A vulture-like creature swooped down on me. I said, "I'd like that one."

"The white Mustang convertible? Yes, ma'am!" Drool drizzled down the man's craggy beard. I filled out the paperwork and paid. Putting the top down, I took off.

"This isn't duty hair," I told Chicken Boy when we met outside Cajun Delights, his gaze steady at my head. "This is Mustang hair."

Chicken Boy carried the yellow head, a heavy-looking appendage with eyeholes. He seemed to be in his late teens. Dark brown eyes, long black hair, too-thin face. A breeze puffed up the feathers of his costume. "Did you know we got other costumes?" he said, holding the head up toward me like an offering.

"At Rent-a-Costume," I said. "Well who would imagine?"

"Yeah, we got a Mickey Mouse suit. And Santy Claus and Pokemon and even a caveman. Lots of women like that one."

"Uh-huh, but I like the chicken."

"Figures." He draped on the head. "Look at those big chickens." His admiring tone echoed from inside the beak, his wing pointing to a gaggle of geese that wobbled up a hill near the pond.

I took a sharp breath and peeked inside the restaurant's front door.

Gil came into view. I exhaled, watching him saunter through the large room with few customers. Mmm, Gil had kept broad shoulders for a man his age. A tapered back. A fine tush that fit well inside my cupped hands. I wanted warm chocolate chip cookies. And sex with Gil before that.

"We goin' in?" Chicken Boy bumped into my backside.

"That's him," I said, losing all sexual desires.

Chicken Boy crouched to peer through the doorway. His beak must have captured someone's attention. Workers turned toward our door and chuckled. "Hate it when they laugh at me," the boy said, adjusting his wing feathers.

"They laugh *with* you," I said, right before he yanked the door open.

CHAPTER 14

Most of the restaurant's patrons snickered while Chicken Boy strutted, his wings bumping the sides of his stout stomach until he reached Gil.

I crept inside. Chicken Boy faced Gil and sang the birthday song. People around them all clapped. In a cracking voice, Chicken Boy added, "And we hope you have many, many mo-o-ore."

Gil's deep-throated laughter erupted. "Cealie!" he said, striding toward me. "I should have known you were involved."

He embraced me. His chest felt warm. Safe. I told myself I should stay here. Gil felt secure. He felt . . . What he felt like made me horny.

"Happy birthday," I said, drawing back, my cheeks heating from what I'd been thinking. It involved a picture of Gil naked. Nice picture. Very nice.

With his hug to me, most people went back to eating or their duties. Gil gave me a smile. "I'm glad you remembered."

"How could I forget?" I again felt only in his space, forgetting others were near. A fake cough reminded me. It sputtered from a hollow space within feathers.

"Excellent job," Gil told the boy in costume while thrusting out his hand. Chicken Boy shook it, muttered thanks and looked at me. I pulled out my wallet, but Gil tipped him before I could. The youth looked about nine feet tall when he strutted out. Gil turned a different smile to me. This smile came with his piercing gaze. Parts of me reacted.

A male customer chuckled. He didn't watch us but conversed with friends at a table. Seafood platters covered its checkered cloth. "I'm starving," I told Gil.

"You've come to the right place." He led me toward his table, and I glanced around to see if I'd find Legs. No sign of her. I pranced beside Gil. If his current girlfriend were here, I wasn't sure what I'd do. But I did know that this time I wouldn't leave without eating.

Gil called a waiter named André, introduced us, and said I was a special guest. Then he told me, "We have crayfish."

"Yum," was all I had to say.

"Please bring her a double serving," Gil said to André. "Two dips to go with it, and a Bud Light."

When André left, Gil peered at me. "Cealie, you look . . ." He may have wanted to say something like great, but his gaze skittered to my hair. I smoothed it, almost saying duty hair. But I didn't want him to know about my teaching since he'd already expressed an opinion about me getting involved in the investigation. "I'm driving a convertible," I said, and he responded with that fabulous grin.

A busboy cleared the table beside ours. Gil complimented him on the way he lifted every condiment and sprayed the tablecloth. "Thanks, Mr. Thurman." Wires on the boy's teeth shone with his smile, reminding me of Cynthia Petre's braces and the complaints I had heard in the lounge.

"Gil," I said and he inclined his head to listen, "when someone is hired to clean a school, would the school personnel hire that person?"

"I believe the school board does that, although someone from the school might make a recommendation. Why?"

Assorted crackers and my beer arrived just in time. "I wondered." I swigged the beer, buttered some crackers and ate.

Gil's face lit with a smile. "I see that you didn't cook again."

"Nope." I guzzled more crackers.

He seemed pleased to sit back and watch me. "Wish I could get crayfish every day," Gil said. "Just for you."

"I'm flattered."

He leaned forward, making my whole torso heat up. "How are things going with Kat?" he asked.

"Ah, Kat." I lost my body warmth. "She went to school yesterday. But not today."

His forehead wrinkled. "Make sure you keep me up on graduation. You know I want to be there. If she decides to graduate."

I promised to let him know, and Gil waved to get his manager's attention. He made introductions between Jim Harris and me. Gil whispered to Jim, who gave me a grin and then strode to the mike on stage and announced, "Joke contest time."

I smiled at Gil. He was having this now for me. "One of these days, you'll have to get up and tell one," he said.

"Maybe I'll be second. Right after you."

"Touché."

A young man wearing a fraternity T-shirt hopped up from a table with other males dressed like him. He reached the mike. "Boudreaux's cat was sick, so Thibodaux drove him and his cat to the vet. The vet put the cat on a table, ran his hand back and forth over it, and gave Boudreaux two pills. 'Give him these,' the vet said. 'That'll be three hundred dollars.'"

We all snickered about the charge and then waited for the punch line.

" 'Three hundred dollars!' Boudreaux cried. 'Just for two pills?' The vet shook his head and said, 'The pills only costs fifty cents. The rest is for the CAT scan.'"

Everyone laughed. The jokester bowed, hopped down, and joined his approving friends.

"That was great," I told Gil, and he agreed.

to join him. Gil, the gentleman, would tell me to stay. But would I want to?

No way. *I* chose to stop being with him, I reminded myself, choking down the anguish balling up in my throat.

"You aren't finished already?" he said.

I mumbled, trying to wipe my mouth, clean my hands and rise at the same time. "This was wonderful. Thank you." I put my hand out to shake his. "Do I owe you anything?"

"Of course not. You're leaving?"

I kept my body distant from his. He hadn't yet noticed his tall lady friend. "I have so many things to do," I said, unable to think of one to mention. "I hope you'll enjoy the remainder of your birthday."

Legs had shifted over. Gil saw her, and they exchanged brilliant smiles. One man and his current girlfriend and his ex would absolutely crowd a table. Before I would hear Gil speak to her in a lovey-dovey tone, I scooted to the front door.

I passed the crowd coming into Cajun Delights without glancing at Legs, and I drove away, feeling my eyes burn. Surely caused by the crayfish's peppery steam? I was probably stuffed and tired from the day's work, I decided, although I couldn't remember when I had put in so few hours in a workday. I also couldn't recall ever having left a job so exhausted.

Daylight was evaporating when I reached the condo. I would call Kat. My weary body told me to rest a few minutes first. I kicked off my shoes and fell back in bed with arms against my sides, reminding myself of Mrs. Peekers on that stretcher. Pictures filtered through my head—bloody car hoods, huge chickens with black nylon stockings on their heads, Gil shirtless.

My right eye cracked open. I shook my head to rid it of unwanted scenes and spied the hands of my travel alarm indicating it was eight o'clock.

Surprised to find my back stiff, I rose to get a shower and then dive into nightclothes. I was thirsty and moseyed to the kitchen for a drink. Bright light popped through the curtains. "It's morning!" I said, almost swearing. Minnie's lone stem leaned toward me. "Why didn't you wake me?" I said, pouring myself water, remembering Harry Wren's warning about not flooding a cactus.

I returned to the bedroom, determining that I'd probably slept without moving. I glanced in the bathroom mirror and groaned. One side of my face looked the same color as crayfish, about the same shade as curdled blood.

I phoned Kat. "Morning," I said. "No arguments please, let's go shopping."

She made a small snicker. Good to hear. "When?"

"Whenever your malls open on a Saturday." Before she could mull on that, I said, "How's your dad?"

"Don't ask."

"Okay, I won't." While she seemed to be considering my suggestion, I said, "I'll take you in a convertible and put the top down. Pick you up about ten." I hung up before she could decline.

Finally, I would be able to talk to her. With Kat thrust into emotional abandon while buying clothes, I could learn more and appeal to her common sense. And away from their house and the school, I'd get to spend quality time with her.

I covered the red markings on my cheek with makeup and put on dressy casuals. "What a great day!" I told Minnie in the kitchen, hoping my enthusiasm might cheer her. Harry Wren knew so much about growing cacti. I wished I'd thought to ask him about plants' responses to conversation. One thing I knew, causing my smile to brighten—I wasn't going around that school again to ask him.

I grabbed flats from the pantry and went outside. Just from a habit of late, I walked around the Mustang, inspecting. The white color remained pure. No dents. No one had ripped the stallion out of the grill.

A great start to a wonderful day.

Roger was washing his tan Ford truck in their driveway. Kat's faded red Chevy sat in front of it.

I strolled up to Roger, and he quit hosing and used one arm to hug me. "How've you been doing?" he asked. I said fine and inquired about his work. "It's all right. Kat's inside," he said, finished with our conversation.

I stepped away, thought and turned back. "What about graduation? Are you ready to go?"

His first expression was that blank, distant look. Then Roger's eyes brightened and he smiled. "I sure am." He knew how important Kat's graduation was to Nancy. He probably didn't know Kat's current plans. He would soon enough if she chose not to go through with the ceremony. But Roger looked cheerful now, with the expectation that she would. I couldn't steal that cheer from him.

"We'll all get together to do something soon," I said.

"Good." He began rinsing his truck.

Kat's kitchen smelled of food, this time baked biscuits. "I knew you'd be hungry," she said when I entered, "so I went out for biscuit mix and whipped up a batch."

"You already went shopping?" I snatched a couple of warm flaky biscuits from the oven and munched, shaking my head. "Kat, you're really something." And she was. Always, she had been the little homemaker. And a quality student. "You look nice," I said.

She'd tucked her reddish-brown waves behind her ears. Her blouse of stretchy material, khaki slacks and backless sandals made her look stylish. "Thanks. You too." I wore a pistachio colored pant set I'd picked up in Dallas.

Kat liked the Mustang. I offered to let her drive, but she declined. She seemed carefree with the wind whipping her hair across her face, her smile almost as happy as mine.

She didn't offer suggestions for which stores we should enter at the mall. I saw Le Boutique and thought the name interesting. "This is pricey. I've never been here," she whispered while we meandered between the shop's racks holding few garments.

The only other people were three female employees, all wearing black tops, skirts, nylons and heels, reminding me of someone I chose not to consider. They raised their chins and gave us snooty expressions that asked "Are you wealthy enough to shop here?"

"Yes, I am," I said to the pencil-thin one nearing us.

"You are what?" she asked.

"I am looking for something extra special."

"Oh!" She did know how to smile.

"I need part of a graduation gift," I said. I turned to Kat. "Choose some things, as many as you like." Her gaze skimmed the floor, and I urged, "Please do it."

The skinny saleslady clutched Kat's elbow. "Aren't these beautiful?" the eager woman said, guiding Kat toward separates that all looked the same, except in different pastel colors.

I headed for a section called Delicate Undies. The woman with wedge-cut hair swooped down on me. Was their commission as much as a car salesman's? "If I find something, you can ring me up," I said, discovering she could smile, too.

Bras in Easter colors dripped from hangers. They didn't have my actual size, with a long cup and space for sag near the armpit, so I grabbed one with the next-best dimension in yellow. Slim slips guaranteed to enhance a woman's entire figure enticed me, but I no longer wanted anything like a girdle. Whatever my figure became at each stage of my life would be fine. My body parts could all expand and droop as they wanted. I did decide to let my cleavage poke out with the little black lace thing I plucked up. I snatched matching panties and six pairs of nylons without control tops in various shades, but mostly sheer black. Was I thinking of Legs again here? I told myself no, this was only for me, whenever I wanted to feel sexy.

Kat's saleslady had her facing cashmere jackets. "Pretty," I told Kat. "Why don't you try one on?"

She tucked her chin. "No thanks. I have a nice jacket." She and her sales rep held no garments. "I don't see anything I want," Kat told me.

"Are you sure?" I indicated leather skirts. "You'd look great in one of those. And you could get some of those pretty silk blouses to wear with it."

"They're called shirts now," the sales rep said, her nose higher.

"What, they don't make blouses anymore?" I considered a moment and said, "How about housecoats?"

She gave me a pained expression.

I wanted to buy Kat a suit, but she refused. "I guess that's all," I told the disappointed young woman at her side. I made my purchases and we left. I scanned other shops that might entice Kat, but she lowered her eyes and shook her head. My rear neck muscles tensed. Kat didn't want to shop for clothes. A horrible sign.

"Macy's," I said, seeing that name on a store. Kat had always enthused about items she bought there with Nancy, and over the years, mentioned outfits she wished she could buy. I'd wanted to send her the money or get her a credit card but her parents had said no.

Inside the store, I grabbed a low-cut scarlet dress off a rack and held it up in front of Kat. "This is you." At least she grinned as she pushed it away. I directed her to sportswear, tailored garments, swimsuits. Kat shook her head. "Oh, bedding," I said, and her step quickened beside mine.

"Pretty," she agreed when I pointed out sheets and comforters. I suggested she choose some things, but Kat said she didn't need any. We neared a bed made up with muted green sheets sprinkled with burgundy leaves. Its matching coverlet was turned back. I kicked off my shoes and stretched across one side. "Come here," I said, patting the pillow beside mine. Kat's eyes widened in horror. "It's okay," I said gently.

A saleslady appeared and asked if I needed help. "I'm checking out the mattresses and bedroom sets. And I'll let you, and only you, know if I find what I want," I added, making her smile expand.

"Come on, baby girl," I told Kat after the woman left. "People do lie on mattresses to check them out, you know."

She narrowed her eyes. "You want a mattress, Gram? But you seldom even stay in one place."

I raised my hand. "I can get anything I want, remember?" Kat smiled and nodded, and I said, "Climb in."

She glanced around, probably to search for anyone she knew from school. She was concerned about appearances, and I couldn't totally change that. But I could try a few alterations. Kat dropped her hips gently to the sheet, and I asked, "How's this one feel?"

"Nice."

I patted her pillow. "Now try this. I'm not sure whether I like these fluffy ones."

Kat looked aghast, but I nodded and she laid her head back, leaving her legs over the side of the bed. I wanted to suggest that she kick off her shoes and relax, but she was Kat. "Soft," she said, head sinking into the pillow.

When Kat appeared totally relaxed, I said, "Tell me about Mrs. Peekers." She responded with a big sigh, and I said, "Is she a mean teacher?"

"I don't think so. She's tall. Some people think she and Miss Hernandez could be sisters." There was love in the way she said Hernandez's name. I thought I also heard bitterness.

I laid my hand over Kat's. "What would make anyone think your friend—" Kat's eye flicker made me pause, but I needed to ask it— "Why would they think Miss Hernandez could kill?"

Kat sat up. She faced away from me. I shoved up to sit and noticed shoppers staring at us. I gave them big waves, and they turned their gazes aside. Kat had started to walk off when the saleslady came. "I don't care for this one," I said, indicating the bed we'd been on. The lady's falling expression almost made me tell her I'd take the entire package. I glanced at the exquisite bedding. I could have the whole ensemble shipped to the apartment I kept, I considered, jaunting after Kat. Nope, I already had new mattresses and sheets there.

Kat didn't speak when we left the store. Eventually she slowed her pace. I led her to the food court, tempting with the scent of fried chicken. We stopped at a Greek counter instead and then sat picking at meat wrapped in grape leaves. Families ate around us, their voices and presence making our silent meal more solemn. I asked Kat how her food was, and she raised her shoulders with indifference. The entrée was bland, not at all like Cajun cooking. My thoughts flitted to Gil and left him. A carousel's music attracted me. I eyed sparkling diamond shapes circling, along with little kids on rising and falling animals. "Let's ride," I told Kat.

"Not today."

I stood in line, straddled a stiff tan rabbit, and waved to Kat each time the merry-go-round circled. She regained a half smile.

Afterward we strolled through the central corridor, Kat's smile fading. This problem with her beloved teacher was making her almost as sullen as she had been during the end with Nancy.

Motion at a store's entrance sought my eye. A stuffed ferret on a table tumbled over a ball. Amused, I moved Kat closer to watch. A toy dog strutted, barely missing the ferret. A monkey opened its mouth and sang the Macarena.

"Let's go in," I told Kat, needing to soften her mood and ask more questions.

"A toy store?" she asked.

"Why not? We can play."

CHAPTER 15

"Look at this," I said, entering the store and grabbing a hula hoop. I thrust it over my head and tried to lasso Kat with another one, but she backed off. My hoop swiveled around my hips. "I'd forgotten this was great exercise."

Kat looked away from customers who watched, suggesting she was highly embarrassed. I kept my hoop going a while and then it struck my knees. "Very good," Kat said.

"Thank you very much." I lunged for the next thing that enticed me.

Kat snickered. "You remember how?"

"Just like riding a bike." I whipped the jump rope out of its container and clasped the wooden handles. "Such great memories." I flung the rope around and tried to jump, but the rope caught toys on a shelf. Dinosaurs tumbled to the floor, and something shattered. Kat's hands covered her mouth. "Of course," I said, "I never did learn to ride a bike."

A grim-faced man stomped to us, eyeing the scattered items.

"Sorry," I said. "I'll pay for them." I replaced the jump rope, and Kat and I scooped up the remains of a piggy bank. "I'll take care of it on our way out," I told the clerk, and then I led Kat toward the store's rear. Unseen by others, she giggled. A woman with bluish hair appeared and stared at her. My granddaughter and I smirked at each other and shuffled around corner shelves. We became like two bad girls, ready to pull something off.

"This used to be so much fun," Kat said, drawing a box down from a counter.

"Oh, an Easy-Bake Oven. Would you like one?"

She frowned. "I have enough with my real stove."

"Take this one just so you can play again. I'll play with you."

She slipped the carton back into place. "That's okay."

Getting Kat to lighten up was proving most difficult. I glanced at her serious face. Engaging Kat in play might distract her so that I could discover more. How could I get her to tell me what she knew about people who might be involved in a killing? Or anyone who might want to harm me? Surely no one would try to hurt her. Would they?

I shivered. Nobody from Sidmore High had given straight answers to all I wanted to know. And Kat balked every time I asked outright about motives of people connected with the school. Should I push her to return—or make certain she wouldn't?

We needed to play.

I guided her to another aisle empty of people. Kat opened a book that played a tinny version of "Mary Had a Little Lamb," and I pulled up all the ladders on a fire truck and made its little driver climb them. We touched fluffy stuffed animals and I offered to get some for Kat's bed, but she declined.

"Now that's great fun," I said, spotting familiar boxes. Kat agreed. I opened a box, spread the Twister mat on the floor and spun the arrow. "Right hand, green," I read. I placed my hand on a green circle. "Now your turn."

Kat shoved the arrow. "Left foot, yellow." Finding no spectators, she slid off her shoe and stepped on that color.

I spun right foot, blue. Kat took her turn, and we worked at getting ourselves into bent positions while not losing our footing. Once Kat was involved in the game, I said, "Yesterday medics took Mrs. Peekers away from school."

Her face shot up toward mine. "What?"

"It was an accident. Probably." I explained what I knew. From my twisted position, I raised a hand, pointed toward where her left foot should be, and almost fell over. Kat automatically shifted her foot. "Baby girl," I said, "I like Miss Hernandez."

Kat's expression warmed. She almost smiled.

"Your turn," I said, getting her attention back on moving her body. While she made the next move, I asked, "What connection did she have to Grant Labruzzo?"

Kat exhaled. "Miss Hernandez was at school late on the day he died."

"I've noticed that many people stay around after the bell rings. Although I can't imagine why anyone would want to do that."

Kat didn't grin as I'd hoped. I took one turn after another, striving to keep her distracted.

"All of the practices were over that afternoon," Kat said, "and there weren't any games the evening he fell."

I didn't want to move lest I jolt the scene playing in her head. I tightened my shoulders to make my arms quit wobbling.

Kat said, "Mr. Labruzzo yelled at her that day."

"The custodian yelled at a teacher? Why?"

Kat stared off. Wanting to keep her with me, I stretched to spin and wound up bent like an aging pretzel. Kat spoke in a quiet tone. "Some kids in Miss Hernandez's class said she asked him if he'd hang some things from her ceiling. With a long ladder, he could reach." Her unfocused eyes slid to Sidmore High. "Before homeroom that day she'd told me she had an idea for displaying her students' work. Their projects would make the room colorful, and if the students who needed incentive saw their accomplishments, they might work harder." Kat took a breath. "That's the last time she really spoke with me."

"Do you know why Grant Labruzzo yelled at her?"

"She had stopped him when he was passing her room and glancing in it. And after she asked him to hang the pictures, he hollered that teachers needed to start doing their own jobs, cleaning their boards and desks, and taking care of stuff written on their walls."

I shook my head. "So why would people think she killed him? Just because he yelled?"

"Miss Hernandez never got mad at anyone. And she was there late that day, doing things in her room." Kat spoke lower. "She seldom stayed after school hours. It's one of the things they've questioned."

"They?"

Kat's gaze flickered. "The police. Some kids in her class said she'd looked so humiliated when Mr. Labruzzo yelled at her in front of them. Her face turned kind of purple." Kat stared off. She didn't want to talk but needed to. "He just walked away, and Miss Hernandez raised her arms and made fists. She slammed them down, like she'd like to slam him, the kids said."

"And then what?"

The portion of Kat's face that I saw went blank. "And then the bell rang. She stormed out of her room before the last students left."

Neither of us cared about spinning. I felt a catch in my groin. "So some of the students who saw that incident suspect her. At least one of them told the police, and they've questioned her. But they haven't made an arrest."

Kat's knees lowered to the floor. "Ever since then, it's like she doesn't want to talk to anybody. She teaches her classes and that's all." Kat unfolded herself on the mat and sat, her inner pain almost palpable.

But she's not your mom, I wanted to say. *If the woman did something horrible, your life hasn't ended.* I couldn't tell that to Kat. I wasn't in her position and wasn't even living close to her.

"Miss Hernandez seemed hesitant about speaking to me yesterday," I said, sitting on the mat, "but she spoke."

Kate smiled wanly. "People have to respond to you, Gram."

I grinned. "She said to tell you she'll be okay." But I considered the varying responses I'd received at Sidmore High and shuddered. Was the school a place of higher learning—or violence? "Kat, are you afraid of any kids at school, like Roxy or Sledge? Or anyone on the faculty?"

Her lips tightened. She shook her head.

"Was Grant Labruzzo a flirt?"

She made a rapid eye blink. "Not really. But he had that look."

"What look?"

"Like when a guy kind of likes somebody."

I let that image sink in and didn't especially like it, but he was a young man. "So he gave you that look, and he'd looked at Miss Hernandez that way too, right?"

Kat swallowed. She made a slight nod.

"Did he flirt with everyone?"

Kat sighed, her eyes shifting. "I don't know, Gram. I'm ready to leave when you are." Her clenched mouth told me she wouldn't disclose more.

"Final averages are important," I said. "And exams contribute a lot to those averages." Kat didn't seem to be listening. She looked at a young woman and her daughter who entered this section but didn't seem bothered by their presence. She helped me replace the Twister in its box. "I guess your daddy leaves for work before you leave for school," I said, "so he probably wouldn't know if you were missing any days. Unless somebody told him."

Kat's eyebrows shot up. "Don't you think he worries enough?" Her firm gaze steadied on mine, warning me not to interfere. "And the school doesn't contact parents of seniors.

They know we're old enough and mature enough to make our own choices."

I swallowed, responding with the smallest nod. I remembered that I had to pay for the broken piggy bank. Kat went outside to wait, and I grabbed something on the way to the checkout line. Joining Kat, I said, "You haven't chosen anything, but this is a start on your graduation present."

"Oh, Gram." She took the panda and held it at arm's length. The glittering in Kat's eyes came from tears. I knew they weren't for the bear. As much indecision as I bore, how much more did this child carry? Should she return to school or not? Go and take exams? Was her good friend a killer? Kat rubbed the soft bear along her cheek. She clutched him in her arms, and I was especially satisfied that she had accepted something to cling to. "Thank you," she whispered.

"Kat!" a male shouted.

She and I turned to see John Winston pumping his arms, storming toward us.

"You bitch!" he yelled at her.

"What?" Kat and I said in unison.

John Winston headed toward us, red-faced with anger, a husky buddy at his side.

"Don't speak to a lady like that," I told John.

He jabbed an index finger at Kat, his aqua blue eyes flaring. "You started a crappy rumor about me."

"What rumor?" she said.

"You told everybody I wrote a note about the police arresting Miss Hernandez."

"I didn't tell anyone that." Kat stopped. She turned abruptly and flung an infuriated gaze at me.

I felt the blood drain from my face. I raised my palms. "I only asked him. But now we know it wasn't even true. They didn't arrest her." Kat's glare pierced my heart. "It wasn't even true," I repeated, squirming under her accusing eyes.

"But that's just fine," John told Kat, "because now I'm telling everybody in our class not to trust you. And nobody ever will!"

John hustled away, his buddy giving us a smirk before he followed behind.

Kat's green eyes nailed me. I shook my head. Raised both shoulders and palms. Cried inside.

We remained silent on the long ride home. Needing sound, I raised the radio's volume. Kat's gaze shifted toward me, and I said, "You can change the station if you'd like."

She turned away.

We reached her house, and she shoved her car door open. "I didn't mean to hurt you," I said, my tone pleading. Kat slammed her door. I yelled, "You forgot your panda."

She yanked the bear off the seat. "Thanks." Kat ran up the front stairs and dashed into her house. The door reverberated with its slam.

Tears building behind my eyes rushed out. My arms quivered while I drove. I slunk into the condo and tumbled onto the recliner. Cocking it back, I remained still, exhausted. My forearms and hips ached from twisting. My spirit's pain was my main concern. Everything in me felt drained.

I had butted in. And made my granddaughter hate me?

My eyes felt as if they dropped farther into their sockets. I stared at shadows lying across the den's rented furniture. Was this my whole future? When I gave up my home to go seeking the uncertain—was this what I wanted to find? Neutral leathers and floral prints surrounded me. Attractive rugs, sleek ceramics, and woods. Everything glistened. In all the places I stayed, I always left floors and kitchens looking like I'd found them. Barely used. Never tarnished. I'd muss one side of the beds, turning back just my portion of the sheet. At night I returned to that single pillow and space.

Weights seemed to press against my eyes.

I pushed myself up and crossed to the light switch, flipping on brightness. That did little for my mind-set. I strode through the condo, flooding each room with false lighting. Perfect colors still stared at me, each blending with the others, nothing about them human.

Human. Alive? *Leave or die bitch.* Telling Kat that those words had been written on my truck would have added to her worry. I'd already piled enough on her by questioning John Winston at school. Now what if all her peers turned away from her because of me?

"Oh, Cealie," I said with a sigh. How stupid I'd been to think I could remedy all her problems. I'd thought I could learn about a man's death and fix up Kat's life. But detectives knew how to uncover truths. I needed to do what Gil suggested and let them do all the detecting. And, I hoped, soon my grandchild would once again want to be around me.

I strode into the kitchen. " 'Evening, Minnie," I said, grabbing my plant's pot. Her slender stem leaned against its side. I'd messed up enough. I had alienated Kat. I could have stayed with Gil months ago but left and now felt responsible for thrusting the young woman with long legs onto his lap. Gloom set in, heaviness weighing on my shoulders. I needed to get something right. I had a dependent again. Minnie depended on me for survival. And I didn't even know what type of cactus she was. I had to let other people live as they chose and keep Minnie alive.

School counselor Harry Wren had mentioned on-line sites concerning cacti.

I studied Minnie. One short triangular stalk formed her torso. Bumpy nodules on her ridged sides showed lighter spots where thorns might have been shaved. Out of all the cacti in the nursery, she'd seemed dainty. Attractive without being showy.

Those tiny pink sprouts grew out from her pink head like old-fashioned hair curlers, giving the suggestion that she didn't give a damn. She was my kind of lady. She didn't stick and would fit perfectly in my hand for jet travel. In cars, she'd snuggle in cup holders. I had immediately known her name should be Minnie. She'd had no label to tell what type of cactus she was, and the salesclerk hadn't even known.

Okay, I could surely take care of this sweet plant.

I carried her to the den, set her beside me, and typed "cactus growing" on my laptop's search engine. The results offered me 39,145 sites. I blinked. Was I the only person in the country not already raising cacti?

I hit on general plant care. *Plants like to be talked to,* an expert advised. "I'm in the mood for love," I sang, hoping Minnie would also like songs. I liked this search already since I enjoyed learning new things whenever the subject interested me. My gardener had planted and tended all those lush plants in my gardens. I supposed he also spoke to them, for my flowers and bushes thrived. Maybe he also sang. I hummed a few bars of the love song, my thoughts encompassing Gil. Without clothes. Hmm.

Shoving those ideas away, I continued my search. I clicked on Cactus Mall and flipped through screens, searching for a cactus that looked like mine, while an idea came.

"After I learn about you, I'm going to search for chemicals that give off noxious fumes," I told Minnie. Why had someone spilled—or poured—cleaning fluids under the door of the custodians' room? And had it really been locked? Why try to harm that teacher, Mrs. Peekers?

She did resemble Marisa Hernandez.

I spoke while watching the wrong cacti spring up on my monitor. "I doubt that I'm any closer to getting Kat to take exams. Should I push harder, or let her decide?" I glanced at

179

Minnie but saw no inkling of a reaction. "Nancy would know."

Maybe plants that were spoken to would hint at a problem's solution? Minnie only bent a little, possibly to listen. Ponder? More conversation might help. Her and me. I scanned more cactus pictures and spoke. "The first little house my husband and I owned had no flowers, except plastic ones. Freddie and I worked so hard at being Mom and Dad." I mentioned Roger, our currently brooding son. "A lovable child, he always wanted to be cuddled." An urge came to cuddle him now. He didn't want me to. My eyes warmed, and I tried to focus on Minnie instead of my son.

"The main thing that grew in our lawn was grass," I said, scanning photos of cacti with spectacular flowers and some coated with fuzz. "We took turns shoving our rickety lawn mower through that. I was glad when it snowed and everything froze." I winced, not having planned to tell Minnie about wanting any plants dead.

To my relief, she didn't seem any worse from my comment. I nudged more dirt against her side and noticed a tiny sprout of pink. "You have a new button," I said. Smugly, I determined my plant was prettier than Harry Wren's. And he'd looked conceited, telling me about all his cactus knowledge.

My Web search for cacti took me to the Adenium species, a cactus that looked like a regular plant with flowers. I found Grumbley White, a Red Everbloomer, and an obesum that resembled a pink-blossomed tree as tall as the man standing beside it. The *Ferocactus stainesii* showed what I'd always thought of as a cactus. The plant was eight feet tall, its clump ten feet in diameter. "Its attractive red spines," I read to Minnie, "makes this plant deservedly popular. In cultivation in the UK, the plants are quite slow to mature. They need to be moderately large before they flower."

Mmm, a challenge. I was beginning to see why so many

people were interested in cactus cultivation. And this site gave the exact areas where these plants were found—the mountains east of Illapel in Chile, another in Brazil in Rio Grande do Sol—but both of these always grew alone. "Poor things," I told Minnie. "I hope your type doesn't always grow all by itself."

I viewed cacti from Bolivia, Peru, Argentine, Uruguay, and Burma. "Maybe we could travel to those locales to see them growing in the wild," I said, trying to get more enthusiastic. I was alone. I glimpsed at my plant. So was she.

Kat's tumultuous situation rooted through my brain. Could I solve her problem? Should I try?

I scooted Minnie closer to my laptop. "Look at this." From Kenya and Tanzania, the cactus looked like a star wearing a zebra print. "It will grow in the middle of the freeway," I read. "But its flower stinks of death and it is pollinated by blowies." I didn't know what blowies were and didn't want to find out. The next plants reportedly also stank, one like old socks, another of dead meat. A Dutch missionary named one of them in 1809; he couldn't spell, so his error remained immortal. Interesting. The Cero, developing into a large tangle of leafless vines, was once marketed in Australia as The Condom Plant. The man who coined that phrase supposedly made a fortune.

I grinned. My smile faded. "Cero." *The thing just looked like a bunch of vines,* Brad McClellen had said.

My heart went out to this leafless plant. It was one such as this that Grant Labruzzo knocked over and killed in Harry Wren's office. And Harry had mourned. He still did.

"Ha, look at this." I indicated what resembled a reddish ball and read, "This cactus needs to be kept awash with water, and the occasional shot of Jack Daniels will keep it in a good mood." Maybe a good shot of Jack Daniels would perk up Roger. Or, lately, me.

"I'll find your relatives soon," I told Minnie. And how about

181

mine? Troubled, troubled, troubled.

As soon as I learned exact care for Minnie, I'd search for those deadly chemicals.

"We'll probably even get to discover where you come from," I said, interested now in the history I was learning about plants I viewed. "Oh, this one's lovely." The stately cactus with yellow ruffled flowers was a *Notocacti*. "This beauty," I read, "was unfortunately lost—" *Uh-oh*. It rotted due to being overwatered.

Immediately, I changed screens. "Hm," I said, "where are you on here, Minnie?" I saw a *Pedilanthus* with two stems, each looking like a penis with an orange flower on the side. (Need I think of Gil again?) A thin nine-foot plant with pink flowers grew in a greenhouse. In the wild, this specimen was pollinated by bats. I imagined scores of dark creatures closing in on one plant and considered threatening people closing in at Sidmore High. Was one of them actually deadly?

Maybe not, but all of this week's happenings pointed toward a person who yielded a definite threat. To my grandchild? I didn't think so. But that person had implicated me with the warning on my mail truck. Should I take those scrawled words seriously? I doubted it, yet . . .

I didn't know if you should tell plants problems, but I had to mention my concerns. That was talking. "Kat will be destroyed if the woman she loves proves to be a killer." I rose and paced, scenes swelling in my head. Marisa Hernandez, tall and flat-chested, but so pleasant, raised both arms, threatening. The young man Grant Labruzzo tended to his job, pushing a wide dust mop. He emptied trash cans from classrooms, but not most of them.

When he reached in Marisa's room for her overflowing gray can, she held students' colorful posters and screeched, "Hang these things for me!"

"Way up there?" Labruzzo said, pointing to her high ceiling.

"Yes, there. And do it now!"

In my mind the ceiling rose. "I won't do it!" Labruzzo said. He swore about dumb teachers and strode out, leaving her trash behind.

Heads of seated students whipped back toward Hernandez. She turned all colors of the rainbow and her colors darkened, growing harsh. Fury pumped her up so that the woman resembled a pro wrestler. A bell jangled, and the teens watched her stalk out, a blade growing in her hand. Hernandez crept stealthily behind the custodian.

Kids slunk behind, while their teacher slid on her toes, following handsome young Labruzzo. He entered the auditorium, pushing his mop in sideways motions. Folded seats filled the room. A bare stage stood between curtains. Labruzzo went up the stairs toward the balcony, his wide mop circling. He didn't notice from behind—a flash of silver swerved up.

Marisa Hernandez appeared, her blade raised.

Labruzzo saw her.

"And then what would have happened?" I asked myself. "He'd give her a flirtatious smile?"

Ridiculous.

No, the children would watch their teacher pounce on him.

My mental scene returned. Labruzzo jumped in time, knocking her knife away.

"You think I won't kill you!" Hernandez screamed, her dark eyes fierce beneath long red-black bangs. "But I don't need a weapon!" She grabbed him and thrust him headfirst over the railing. Teenagers wailed. Kat stood among them, staring in horror.

My breath trapped in my throat. Could Kat know more than she admitted? Had she *seen* her mentor kill that man?

Reasoning slapped away my imaginings. "How could a woman toss that man off a balcony?" I asked Minnie. "And

183

would a person kill just because she'd been embarrassed?"

Hernandez's hair was blond, and she didn't wear bangs. Grant Labruzzo hadn't been stabbed.

I had witnessed many unpleasant happenings at Sidmore High the last couple of days. Besides the obvious, a small event kept niggling with my mind. I needed to decipher what it meant.

CHAPTER 16

I struggled to grasp the importance of an incident that had seemed ordinary yet unusual at Kat's school. Envisioning students and the staff, I recalled words I'd heard and threatening movements I'd seen. Scenes with too many faces and events crowded my inner vision. I tramped to the lavatory and soused my face with cold water, unable to bear considering that Kat's new mother figure could have committed a murder. Unless Marisa Hernandez was someone she didn't appear to be.

I yanked up my phone and punched the new number I'd stored in memory.

"Cajun Delights," a cheery female voice answered.

My breath caught. "Sorry, wrong number," I said like a schoolgirl and then disconnected. I'd reverted to previous behavior, turning to Gil for help in reasoning out thoughts that confused me. But I couldn't turn to him any longer.

"I am woman!" I said, facing Minnie but reminding myself. "I can do anything—alone." I didn't need anyone to fend for me or make my decisions. I was quite capable of handling problems on my own. A sensation rose above my diaphragm, my chest filling with . . . regret?

I shook my head. I could go through life without being half of a couple. That's what I wanted. "It is," I told Minnie.

What had I heard at Sidmore High School?

Cactus Growers Society came to mind, along with a knowing that something there I couldn't directly put my finger on had clashed. I did a new search on the Net for the society, while an expletive I'd overheard heard at school came to me. I wanted to shout the word (it started with F)—because I knew I'd go back to that school. But at least this time I wouldn't teach.

My doorbell rang, and I jumped from surprise. Scooting to the door, I peered through the peephole. "What a nice treat," I said, letting Kat in.

"I thought you'd want to know. Mrs. Peekers will be all right."

"I am so relieved. Do you know what happened?"

Kat remained inside the doorway. "Somebody locked her in the supply room. Boxes of cleaning supplies had been delivered and left outside that room. Then somebody took bottles from two of the boxes and poured stuff from them under the door."

"What was in the bottles?"

"Ammonia and bleach."

I gasped. "Even I know that those cleansers can create a deadly combination."

Kat nodded grimly. "Especially if they're inhaled in a small enclosed space. Mrs. Peekers was lucky. She got weak right away, and everybody was in class. But a guy was cutting his class and passed that room and heard her yelling for help."

"Thank goodness. How'd you find out?"

Kat's eyes flashed. "I still have a couple of friends." Her comment and tight lips let me know the chill between us remained.

Without moving closer, I said, "Did you talk to Roxy?"

Kat glanced across the den. "Nice place." She looked at me. "I've gotta go."

"Oh, come in. Sit down."

"I have things to do, Gram."

"This late?"

"I'm not a kid anymore." She opened the door. "Just do me one favor. Please stay away from my school." Kat turned and left.

I watched the door, hoping she would return. When she didn't, I lolled through the condo, considering. Someone had tried to kill that teacher. I quit walking, my arms still moving with trembles. Had the same person tried to kill me? Locked in a room, spilled chemicals.

I'd thought I smelled bleach in the hall near the custodians' room. And what was that substance I had seen written on the label of the vial that broke in my classroom?

Sulfide. I ran to my laptop and did a quick search for that word.

The results offered me 103,000 choices. Drat. I had such a limited knowledge of chemistry. Still, I began to scroll some articles. Selenium sulfide, used to treat dandruff. Pyrite, the most common sulfide mineral, is fool's gold. Ah, Toxic Sulfide.

"Sulfide can kill miners," I read aloud. "And hydrogen sulfide gas can kill sewer workers. The colorless gas reeks of rotten eggs." Yes, that had to be what spilled in my classroom. Although a liquid had wet the floor. Toxic sulfide, I read with interest, could be harmful in hydrothermal vents, deep-sea vents, seeps, and estuarine mud.

Oh, not quite the situation I'd been in. There were other sulfides, and even this hydrogen sulfide was sometimes used in water supplies. I quit reading. This search was only making me more confused.

I walked to the kitchen and poured a glass of water from the sink. I smelled it. No fart-rock odor and no rotten egg stench. I was grateful that police and maybe even scientists would be solving the mystery of what had transpired at Kat's school. Maybe what Kat needed to do tonight included studying for finals.

I sipped my unscented water, sharing it with Minnie in the den. I also repeated Kat's good news since I'd failed at discovering Minnie's type on the Web, and positive comments were

probably best for plants to hear. "Mrs. Peekers will be all right."
But someone had locked her in that room. Poured potentially
deadly substances. I had only Abby's word that the substance
spilled in my classroom hadn't been lethal. Suppose someone
was really out to harm me. And Kat was close to me—really
close.

I needed to do something that might help this troubling situation. I flipped through the phone book, found the location of
the nearest police station, and drove there.

Detective Dantin, a uniformed man of medium size and age,
guided me down a grimy hall where I spied a handwritten note
taped to the wall. *Fruit break at 9 and 2,* the note said.

"What's a fruit break?" I asked, following Dantin into his office.

"Some of the guys went to a class to stop smoking." He sat
behind his desk, while I took a chair. "They used to go out back
for a smoke break at nine and two. Now they bring fruit trays
out there instead."

I grinned and leaned forward. "Can you tell me what happened yesterday to a Mrs. Peekers at Sidmore High? My granddaughter goes to that school."

He made a half smile. "We have the incident under full
investigation. Right now, we can't give out further information."

"Well, I was there, and I saw the police wheel the woman out
of that supply room."

His smile lessened. Still no comment.

"I was subbing, and somebody tried to kill me."

That statement got his attention. Dantin typed my information on his computer. I told him I'd been locked in the
classroom. Maybe. One of his eyebrows lifted. I explained that
Abby said my door wasn't really locked, but I was certain it
was. Of course, John Winston opened it. He said the door just
opened when he tried the knob.

"John Winston," the cop said. "Is he a student?"

"Yes, but only for a few more days, just like my granddaughter Kat. She used to go out with him, but they broke up. Now they're about to graduate."

"I'll send someone out to school Monday to talk to this John Winston."

"Don't do that!" I explained about Kat already being mad at me for insinuating that John had caused a problem, and John told her he'd get everyone to stop being her friend.

"Sorry about that," Dantin said, although he didn't look like he was. "But we can't rule out a connection between these incidents until we investigate every lead. Thank you for bringing us this information, Mrs. Gunther."

Dammit. I wanted to kick my interfering butt while I drove away. I should have listened to Gil and stayed away from the school. Sadness swept through me. I really needed Gil's comfort. I told myself not to, but turned around and headed toward his restaurant.

Anticipation built as I neared his place.

Cajun Delights was all dark. The lot was, too, except for two vehicles parked near the rear. They rested close to each other.

Gil was probably inside, alone with Legs.

I accelerated past the restaurant. It had shut down early, maybe so he could have a grand celebration with his girlfriend. *Grrrr.* If he was having sex with that woman, well then I could have sex with someone else, too.

I drove around, looking for barrooms. Passed one. Undid my top button to show some cleavage. To hell with Gil. I'd find another man. Mature men and even much younger ones often gave me sidelong glances. I could pick up a guy from a lounge, take him back to the condo and make mad love all night long. Yes, I could. My sources on sexual behavior had assured me that older women, who were no longer bothered by concerns about getting pregnant, often enjoyed sex more than they did when younger. I shoved up on my underwire to make my fat boobs poke up higher.

I passed another bar. Restaurants. More bars. Spying a brightly lit one with many cars sitting out front, I slowed the Mustang. Pulled into the parking lot.

But making love—and having sex—two entirely different experiences. I wanted one, not the other.

I veered away from the place. "I'll keep my nose out of everybody's business," I told Minnie when I rushed into the condo and swooped her up. "And I'll never make another deathbed promise." I would also stay away from Gil forever, but I needed to quit thinking about him.

Minnie's soil was black from the last water I dumped. I apologized, returned her to the kitchen counter and turned off the light. I needed to hide away in the dark, too. Maybe I needed to avoid everyone. Kat was already furious with me. And now the police would show up at school and question John Winston, and he'd become extra furious. He would take it out on Kat. Maybe she'd never speak to me again.

I didn't know how to correct that situation. And now it seemed I was destroying Minnie. Unhappiness held on like a giant leech clinging to my skin.

A glow came from my laptop screen. I went to power it off.

Results of my last search were up. When I left sulfides, I'd returned to the Cactus Growers site. I sat down to exit the Web, and the words on screen captured my attention. Cacti have ovaries below the petals, I read. The tissue contains a cambium, a woody heart. . . . Oh, Minnie did have a heart. And an ovary. I glanced at the dark kitchen and smiled. Would she give me babies?

Some cacti live for centuries, I saw, skimming more. Some lived a year or two. Uh-oh. New Zealanders can't be trusted with *Lophophora*. Maybe I was part New Zealander. I hoped Minnie wasn't a *Lophophora*. I still hadn't found her type anywhere. This society that Harry Wren mentioned said it was America's organization for growers of cactuses. In the last two years, there had been 77,000 visits to this site. So Mr. Wren certainly wasn't its only member.

I had an urge to order the plants I saw with long hard spines and stick them where they would hurt whoever was causing all the problems with Kat's school. The custodian dead, a sub shot, Mrs. Peekers and I locked in. Chemicals spilled. Leave or die, bitch.

My body stiffened with new knowledge. Absolutely, they were connected.

Policemen were taking care of the situation. That was good. Maybe. And would Kat ever want to see me again?

My fingers trembled while I hit on computer keys. I wrote the cactus society a confession, admitting all the liquid I had poured on Minnie. I didn't know what the Ekkiwola Cacti Vault was, but saw it listed as only being able to operate through donations by visitors to its site. I made an online donation to the vault in atonement for hurting my plant.

I stood up and stared at the door. Everything inside me yearned to dash out there, drive through the dark and find Gil. I wanted to snuggle with him. No, I'd want more than that.

But he was with the sexy woman with long legs. And what would they be doing to finalize the celebration of his birthday?

More emotions rose. Hatred was a sentiment I didn't like to harbor. I struggled but couldn't shake it from my body. I felt the need for human contact. It was too late to call my friends in distant places. Too late to immerse myself in a crowded theater. And plant lovers all over the world were surely angry with me now. I couldn't even go to their chat rooms.

Gil was snuggling with his lover. I could toss on my slut

outfit, drive out, and pick up a man. I could show Gil. Yes, I could.

I shivered. Returning to the laptop, I saved "Beginner's Guide to Growing Cactuses" on a disk that I would take some place to get printed out. I slid the disk into my purse and then checked e-mail. Live people would have sent that.

Nine messages popped up. One promised to lengthen my penis. Three others said their cream would increase my bust measurements. Had Marisa Hernandez ever been tempted by such an ad? Hannah had high breasts for a woman her age. Maybe she'd discovered the Wonder Bra like Millie, who cursed the papers she ran off in the lounge. Anne Little, dubbing herself "keeper of the keys," was a big woman with medium-sized breasts. Tom Reynolds had called in sick yesterday. The only time he'd missed, a few hours before that, it seemed, was to attend Grant Labruzzo's funeral. Who pulled the fire alarm? And who dumped the cleansers? A man died at that school.

Flirtation. Jealousy. Motives for any of those horrible events?

Let's go back to Cairo a subject line on my screen said, and the tension in my jaw relaxed. I clicked for that message, sent by Betsy Tullis. Betsy and I had met while riding camels near each other. Betsy first belted out her contagious joyful laugh when I'd said I wanted to sit up on their humps—I said I always liked to straddle humps. Betsy was someone I planned to keep as a friend for a long time.

Cealie, have you been to Serengeti? If not, you need to rush right over. The stars are brilliant tonight and seem set in a velvet carpet. They look like they're right overhead—I believe I could touch them. I've watched exotic creatures in the wild and yesterday, took a sunrise balloon safari. The wildebeest have been traveling in columns several miles long. They must've spied a sexy female up ahead.

Sexy like you and me.

Miss you, Betsy.

I grinned. I thought of a sexy female, conjured an image of Legs, and lost my smile. I typed up a reply. *Betsy, I'm coming right over! Leave the door open. (Oh, you probably don't have one.) Well, leave a space by your side and I'll be there.* I considered a moment and then wrote *I'd really like to, but I'm near Chicago, about to watch my granddaughter graduate.* Was I telling the truth? *I told you about Kat. (I also mentioned Gil. He's here too, but that's another story.)* I smiled as my message went off toward the stars of Serengeti.

I deleted other messages until the second-to-last subject line said *Come visit us, Cealie.* Wilma Setton, whom I'd met on another trip, wrote it. Wilma had advised me about what to see and places to avoid while in Singapore. When we met on the plane, she'd just left her fourth husband. I didn't want to keep close company. Wilma believed she evolved from a cat, since her favorite activity was stretching up against males and sometimes trying to claw out their eyes. Here she invited me to visit her and her new mate in Denver. I deleted Wilma's message. The final subject line read *YOU'RE IN DANGER!*

Tightness gripping my chest advised me not to read the message. My semipsychic cousin Stevie had sent it. I ignored my instincts and read what she wrote anyway.

Stevie's entire message shouted: *CEALIE, YOU AND SOME- ONE NEAR YOU ARE IN EXTREME DANGER! YOU MUST LISTEN TO ME. MUST—STOP—WHAT YOU'RE DOING. I HAVE HORRIBLE VIBRATIONS. I SEE VISIONS. THEY SHOW THREATENING PEOPLE AROUND YOU. LEAVE THAT PLACE, CEALIE. I'M NOT KIDDING!*

YOUR FAVORITE COUSIN, STEVIE.

CHAPTER 17

Stevie's warning dried my mouth. I touched the delete button, not wanting to believe her e-mail message. More often than not, my cousin's foretelling missed the mark. But she had helped her local police solve a crime they'd considered unsolvable. And there were threatening people at Kat's school. What if Stevie was right this time?

My mail truck bore a message: *Leave or die.* How clear was that?

Who else around me might also be in danger? My arms hit my side with their shaking, and I said, "Kat."

A person had died at her school. Another had been taken off on a stretcher. I could avoid Sidmore High forever, but would Kat? Should she? I pondered alternatives, walking out the condo's back door into the dark. How important would graduation really be in Kat's future? Could ending her school years by going to take final exams bring about an end to her?

A knot balled up in my throat. I dropped to a lawn chair, barely noticing that people walked past. Night veiled the surrounding apartments. I stared out, my mind viewing unwanted scenes, trying to sort them to discover what seemed wrong. The threatening Sledge. The nonthreatening appearance of Marisa. Blood covering Grant Labruzzo, draped across folded chairs. Roxy, lips painted brown. The flap-flap of papers running through a copy machine, Deidre's pen bleeding red across tests. Coach's murderous voice. Hannah's jutting breasts, and Anne's

swinging hoop earrings. Abby's eyes hidden beneath bangs. Clashing voices and symbols. *Leave or die, bitch.*

All was silent now in the dark. I stood and found my legs unsteady.

Dashing into the condo, I slammed the sliding door to the courtyard. Turned the bolt lock. My pulse pounded. Who might threaten Kat? She was a child. I needed to protect her. I needed help.

I ran out front and took off in the Mustang. I drove, veering through Saturday-night-out-on-the-town traffic, and neared Cajun Delights. Staring ahead, I passed by it. I tore through streets while Stevie's warning bounced through my mind.

Kat's car was gone from the driveway when I reached her house. I parked behind Roger's truck. Lights were on in the kitchen and his bedroom. I shoved the bell at the back door.

A flicker of surprise crossed Roger's face, and then the smallest smile appeared. "Hello," he said, looking weary.

"Hi." I attempted a chipper tone, pecked a kiss on his cheek, and walked in.

He looked askance toward shiny appliances. "Can I get you something? Tea? A beer?"

I dropped to a chair, and Roger shifted his feet. "No thanks," I said. I forced myself to chitchat first. "Kat and I had a nice morning shopping."

"I saw the panda." He glanced toward the door. "Kat's at a movie with a friend."

"A girlfriend?"

Roger nodded, and I leaned forward, unable to keep up any pretense. "How do you think she's doing?"

"Doing?" He gave me a blank look.

"Toward graduation. Life in general." I wasn't exactly sure of what I wanted from my son. But I needed something. Someone.

I required the comfort of knowing that Kat would be supported. And safe.

Roger's response came from the bottom of his sigh. "I'm not sure." Unable or unwilling to express his real thoughts, he pulled out a chair and sat beside me.

"How is she, Roger?"

"Kat seems to be doing all right in school. As usual." His breathing appeared shallow. "She'll graduate. And then go off to college . . ." His gaze shifted toward the far wall. He resembled a man who was lost.

I touched his hand, the realization striking like a blow to my chest. His daughter, just like his wife, would soon leave him. And then he would be all alone. "You're really going to miss her," I said.

He swallowed hard, a small sound coming from his throat. "I will miss her."

"I could stay in town a while."

He made a sad laugh. "I'm a grown man. I don't need my mother staying around to take care of me."

Yes, maybe you do. But I could see his point. Having a mom hovering might make him feel less of a man. But I might possibly help. As the time neared for Kat's graduation, I'd have to feel out the situation.

This was certainly no time to intensify his worry. He had to know that a custodian died at Kat's school, but he didn't seem to have an inkling of how that death was affecting her. I couldn't tell him everything, couldn't make myself discuss the possibility that she might not graduate. I squeezed my boy's hands. "She'll do fine. So will you."

Uncertainty gripped Roger's face. His eyes looked haunted. I kissed his cheek and said, "Can I do anything to help?"

His lips made a shaky, sad smile. "Kat will be leaving home soon. What can you do about that?"

Both of us slowly got to our feet. I hugged Roger and he draped his arms across my back. My eyes burned. With a final squeeze, I went for the door. "You don't need to tell Kat I was here," I said.

Roger kept his semblance of a dazed person. I heard the door lock click behind me.

My chest felt like a heavy weight was in it while I drove. Besides trying to get over the loss of Nancy, Roger had been experiencing this extra grief. He dwelled on knowing he'd soon lose his daughter. I knew of a possible threat to Kat but hadn't been able to tell him. What kind of mother and grandma was I?

Headlights heading toward me all blurred. I swiped a hand across my eyes. They wet my fingers.

I wished the police would tell me what they knew or thought. I returned to the condo and let a long, hot shower sting me. Needing consolation, I powdered with a fluffy mitt and draped on a lightweight granny gown. I sat on the edge of the bed, held up the fabric, and admired the tiny yellow flowers on a white background, and tried to recall when I'd last worn the thing. The months while I'd been shedding my old self, I hadn't put it on. Instead I chose to wear nylons and silks. Especially during my tenure with Gil. I shoved away his image and the picture of what was surely his car, parked in darkness near his girlfriend's.

I sighed. This gown brought me comfort. It had attracted my focus in the closet, drawing me to it as though to an old friend. Bereft of spirit, I stretched beneath the bedcovers. I reached under the sheet, drew the gown's bottom down to my ankles, and curled to my side, willing my mind to shut down. *Sleep,* I said, using self-talk. Don't think of problems. Only positives.

When I couldn't do that, I urged my mind to blank out. No pictures. No faces. No threats. But someone had just warned me again. My mail truck. And now cousin Stevie. The image of Roger's face creased in misery came, and I willed it away, blanketing my mind with a black wall.

I awoke to glowing numerals on the clock near my bed. It was almost two a.m. Stevie would be getting ready to leave for her nighttime workout. I hustled up, grabbed my cell phone, and called her.

"Cealie!" she screamed, answering. "It worked!"

"What worked?" My mind only focused at this hour because of the heaviness weighing on it. Stevie was the only person I knew who purposely woke up in the middle of the night. She'd jump up from sleep, toss on workout clothes, and drive across town. After an hour and a half at the gym, she'd crawl back into bed for a final three hours of deep slumber.

"My message worked," she said.

"Yes, I received it. Oh my God, Stevie, I was afraid of that." My heart thump-thumped as I relived the fearful threat that she'd brought to my attention. I was in extreme danger. So was Kat.

Her laughter sputtered. Stevie's annoying laugh sounded as if she were choking. I used to think I'd have to pull off the Heimlich.

"What are you laughing at?" I asked. "I'm talking about the warning. You know, your message." It dawned on me that I hadn't noticed when she'd sent it. But a threat was a threat. She snorted. Stevie sounded like she was holding her breath between cackles. "What!" I shouted.

"Oh Cealie, I knew that would get your attention. That's why I made it up."

"You did *what?*"

"I don't know why you're mad. I don't even know where you are. But I miss you, favorite cousin. I just wanted you to get in touch with me."

"Stevie, I can't believe you!"

"I'm sorry. But please come over to visit. I have this big prob—"

I'd give her a problem, I promised myself, slamming my phone shut and tossing it down like a hot coal. My ears burned from fury. Fire might've come from my nostrils. My dear relative had made a fool of me. She'd percolated my emotions so that I feared for my granddaughter's life. And all had been done just for kicks. To get my attention.

She had my attention, all right. As far as I was concerned, Stevie needed lots more problems, and as soon as I could come up with a few catastrophic ones, I'd send them her way. What she'd done was unforgivable. Making me fear for Kat?

I stomped from the bedroom, flicking on every light. Sleep wouldn't return during the final hours before daylight. "Minnie," I cried in the kitchen, "you see why I try to avoid most of my relatives? They just get you in an uproar!" I nibbled on cheese and crackers, telling Minnie all that bugged me, especially my cousin. I still wondered about the advisability of Kat showing up for the commencement ceremony, but I was too irate to consider the reasons.

Negative talk might not be healthy for Minnie, but what were friends for, if not to listen? Minnie was a good listener. Daylight broke through the curtains by the time I was done with pouring out misery, and Minnie looked none the worse for it. I showered and then in my undies, did some big stretches. The exercise helped rid me of worry. Stretching loosened the last tightness in my muscles from the hula hoop and playing Twister.

I tossed on pretty clothes—a fuchsia linen dress and pantyhose without a control top—and made plans to have my son and his daughter for a meal. Of course, not on my cooking. And the restaurant we'd go to would *not* be Gil's. First I needed to convince Kat to talk to me. I'd try to go through Roger. But it was still too early to call their house.

From the pantry I grabbed the box holding my New Balance walking shoes. I put them on and went out, finding a misty morning that promised sunshine. I was the only person wearing a dress and stockings during my brisk stroll, but I wasn't bothered. My mind was clearing of murder. Most of the school people I had thought of last night couldn't be killers. I was certain of that now. They were ordinary people: teachers who got angry at teens and teens who acted up to challenge adults' authority. At the schools I'd attended while growing up, there had always been a few vocal teachers who criticized many students, and always a few students who attended, it seemed, only to give their teachers misery. That situation probably still occurred at every school.

My cousin's silly warning washed from my brain, and I pumped up my mind with positive thoughts, deciding I was an all-right parent and grandmother, at least as good as I knew how to be.

I smiled at a barking dog that led the way for his master, a pear-shaped man in navy jogging clothes emerging from around shrubs at the corner. Leaves drifted to the sidewalk ahead of me, sprinkling my path. I inhaled sweet fresh air and loosened my hands from their clenched position, letting my arms swing free, while my pace slackened.

At the corner I spun around, reminding myself that exercise was one of the many things I chose to do or not. Now I selected *not*, at least not so much that I'd work up a sweat.

The sound of a fast-moving vehicle coming up behind made me aware that hair grew on the back of my neck. I sprinted forward and glanced over my shoulder.

Exactly where I'd just placed my foot to turn around, a truck sped across the curb.

That truck had run a red light. And almost hit me.

I stopped, my body shaking like a six-pointer on the Richter scale. How close I'd just come to being run down. Accidental? Sprouting goose flesh told me maybe not.

I rushed back to where I had been. The black truck's rear bumper barreled around the far corner. The truck appeared mid-size, fairly new. Had I seen that truck in Sidmore High's parking lot? I struggled to envision all those vehicles from school jumbled in clumps.

Unable to remember any one truck, I jogged back to the condo. The driver probably only missed the edge of the road, I told myself, stilling my jittery hands to throw the lock inside the door. Maybe the driver fell asleep. The hour was still so early.

Had that driver even seen the red light? Or was he, or she, color-blind?

I leaned against the door, waiting for my heartbeats to slow. Suppose someone had been lurking, knowing where I was. That person could have waited for me to come out. Where had I given this address? Only to the school board and the auto repair shops. But students had definitely noticed what I drove. The avocado mail truck had been parked out front of the condo like an ugly neon sign advertising *Cealie's here.* Anybody from school could have recognized that vehicle. And now, the showy white Mustang convertible was parked out there.

"Dammit, Stevie," I blurted. She had given me those fearful ideas. No one was trying to harm me. I was back in the condo, priding myself on my healthy duckwalk, pleased that I hadn't worked my body nearly as hard as I used to. I mentally patted my back.

A chill skittered along it. Was it possibly that someone from school was coming after me? Yes. But I would go after them first. I needed to locate that black truck.

I grabbed the phone book. I had to find something. *Hernandez, Marisa.* On Holiday Drive. I jotted down her address. Breathing quicker, I flipped through pages, searching for more teachers. My shoulders fell. Not one other adult name that I knew from Sidmore High.

Changing my shoes, I took off in the Mustang. Maybe I'd see that black truck. After all, I was in the suburbs, not the city.

The streets slept during this early Sunday hour. I was usually asleep until after the sun rose, and now was surprised to see how vacant an area filled with moderate dwellings and businesses could become. Cars, trucks, and SUVs sat in driveways. Garage doors were all shut. No motion came from lawns or structures. I wondered about the people living inside. Most homes would hold hardworking parents and children who toiled at school. Some would house singles. A few—I wondered how many—might shelter killers.

"None," I told myself, willing it to be true. I careened around a corner, knowing that what I'd said was a lie. The world did harbor killers. I saw their faces on the evening news. Behind these shut draperies I passed were people sharing a hearty breakfast while plotting their attacks?

I scanned streets, searching for a late-model black truck.

Finding none, I stopped at a convenience store, bought a map showing this area, and a sweet roll and milk. I then sat in a booth with breakfast and scanned the map. Holiday Drive was only five blocks away.

I found Marisa Hernandez's street and saw bikes and plastic toys lying on some lawns. Most vehicles had been tucked into garages of unassuming brick houses, the majority of them one-story. I didn't see a truck like the one that nipped the corner I'd just walked across.

I shook my head, trying to make that picture leave. But fear stuck to me. Murderers might be living in these homes. And one might attend Kat's school.

I located Marisa's house. Attractive white brick, burgundy shutters, freshly mowed lawn. A closed garage. I didn't really suspect her, I told myself. After all, she was Kat's friend. But why would some people believe she was a killer? Even teachers in the lounge seemed to think so.

Grant Labruzzo also used to live down this street, Abby Jeansonne told me.

I drove down Holiday, hoping to find his name on a mailbox, hoping I could discern something by the proximity of his and Marisa's houses.

CHAPTER 18

I circled blocks throughout the subdivision, peering at mailboxes that displayed last names. I didn't see *Labruzzo*. Didn't see a black truck. I made another pass in front of Marisa's house. Still no sign of her or whatever she drove.

I left the residential area and wove through streets with little traffic, nearing a business section. The police station was close. Maybe I should tell Detective Dantin about what happened.

And what did happen? I considered. A black truck ran a red light and rolled over the corner of a sidewalk. A grin sneaked to my face. I sometimes made last-minute decisions while driving, took sharp turns and clipped a few corners myself.

Besides, tomorrow the detectives would question John Winston at school. Then he'd get more furious with Kat. And she'd get more furious with me and probably never want to see me. No way could I involve the police again.

I veered away from the station, sadness cloaking me. I wanted to help Kat, but each of my efforts only gave her more problems. A flashing indicator light on the car ahead made me realize I was creeping down the street just like the string of vehicles I followed. I would return to Marisa's subdivision. Maybe I should leave Kat's situation alone, but I couldn't. The traffic ahead of me appeared to be turning beyond a row of tall hedges. The road must be blocked. I signaled for a turn and followed the others, determining how I'd get back to Marisa's street from here.

"Silly, Cealie," I said with a laugh, noticing that I'd pulled into a church parking lot. Foolish me, a lamb trailing its leader. I headed toward the lot's exit. A second thought made me slow. My purse held my computer disk. Maybe I could pay someone in an office here to print out my instructions for the basics of how to raise a cactus. I circled the lot, saw lots of vehicles but no office. The only structure was a tall yellow warehouse with a marquee: *All-Believers' Church. Enter All Who Believe. We Especially Invite Those Who Don't.*

All-Believers. This was Grant Labruzzo's church. I hadn't thought to look for it in the phone book, but now here I was. And maybe I fit into their sign's last category. I parked beside a rusty minivan, determining that at the moment, I almost didn't believe in people, even myself. I hadn't found Labruzzo's house, but maybe I could learn more about him in here.

"Welcome, Sister!" a man's voice boomed when I entered the vast structure. A small person with suspenders, he had little sprouts of white hair on his head and a tremendous smile lighting his face. He caught me in an embrace.

"It's nice to see you," I said on a tinny breath once he let me go. Another greeter caught me. The barrel-like woman squeezed away the last air remaining in my lungs, and I tumbled into a nearby pew. Any other well-wishers would make me need emergency oxygen.

The large number of people who chatted in the refurbished building that smelled of incense surprised me. The varnished pews appeared new. Thick dark wooden beams ran up the walls and across the ceiling. The concrete floor chilled my feet. In front of all the pews stood a stage, the only thing on it a high-backed chair covered with royal blue velvet.

I tightened my shoulders, feeling out of place. My parents had brought me to church, but after I grew up and left them, I knew their choice hadn't been mine. In adulthood I perused other religions but neglected getting attached to any.

Voices swelled in the church cavity, filled with faces with tremendous smiles. "Good to see you, Sister," a youthful female voice said from my right. A teenage girl in a plain brown dress with an apron top clasped my hand. Her skin looked fresh with not a trace of makeup.

"All of you are so sweet," I said, taken with these people who seemed to honestly care. And Millie in the teachers' lounge had complained that churchgoers here were all crazy. Little did she know. Grant Labruzzo had probably been as caring as these people.

"This is my mother," the girl said, indicating a gnarled lady seated at her side. The lady looked much too old to be her parent.

"Happy to meet you," I said, stretching my hand out and flashing my largest smile.

Mamma's raisin face didn't leave its study of the pew in front of us.

The teen whispered, "She can't see or hear you or speak."

"Ah." I folded my arm back.

"She's here to get the spirit," the girl said, her voice having to rise with the upsweep of surrounding voices.

"I hope Mamma gets it," I said. Cheerful men, women, and children made me want that spirit, too. Babies asleep on some shoulders enticed me to want to hold them. I asked the teen, "Did you happen to know Grant Labruzzo? I believe he came here."

The girl's eyes glazed. "Brother Labruzzo."

Other voices dropped off. The girl peered toward the front, her countenance taking on a glow. I glanced forward, as all alleluia broke out.

"Alleluia. Alleluia, alleluia, brothers and sisters!" a preacher called out as he erupted from a door near the stage.

"Amen! Alleluia!" the congregation shouted. I said a quiet alleluia, wanting to replace my doldrums with these people's contagious joy. I was ready to hear their message. I especially liked seeing wholesome-looking teens in positive action.

"God loves you," Preacher called. Like a Broadway dancer, the agile man swooped down the center aisle, pumping his arms from beneath folds of his coral-pink gown. "He loves *you.*" Preacher stopped, his wrist cocked, his outstretched finger appearing to count every person in the warehouse. His statements drew more alleluias and many yeses. His finger-pointing toward the faithful made everyone start hopping. Preacher's fingertip found my area. Nearby bouncing bodies drew me out of reverie. Caught up in the energy, I felt special.

Believers began scurrying to the center aisle. People of all ages gathered, stretched their arms, and swayed.

I hoped I wouldn't have to join the jostling. But then I determined, as more of the congregation filled that area, I'd surely done worse. And their stretching and bending with arms flailing must be excellent exercise. Fun, but not strenuous. Kind of like a Richard Simmons workout.

The teen girl beside me screamed, "Oh, yes, yes!" and fell over sideways.

I gasped and reached for her.

"Alleluia!" Mamma yelled near the girl. Then the prune woman slumped.

Mamma could talk! I'd witnessed a miracle, I realized while rooting through my purse for my cell phone. The 911 lady answered. "Yes," I said, breathless, "I'm in a warehouse church." I started to explain the crisis—two people down in one family— when rising voices and thumps of falling bodies made too much noise for my voice to be heard. More people fell. Others tossed out their arms and shouted. People swayed. They slumped and fell to the floor. Had Legionnaire's disease filtered in through the vents?

"And He wants you! And you. And you!" Preacher called, his finger selecting for God. And once God chose, His elect tumbled, one after the other to the chilled cement floor.

"What's your emergency?" the woman on my handset yelled. "I'll send paramedics or firefighters or police. But you'll have to tell me what's happening."

My eyes expanded to take in the falling bodies. Beside my feet, the teen girl lay crumpled across a kneeler. She didn't appear to be breathing. My pulse raced. "People are passing out. You might need to remind me of how to do CPR," I hollered to my phone, which I set down on a pew while I knelt beside the girl.

As I went down, I spied a man from Sidmore High. Three rows up. Skinny vice-principal Tom Reynolds. He'd missed school Friday. His arms weren't flailing when he saw me. His eyes widened, his mouth opened, his face looked pale.

I folded down into position and clasped the girl's chin. Her cheek was cherry red from where it hit the kneeler. "You'll be all right," I said, hoping she could hear. I turned her nostrils so she could get air and hoped I could hear the 911 woman giving me instructions. I'd try for Mamma next. But she was lying so still. My mouth neared the teenager's, and her eyes popped open. "Alleluia, you're alive," I cried. Here I was, saving a person.

The aqua eyes of the girl with an angelic nature glared at me with such harshness that my hands shrank away. Her glare reminded me of Sledge. Her eye color made me think of another boy. "Your eyes resemble a student's," I muttered. "John Winston's."

She stared at me. "That darn John passed the note, made us believe Miss Hernandez was a killer."

My pulse stilled. I glanced at Mamma. She lay motionless, her big blue eyes peering at mine. Another miracle from Preacher. I let the teen go, and Mamma's lips curled into a grin. She shut her eyes, and her arms again slumped over the pew.

The sweet teen girl watched me sit back. When she seemed certain I'd remain there, she released a loud sigh and turned her face back against the kneeler.

"Hello! Are you still there?" the frantic words shouted from my phone.

I peered at people swooning everywhere. Preacher's well-fed face beamed. Bodies were falling around him like garbage being dumped into a heap. "I'm sorry," I said into my phone. "It's not an emergency. It seems there's a party going on." The 911 lady hung up. I peered around for Tom Reynolds.

No sign of him bent over a pew or sprawled on the floor. Maybe he'd been smart and done what I now knew I must do. I needed to get the hell out of this place before heaven surrounded me with more crumpled bodies.

"Come again, Sister," called a man who rose from a death-like trance when I ran past him, hitting the church doors on my way out. To my relief, they opened.

These people were like cult followers, I determined, veering my Mustang out of the parking lot. This had been a new experience I could add to all the others I'd had since I became an evolving woman, discovering the varying essences of life, selecting those from which I'd want to partake. Membership in All-Believers Church wouldn't be high on my list.

I hadn't seen Tom Reynolds outside the church. Obviously he was a member. No wonder he had accompanied Hannah to Grant Labruzzo's funeral. As principal, she would've represented the school. No other staff member attended the services. And Miss Gird said that Tom Reynolds had gotten Labruzzo hired for his custodial job, which he'd carried out so poorly. Why had Tom Reynolds run out once he saw me?

I didn't know but now developed definite ideas about what happened to Labruzzo. When he was up on the school auditorium's balcony, he probably swooned out of habit, like all those people who fell over the pews. He could have fallen. Yes, he could have.

I drove, getting vibes, but not good ones. I wanted to cook a six-course meal even more than I wanted to return to Kat's school. But I needed to go back there tomorrow. I had to find out why Tom Reynolds left the church so quickly. And I'd search the parking lot for black trucks.

The picture of a male falling brought to mind something I'd recently read. Maybe Grant Labruzzo took one of those post-Viagra pills that caused a few men to pass out. One man had cracked his skull and required stitches. An authority said some males might die because of taking that pill. "Wow," I said, suddenly envisioning Labruzzo as a lover. He'd certainly been young enough. But at that age, needing a sexual stimulant? Not from what I remembered about men. Yet the ad had said that even some males in their twenties started taking those pills. Gosh, hard to imagine.

I turned onto Holiday Drive, punching Roger's number in my cell phone, slowing before I reached the white brick house. Kat answered on the third ring. "Don't hang up," I said. "Kat, we were right. John Winston did write the note that said the police arrested Miss Hernandez. He wrote it and then sent it around your class just to get you worried."

"How would you know that?" Kat raised her tone. "You didn't go around asking people again, did you?"

"A girl from school was at a church service. I didn't ask. She just told me."

"Gram . . ."

"I promise."

I watched the garage door on Marisa's house sliding up, anxiety tightening my chest. I didn't want a black truck to roll back on that driveway.

"You really went to church?" Kat said.

"I was up real early and found one." My tension loosened as a blue compact car emerged from the garage. "Kat, do you know Tom Reynolds very well?"

"He's the vice-principal that mainly deals with discipline problems. I haven't been sent to him often." She made a small laugh, and I did the same.

Marisa backed her car toward the street. She glanced at my vehicle, but not at my face, and waited for me to pass.

"Who might know him?" I asked Kat.

"Mr. Reynolds is good friends with Miss Hernandez." I braked at the end of Hernandez's driveway. "But Gram, don't even think about talking to her. Promise me."

I inhaled, considered what I should do, and accelerated. "Baby girl, you get me to make a lot of promises." And if she only knew where I was . . .

The blue car headed in the opposite direction. I moved out of the neighborhood. "Kat, I want to take you and your dad out for dinner." *But surely not at Gil's place.*

"Sounds good. Let me ask Dad." She was gone for a minute and returned. "He said that's fine."

I recalled a mission. I had rented vehicles and needed to get them back to their dealers. "I'll need your help for a little while before we eat. How about if I pick you up early and have Roger meet us?"

She said she'd be ready. We hung up, and I relaxed. Kat was my friend again.

I drove back toward the church. Maybe I'd spot Tom Reynolds. I had left there so quickly that I hadn't taken much time to look outside. And I hadn't promised Kat I wouldn't talk to *him*.

Remembering all those swooning people made me reconnect with the idea of Grant Labruzzo as a lover. I considered sex. Dr. Marie, who'd examined me a few months ago, told me that many women weren't interested in sex after they reached a certain age.

I assured her I hadn't reached that age yet.

From her stool near my knees, Dr. Marie glanced up over pretty eyeglasses and said, "But not men. No matter how old they get, men never stop trying." I liked her immensely for telling me that story. I also liked her office, with wispy cheesecloth curtains in the old converted house. Antique dolls sat in small rockers, and lace doilies covered arms of overstuffed chairs. Used buttons created interesting patterns in picture frames on fireplace mantels. I enjoyed Dr. Marie so much that I could've brought her along with me. Or instead I could fly back through New England to see her each fall while the foliage displayed its splendor.

That would help Sidmore High, I decided. Cheesecloth curtains, a few antique furnishings. Maybe Mozart playing from hall speakers. More flowers and trees. If the kids had a place that felt grounded, maybe they'd be content and not get into those violent moods.

I smiled. I'd suggest those changes to the administrators come morning. I grinned harder, deciding that a woman had surely invented the stirrup system in Dr. Marie's office. So unlike those stirrups at the end of straight beds, hers were attached to a comfortable lounge chair.

Again I considered what I'd read. Had Grant Labruzzo had a problem with penile erection? And if he did, like Dr. Marie said, he surely wouldn't want to give up. "Try this new medication for men," some aging doctor could have told him. "It might make you weak, but it's worth a try." I imagined that doctor winking. Man-to-man stuff.

Grant Labruzzo tried the medicine. He climbed to the school balcony to clean. Got weak and fell. Cracked his neck. Died.

Was that possible? Plausible? *Come on, Cealie, you can do better than that.* Of course an autopsy would've proven whether any drugs had been in Labruzzo's system at the time of death.

I located the church and found its parking lot still filled with vehicles. Driving around every row, I saw no late-model black truck, no sign of Tom Reynolds.

I returned to the condo with no definite idea about what happened to Grant Labruzzo. The police would be solving the mystery concerning his death. Maybe by now they'd discovered he'd only fallen. I needed to shift my mind away from that problem.

With much time to spare before taking my family out to eat, I decided to spend that time doing as I pleased. What pleased me at the moment was reading. My cookbooks were only for putting me to sleep, and I didn't want any sexually stimulating material from my newsletter now, so I flipped through the novels I'd purchased at the airport. The cover of *Lover Killer* promised "A humorous romance with murder."

I shoved that book under my arm and dropped a Bette Midler CD into my personal player. Carrying the sound system and a cup of steaming instant mint tea to the patio, I considered the novel's premise. Lover. Killing. Grant Labruzzo's young face. I had thought of him as his job title, custodian. Yet he did have another life. Abby had suggested and Kat confirmed that he'd been a flirt. Suppose he'd had a sweetheart? He wasn't married, I'd gleaned from his obituary. So suppose a disconcerted lover showed up at school after hours.

A student? Some teenage girls adored older men. And what if

they'd had a heated argument, way up on the balcony? This young woman, I envisioned in a growing picture of the dark auditorium, went into a rampage. She swore at him, displaying a violent temper, and then—What? Picked him up and tossed him over the railing?

"Silly silly, Cealie," I said, sliding the glass door shut. I'd probably just reconnected with that image of Miss Hernandez going after the custodian. Or maybe I had already read too many mysteries.

More people were out than before. I set my CD player on a small table and noted a floral fragrance wafting on a breeze. Shrubs and leaves of trees appeared to be dancing. The brick wall that separated the patios back here looked extra red in the sunlight. I stretched on a chaise lounge and enjoyed the lazy way vehicles moved beyond the hedges on a Sunday morning, much less rushed than on weekdays. Two women jogged past. "You're doing great," I called.

"Thanks," the first one replied. The straggler behind her resembled a wrestler. *She* could have tossed anyone off a balcony.

I tuned in to birds' songs, admired the condo's manicured flowerbeds, and got in touch with the slight warmth from the clear azure sky. A thumping sounded from a basketball bouncing nearby. I felt at peace with the world and its inhabitants, and took sips of my tea. Happy to take a break from worries, I set Bette crooning softly in my earphones and started my novel, ready to laugh.

On page one, a woman died. Drive-by shooting. Kidnappers snatched her son on page two. This wasn't funny. My pulse sped. I didn't want these bad things to happen. The kidnapper who'd shot the mom made smart comments to his partner. Was this the humor? Thugs began to threaten the boy, shoving a gun to his nose, while their truck sputtered, running out of gas. The truck's sputter. The pistol hammer's click.

I shut Bette up, slammed down the book, and stood.

A *pow* like a gunshot had come from the road. A truck, similar in detail to the one in the novel, puttered by. That rickety truck had problems and had probably backfired. And if I hadn't heard that old model, I wouldn't have noticed the mid-sized black truck. It moved before me much more quietly than Bette's voice. It was beyond the brick wall.

I dashed toward the street. I could see the far corner, where the black truck whizzed into a heavy flow of traffic. An instinct told me to run to my car and try to follow.

Come on, Cealie, you've seen too many cop movies.

A young woman jogged toward me. I flagged her down, and she slipped off her earphones. "Did you see who was driving that black truck?" I asked. "A man? Woman? Teenager?"

"Truck?" She glanced at the road, turned and gave me a blank stare. "Uh-uh." Reconnecting her earphones, she jogged on.

Tomorrow I would definitely search Sidmore High's parking lot for that truck. But the rear bumpers of most vehicles there had had school parking stickers. This one's bumper had no sticker that I'd seen.

My heart continued to make knicky-knack jumps when I returned to the patio. I bent to retrieve my CD player and noticed that three feet beyond, between potted plants, something small glittered.

I walked there and lifted a bullet.

CHAPTER 19

I dashed into the condo, slammed the door, bolted the lock and leaned against the door, my heartbeats thrusting into my throat. But bullets could pierce doors. I jumped aside and moved deeper into the condo. Yanking up my cell phone, I saw I'd missed an incoming call and punched nine-one. I stopped before hitting one again. Exactly what was I going to tell the lady this time? That a black truck, possibly the same one I'd seen before, drove down this road? "So what?" she'd certainly ask.

"Somebody in it shot at me," I'd say, insisting she do something. Send the cops. I opened my hand and stared at the bullet. Without the sunlight, it no longer looked shiny. In fact it could've been old. Maybe the bullet had been lying on the patio for quite some time, hidden as it was by the pots holding plants. "But suppose it wasn't?" I might ask the woman who'd answer my emergency call. "What if someone tried to kill me?"

I'd read many mysteries and knew how the plot could go. Deadly plots. I lifted my finger and touched the numeral one again. Then I hit *off.* This was real life, not a story. And I was sure that old truck had backfired and made the noise. Still, my shivering body yearned for comfort. I envisioned Gil, his compassionate gray eyes, broad shoulders, and warm embrace. Should I call him?

I shook my head. I had no idea whether I was now threatened. And we were no longer a couple. I decided to bounce thoughts around to a new friend. Flicking on the light above Minnie, I said, "Cousin Stevie's ridiculous warning sent my imagination into overdrive. And at this church I saw the believers dropping like shot birds. Then this novel I started to read gave me creepy ideas." I considered a moment. "So should I call 911?"

I didn't fear making a fool of myself. I had done that many times and surely would again. But I wouldn't ask for help unless there was an actual emergency, like I thought I'd seen at All-Believers warehouse church. If people were dying, I'd need medical assistance for them. And if someone shot at me, I'd call the police. Other than that, I could take care of myself. I walked, cloaking myself in my mantra—"I am woman. I can do anything—alone." No one actually died at that church, and I had no idea whether anyone shot at me. I dropped the bullet into my purse. Tomorrow I'd try to find out what type of gun had shot that substitute teacher, Jayne Ackers, whose murder might not have anything to do with the school. After all, people got shot every day. This was the U.S. of A., wasn't it?

I recalled that talking to my friend Minnie would make her happier and told her a little about the mystery I'd begun reading. I believe she enjoyed it, for her body seemed straighter. With all of my recent horticultural knowledge, she'd be thriving soon. She would be my companion for a very long time.

Leaving her, I checked to see whose phone call I'd missed. The number came from Cape Cod, but not my office. It was the home number of my manager, Bud Denton, and he never phoned me from home. Fearing bad news, I returned the call. "Bud, how are you? What's wrong?"

"Cealie, I know you can't put a colon after *are*, but I'm not sure why."

The anxiety I'd felt left.

He said, "A client from the Chamber asked me that after I deleted the colon from her copy. I tried to look up the rule but don't have any of the books at home, and my Internet server's down."

Another question similar to the one from Brianna with no hips? I said, "It's because you can't place a colon in front of a predicate nominative."

"Oh, and that would be any noun or pronoun that follows a linking verb."

"Exactly."

"Thanks, boss."

"How's the weather, Bud? And your family?"

"The weather's terrific. Fifty-four today. And Lilly and kids, well, you know how they keep me busy."

"I know. Please tell them hi for me. And everyone at the office." Before we rang off, I thought about my gynecologist, Dr. Marie, up in that area, and knew I'd soon be around her office and mine. It seemed time to help some people brush up on grammar. Our copywriting agency did so much more than write proper sentences. We often broke rules of grammar, but everyone first had to know them.

"I'll tell them. Thanks again, Cealie."

"And Bud, please don't take any work home. Keep the evenings and weekends free for your family." We clicked off. Bud Denton was a good manager. The rest of the staff liked him. His wife seemed a flighty woman, or maybe I just thought that because she was blond to the roots. My own hair would need a touchup soon—of natural burnt sienna. I slipped my phone into my purse, glad my cousin Stevie hadn't called. If she'd had caller ID, she would have my cell phone number and probably call every time she had a funny notion to scare me.

I stretched out on the couch to totally relax body and mind. I napped for some time, and when I awoke, remained lying there on my back. Setting my CD earphones on, I listened to Bette singing "Wind beneath My Wings," my mind summoning an image of Gil. Like the wind, he had carried me through numerous days and nights, giving them meaning. And like the man in the song, Gil was my hero. But Gil was—gone from my life. I replaced Bette with the upbeat jazz of Harry Connick, Jr., trotted to the kitchen, and grabbed my red pumps with stiletto heels. Time to get Kat. And then to eat, avoiding Gil.

I swerved the Mustang to the road, my late husband coming to mind while I drove. Freddy had been a good man, kind and strong and always there when I needed him. And Freddy died. I'd needed him, and he left me. Fear made itself known by the way my body tensed. Fear from reliving the end with Freddy? Or keeping my eyes swaying toward side streets and my rearview mirror, searching for a black truck that might dart out at me? Street traffic had begun to thicken. On that horrible morning with Freddy, I had awakened with him patting my left arm like always, and then when he strolled from our bed, he crumpled. I shrieked, crying out his name, felt for a pulse and found none. With shaky hands, I clasped the phone, yelling what happened. Men dashed in, following their blaring sirens. A fellow with kind eyes pulled me away from Freddy.

I needed Freddy. Cherished him. He abandoned me. And dammit, I wouldn't depend on another man. Wind swept over me from the open top of my Mustang, and I wiped scorching tears from my cheeks. No, I didn't need to go around Gil. No man in my life again. Too much dependence, and then too strong a loss. You are a couple. And then you're . . . what? Who? I had forgotten, but was trying to find out. And I didn't need Gil Thurman's presence mucking up my intent! I grabbed Bette's CD from the seat and tossed it to the highway. Smiling, I imagined I could hear all the tires behind me crunching across her song.

A police car came up on my left and I tapped my brakes, giving its driver a friendly wave. My head whipped back. I had also traveled beside a black truck, heading in the opposite direction. Worry tightened my spine. I floored the accelerator, keeping an eye out for police cars but especially for a truck that might turn around to follow me.

Traffic was lighter by the time I approached Kat's subdivision. No dark trucks in sight. I wanted Gil and shunned that thought, wishing I'd kept Bette's CD. Then here, with fewer cars around, I could toss it out and roll my car back and forth over it, making sure to squash the notion of needing a man. I forced on a smile and was singing "Blue Suede Shoes" from my Elvis CD when Kat answered the door.

"You like Elvis?" she said, grinning. "I'd almost forgotten that song."

"Well, sing it with me, girl." I placed an arm around her waist, and we sang while I ushered her through the dark living room. I changed *blue* in the song to *red*, pausing to wriggle my stilettos in front of Nancy's picture. She'd like that, I told Kat, who smiled and agreed.

"Baby girl," I said once we reached the kitchen. I quit wiggling my body and clasped Kat's shoulders. "Sometimes sad thoughts come that I don't want in this noggin." I tapped my head. "So then I rummage to find other things to think about. Or to sing." I told her because Kat needed suggestions for what she might do when things weren't going as she wanted them to. And I wouldn't be around her much longer.

She said, "And your voice . . ." Kat appeared to be trying to find nice words to say, but she couldn't.

"My singing could make infants cry," I conceded. We both chuckled. Then through the bay window, I spied Roger spading in his flowerbed. His back was toward me, so I couldn't tell his mood. Kat watched him with me. "Sometimes it takes a long time to find the right thought or song," I said, and she leaned her head sideways, down to my shoulder. I stroked her head. "But when you need to change something bad enough, you'll find the right lyrics."

She straightened, smiled gratefully and kissed my cheek.

"I came early," I said. "Are you ready?"

"Ready."

"You look pretty. Gorgeous really." Kat's gold-toned dress accented her reddish hair and brought out her curves. Some of her upswept hair fell loose from its tortoiseshell comb. "I messed up your hair when I rubbed it," I said.

She felt the tendrils. "I'll go fix it."

When Kat went off, I walked outside. "Hi, Roger. Isn't today a beauty?"

My son turned, shovel in hand. "Is it already time to go?"

"Not quite. I have an errand to run and thought I'd get Kat on the way."

He cocked back his head. "And you'll want to eat at Cajun Delights?"

"We don't have to." *Yes, we do.* "We can eat any place you'd like."

"Gil's place is good."

"Or how about Polish food? Or Chinese?"

"We'll do Cajun. I'm almost finished here." He wore dress slacks and a plaid shirt and hadn't worked up a sweat. He stared at my shoes, and his brow wrinkled.

"You don't want me to grow frumpy as I age, do you?" I said, and he almost smiled. "See you in a few minutes," I told him. Whether he liked it or not, I chose not to look dowdy. I spun on my red heels. Felt the grass twist around them. Roger eyed me while I lifted each foot out of my shoes and tugged at the grass to make it let go. Then, smiling at Roger, I slipped my shoes on again and went inside.

Kat had every strand of hair back in place. "What about if we

221

eat Mexican tonight?" I suggested.

"I thought we'd go to Mr. Gil's place. I love all the food in his restaurants." Her smile widened. "And you never know, he might be there."

Anticipation swam through my stomach. We walked outside, and Kat glanced at me long enough to let me know she wondered about my reaction. Did I want to see Gil? She liked him. I always knew that. So did Roger, I believed. I kept my lips tight, my face noncommittal. I wouldn't show her the turmoil of my own feelings. She smirked, and I sang about red shoes, putting the Mustang's top up so I wouldn't mess her hair.

My ideas rounded away from lovers. I wanted to ask whether Kat knew of anyone who might have a motive for killing the custodian, but I needed to make only happy talk. She and Roger needed their spirits lifted. And Kat also needed—to take her exams? She hummed a solemn tune. To stop her, I said, "Sweetie, do you know what I need now?"

"Gram, with you, I have no earthly idea."

"Take your pick." I pulled into the repair shop's parking lot. "Decide whether you'd like to drive this Mustang or a Lexus." Kat snickered, and I said, "You have about three minutes to decide."

She remained in the Mustang while I went in and paid the bill for the work done on the Lexus. "Looks like new," said long-haired Johnny, who led me out back to the car. The kinks from where someone had kicked in the driver's door were gone. No more scratches across the trunk from where it had been keyed.

I trotted out to Kat, holding two keys. "Choose." She chose the Mustang. "Follow me," I said, getting into the Lexus. I led the way a few blocks down to Dickers Rent-to-Own.

"I decided not to buy this Lexus," I told Dickers, whose exuberance vanished. He wanted to show me other vehicles in the same price range, but I declined. I almost said I had a rented Mustang outside and a mail truck in another repair shop, but doubted the advisability of making that comment. He followed me to the front of the dealership, still trying to convince me to buy an expensive car. We neared the Mustang when his angry tone rose. He seemed a different person, not a nice one. "I won't be back," I said. "Young man, when you're in a business, you don't act one way to a customer when you think she'll make a purchase, and another way when she doesn't."

His puffing face reddened. "I don't do that."

"Yes, you do. And it's wrong. It's also bad business." I spun on my stilettos. "And I won't even charge you for my advice."

I rounded the Mustang and slid into the passenger seat. "Let's go," I told Kat.

She started the car. "Why did you have that Lexus in a repair shop?"

"It didn't have enough power." Kat giggled, and I said, "Do you know where Gil's place is?"

"I watched them building it, hoping I'd get to see Mr. Gil outside one day. But I didn't." She glanced at my face, and I tried to refrain from thinking of Gil. We were going to his place, so if he was there, I'd probably see him. I offered Kat a tiny shrug before she took off.

We found the restaurant's parking lot nearly filled and met Roger near the pond. Kat wanted to watch the ducks swimming. "Mm, that smells yummy," she said, peering at the front door when it opened. The scent of fried and boiled seafood made my belly joyful that we'd chosen this place.

"Gil sure does a nice job with these restaurants," Roger said, glancing at our surroundings as we walked. Like me, he probably felt as though he were out in some quiet place in nature instead of the vicinity of a large city. "Nice stained glass," Roger said, opening the door for us. I let Kat go in first. If she spotted Gil, she'd react.

I followed her, my head swiveling. Customers everywhere. Some rising from chairs with their doggie bags. No Legs. And no sign of Gil. I silently cursed. A woman led us past the table where Gil had sat when I'd first seen him. People ate there now and had left no empty chair for him. Soft music played from a jukebox, and people chattered. Dishes being set down or lifted made soft clatters. The young woman who guided us glanced at me. "Nice to see you again," she said. "How are you?"

"I'm great. And you?"

"Never better." She stopped at a table beside Gil's. "Will this do?"

"This is fine," I said, and we all sat.

Kat raved about this new place. She'd have to come often. She peered at Roger. "All right, Dad?"

A hooded look came to his eyes. "If you're around much after graduation."

That was it. Gloom rained down on our table. Kat's smile faded. Roger's usual somber expression replaced his earlier pleasant one. I yearned to shout and shake them. Where had my family's happiness gone?

But I knew. Even as Roger had doubts about what life would be like after his child went off to college, Kat wondered, too. She'd miss him. He would miss her. I was already missing both of them. But what could I do, hang around with my adult son? Go off to college with his daughter?

At least for the moment, my attention spun away from murder. Right here, right now was most important for the three of us. "Things will be different when you leave," I said, placing my hand on Kat's.

Her gaze clouded. She turned to Roger and with her free hand, grabbed his. My son's fingers slid back, almost shrinking from her clasp. Then his hand moved up, and he allowed Kat to hold it in place. Roger's eyes moistened.

"Are you ready for jokes?" the manager called through the microphone, and customers clapped in anticipation.

A waitress came. "Would you like to give your order now, or do you need more time?"

"Ready," I said. Kat wanted everything she loved from these menus, but today would take fried scallops and crab claws. And French fries. I didn't especially like to feel my rear end wobbling behind me, so I normally ate light evening meals. But this one was special. "Ditto," I said, "but instead of fries, I'd like a baked potato. All dressed, please."

"I'll have fried frog legs," Roger said without opening his menu. Kat and I smirked. Apparently she also remembered when Gil convinced Roger to try them. But he had warned Roger that after he ate one, he'd be hooked, and he probably wouldn't be able to find any frog legs around Chicago. It had been the time when Kat and Roger came down to Vicksburg, about six months after Nancy died. They needed to get out of the house and try to escape grieving. The apartment I'd rented had ample bedrooms, and Gil moved his things out before they arrived. During our days together, we sometimes all laughed. Especially during the joke contests and on that evening in the restaurant when Gil convinced Roger to try the frog legs. After his first nibble, Roger asked for forty more. Of course he was kidding, but he ate them every evening after that until he and Kat flew home.

He must have also recalled the trip. Our waitress left the table, and Roger turned to Kat and me with a shy smile. "Do you think twenty legs are too many for me?"

"Naw," we both said, knowing his entrée would hold about half a dozen. The mood at our table had defrosted. We all adjusted our chairs to see the stage, and Kat giggled loudly at the jokesters. I was especially pleased to see Roger seeming to forget his worries. He smiled at people telling the jokes. I liked the way his cheeks crimped when he was happy. But I couldn't get involved in the contest. My interest held on the pair sitting with me and swayed to the table immediately behind me. I tried to face forward but often glanced over my shoulder.

Kat said, "Do you think Mr. Gil will come in tonight?"

I shrugged, attempting a look that said I didn't care. Roger eyed me, and I couldn't tell if he cared whether Gil showed up or not. With Roger lately, who knew what he cared about or if he cared about anything at all? Except that his daughter would soon leave him all alone. Fear of losing another beloved person had overtaken his loneliness from losing Nancy. I understood. My security had come from being Freddy's wife. A while after he vanished from my side, I found Gil. Parting had been painful, but still, I left him; therefore, he couldn't leave me. *Damn,* I thought, *why is it so difficult to understand the stages of love and life?*

I had to shift my thought pattern. "What university do you think you'll attend?" I asked Kat. Nibbling on a cracker, I tried to make the question sound unimportant.

Roger watched her, waiting for her answer. She sipped a cola, her eyes turned away from his gaze. "I'm not sure yet."

Roger set down his water glass. "Kat has choices. On Class Day she received different scholarship offers." He feared her leaving, but looked proud of her achievements.

"Wish I could have seen that," I said.

"You can't be everywhere," Kat said, "and it was no big deal." Relief washed her face. I couldn't tell if it was from the cup of corn soup with shrimp being served to her, or from not having to continue this area of conversation.

I pursued it anyway. "I'm sure your final average needs to remain close to where it's been for you to receive total coverage of those scholarship offers."

She ate, pointing to her mouth to show us she couldn't talk.

Roger leaned toward me. "Why shouldn't her average stay the same?"

I tipped my spoon into my duck gumbo. Kat quit chewing. Her head made a deliberate turn toward me, and then she looked at her dad. "It shouldn't change," she said.

I felt her stare. But my deductions had made me fairly certain that she'd be safe at school the next few days. And I wasn't backing down now. "So what exams do you take tomorrow?"

Her nostrils loudly blew out air. "Chemistry. Advanced Placement English."

"Those exams shouldn't give you major problems, should they?" Roger said.

Absolute silence set upon our table. I clinked my spoon around inside my dish to insert sound. Kat cleared her throat. "No, Dad, they shouldn't."

Ah, that's what I wanted to hear. "Good luck with them," I told her.

"Thank you," Kat said, her tone frigid.

I almost asked if she'd heard anything new about the condition of Mrs. Peekers, but Roger would have questioned my knowing about school. I doubted whether he'd believe I subbed because I needed money. And I doubted whether Kat had told him anything about her recent concerns. "Kat likes her Spanish teacher," I said between bites of gumbo. I glanced at Roger and could see Kat's head snapping toward me.

"Kat finished taking her Spanish classes last year," Roger said. He looked at Kat. "You used to talk about that teacher. What was her name?"

"Miss Hernandez."

Roger nodded, and a waiter served our entrées. Conversation turned to how good all our food looked and tasted. The glint off

Kat's fork when she lifted it made me think of the bullet in my shoulder bag. But she didn't need more worries at this time. And Roger—well, he was Roger, with his mind aloft in some neverland. I bit into golden crab claws. The batter crunched, and sweet meat flaked into my mouth. The chewy scallops were tasty. I offered Roger some of each, but he was so busy gobbling frog legs that he said nothing else would fit in his stomach. Nonchalantly, I said, "Have you done any dating, Son?"

Both his head and Kat's swerved toward me. Roger appeared to choke while he stared at me as though I'd poured burnt coals on his head. I couldn't help myself. I snickered. Kat remained silent a moment. Then she giggled.

Red flamed up to Roger's cheeks. Anger struck his eyes. His lower lip spread up over his top one. I gripped his arm. "We all miss Nancy. You and Kat and I adored her. But Nancy left this world, and no amount of mourning will bring her back."

Kat's expression seemed a combination of pain and gratitude. At least on this, I felt she was with me. I couldn't let Roger go yet. "Son, you're still a young man. Nancy wanted you to keep on living, and Kat needs you to do that."

Kat sat motionless.

Roger threw his napkin down on his plate. "I'm done here." He waved to call our passing waitress and said, "We need the ticket. Now."

"I'll get it," I said, but he insisted on paying.

Kat and I rose to leave, and the waitress who'd recognized me earlier touched my shoulder. "You were here with Mr. Gil for his birthday, weren't you?"

I smiled. "Yes, I was."

"He's such a nice person to work for. The employees got together to get him a gift. Then yesterday, as a gift to us, he let us close early." She shook her head and started away.

"Wait," I called. "He isn't here tonight, is he? In an office or something?"

"I'm afraid not."

Disappointment struck me, and I bit it back. I said, "Oh, and I've seen this attractive woman around here. Young thing with black hair, big bazookas." I reached far out in front of my breasts and cupped my hands.

The waitress laughed. "She isn't here either."

"I just wondered." I hurried toward the exit.

With some delight, Kat came to my side. "It would have been nice to see Mr. Gil again."

"Maybe so." I rushed out the door. Spotlights lit the bridge. I waited there and bent my neck as if I were especially interested in anything swimming in the black water underneath.

Kat nudged my side. "So tell me about you and Mr. Gil."

"I stopped for a meal, and he happened to be here. That's it."

She made a huge smile, and Roger came out, his face stern. "Kat, are you riding home with me?"

"Did you need me to drive anything?" she asked me, still smirking.

"No, thanks." The kid was digging it in. She thought something was brewing between Gil and me again. Her little secret. "Thank you for the meal," I said to Roger, and he grunted. To Kat I said, "Good luck with those exams you'll be taking tomorrow."

Her grin vanished. She scooted off with Roger, and neither of them said another word to me. Still, I was happy. Kat would return to school and complete her work. No one would bother her there. She'd be safe. And before this week ended, she'd be finished.

I trotted to the Mustang and felt my smug expression fading. Where was Gil? Off with that woman? Even if I wanted him back in my life, could I get him?

Gil wasn't here. An unbelievable tidal wave of grief washed through me.

CHAPTER 20

Returning to the condo, I mused. Kat would take those finals—
I hoped. She wasn't happy and might not want to speak to me
again. But that was probably okay, as long as she took exams. I
could get Kat to talk.

I walked restlessly and reentered the dark den, my apprehension returning. Kat and Sidmore High. John Winston would
become livid with her tomorrow when the police questioned
him there because of me. My knees wobbled, possibly from the
stiletto heels I kicked off. Little good they had done. Gil hadn't
been around to see. Neither had the woman with black stockings. . . . *Black.* A black truck had come near twice, each time
for its driver to possibly hurt me. The same truck? I wasn't sure
but somehow needed to get the bullet checked out.

I used up nervous energy by buffing the stovetop with a thick
dry towel. I drank water to moisten my throat. I poured a refill
and automatically dumped it on Minnie. "Oh, no! I'm sorry," I
said, grabbing paper towels. I wadded and pressed them against
the soil. I carried Minnie to the sink and tried to hold in the
dirt while I turned her pot sideways. Clumps of black dirt fell.
No water ran out.

I was doing as badly as Grant Labruzzo had done with Harry
Wren's prized Cero plant.

Apologizing profusely, I attempted to right Minnie to her
former erect position. "That's a girl," I said, urging her
straighter. Her little pink head refused to stay upright. My damp

eyes stung. I was envisioning Kat's hostility and Roger's grief. Gil hadn't been there when I wanted him.

Sniffling, I set Minnie on a counter far from the sink and said, "I'll try to do better." I needed to get thoughts away from family and fears and my former lover, so I went for something that would make me content. I couldn't dwell on problems I couldn't solve. I was a positive person. I was positive the police would discover who'd hurt people from school and with the swift hand of justice, punish them. And I'd do whatever I could to help Roger and Kat.

I located relaxing reading material in the dishwasher, then drizzled lavender-scented oils into my bath water. On the corner of the Jacuzzi, I lit vanilla-scented candles, slender to chunky ones. I set the overhead light on dim. The candle flickers created a pleasant illusion while I stepped into swirling tepid water. I laid my head back on the bath pillow and skimmed my cookbook from Georgia. Not the culinary capital of the country, I decided. But after I'd first dined at Gil's restaurant, no other foods could compare.

Antipasto was the first entry I read. Mm, good dozing material. To create this appetizer, you'd have to shop for seventeen items. Seventeen! Any silly woman who fixed this dish would need a can of mushrooms and one of artichokes, some Spanish olives, ripe olives, bell pepper, celery, white vinegar. . . . I wondered what would happen if you used dark vinegar instead. Snickering, I felt superior to any person who might actually attempt this chore.

You'd serve these hors d'oeuvres and then have all those empty jars and cans and dirty dishes in the kitchen. And this was only to give guests an appetite! Next item: *Antipasto II. Easy.* Ah, a wiser person created this recipe. But it required ten items.

My body relaxed, growing weary from imagining having to

shove the huge grocery cart out to a car, lug all those bags inside, follow each step in order to prepare the dishes. *Cheese Ball I and II.* Didn't everyone know you could purchase balls of cheese? *Curry Chutney Mold.* Yuk.

My eyes shut. I willed them open so I wouldn't sink. I watched the candles flicker, and eyed wall shadows that created interesting dancing figures. Shadowed figures. One approached me. And Grant Labruzzo. I thrust my attention to the book. *Mrs. Jackson's Cheese Straws.* Oh, come on now. Surely these recipes had been written to calm their readers into sleeping. *Cheese Wafers I:* flour, garlic salt, shredded American cheese. Ridiculous. No kitchen today would still hold a shredder.

I thought of Gil and my family. My gaze shifted to the squat candle. I watched its flame shift and yielded myself to a meditative condition. My family would be all right. *Give yourself totally to this moment,* my wise thoughts said. My eyes rolled toward the cookbook. *Jalapeno Cocktail Pie. Rolled Cheese Fingers.*

Gil's warm fingers. All their wonderful magic I was missing. Streams of water pulsated out the sides of my tub. Enticing warm bubbles. I shifted my torso, and the water jet gave my thighs a little quiver. Mmm. I shut my eyes and replayed mental pictures of Gil. His deep gray-eyed gaze penetrating mine. His body, nude. The hot water surrounding me helped me relive how I felt pressed against him . . . I shivered. Jet bubbles sent relief washing through every inch of my body.

A strident rattling sound made me jump.

My eyes snapped open. The noise, I determined, had been my snores. I'd sunken to my shoulders, my nostrils filled with the scent of the lavender water that was tickling my lower lip. The bottom edge of one my favorite cookbooks had turned dark from touching the water.

I climbed out the tub and spread the book's pages to dry.

Dressed in my softest nightgown, I crawled into bed. Sleep overtook me in seconds.

I awoke hungry, entertaining visions of lavender-colored foods flavored with vanilla. My hair needed washing but not my body, since it had been totally cleansed. And sated.

The sun hadn't appeared yet when I leaned over the lavatory, pouring strawberry shampoo into my hair. Its scent made me famished. I'd fix a bagel. Glancing in the mirror, I found the burnt sienna had inched more of itself from my roots. I liked to blame my hairdresser for putting that gray at the base of each hair shaft. Surely it wasn't caused by age. Maybe I'd go platinum blond next time. I grinned, considering what Roger might say to that.

I shampooed my hair, singing about platinum hair to the tune of "Blue Suede Shoes." I laughed, in such a jovial mood this morning, knowing I'd sing my new song to Kat. Last night Roger had asked her about exams. She'd take two of them today. Would she really, or would she back out? Would Roger even know before final averages were released?

I had promised myself I'd go to Sidmore High. Now I quit singing and uttered expletives. I hated any kind of promise. I would go to that school. But under what premise? I tried to create one while towel-drying my tresses. Unsuccessful, I entered the kitchen.

Poor Minnie slumped, her soil still black from my dousing. I carried her to the patio and set her beside my back door. "You'll feel better in the sun, and you'll dry out here." I considered bouncing my ideas for the day off her, but her torso slanted, and the pink poufs on her head looked spread out. Maybe she was catching something. Were plant medications available? I'd have to return to that nursery to find out. Or at Sidmore High, I could ask Harry Wren.

Ah. Was that enough of an excuse for returning? Probably not. I doubted whether a person could just drop in and disturb a teacher's class to inquire about horticulture.

The day promised a clear blue sky. I took time to smell the flowers, which gave off no scent from their beds. They did look pretty—pinks and yellows and reds—and I mentally praised whoever tended them. If I saw that person, I'd get pointers.

A prickle of fear touched my spine. I slowly turned, glancing toward what I'd spied on the street.

A black vehicle approached.

I clenched my fists. I loosened them slightly when I saw it was a car. No other vehicle rolled down this street. Yet. I turned to go back inside. On the cement against the wall lay a chipped piece of red brick. I lifted the piece, found it sharp, and noted the gouged section of wall it had come from. A bullet had nicked that wall. I had a bullet in my purse. It would become evidence if needed, just like this. I set the shard of brick down where it had been. Had someone shot here some time ago? Or yesterday, while I sat outside?

I grabbed Minnie, darted into the condo, and locked the door. I set her down where she would be safe. Nervously, I wiped the stovetop, considering options. I should contact police. But I also wanted to get to Kat's school. I needed an excuse.

Some people would already be arriving there. Maybe I could offer to help Cynthia Petre and the other secretaries take phone calls. *Naw.* Tell Anne Little I was stopping by to see if they needed a sub? *No way.* I glanced at Minnie. "I could go in wearing coveralls and tell them I want to apply for the dead custodian's job."

I gave myself a light cheek slap for thinking of such a thing. My phone rang. Who was up so early? Telemarketers were intelligent people. They didn't rise until seven in the evening, it seemed from their calls. Gil? "Good morning! I hope you have a fantastic one," I said in a sugar-coated tone.

"Gram!" Kat screamed. "I need you!"

"Kat, what's wrong?" I shrieked into the phone.

"My car . . . somebody blew up my car!"

I panted, clutching my phone. "Where are you? Are you hurt?"

Her quiet moment seemed to extend to an hour. The clack-clacking I heard sounded like teeth chattering.

"Kat, tell me!"

"I'm okay. I'm at school."

"I'll be there."

"Gram, I . . ." She exhaled heavily and then seemed able to speak again. "I couldn't get Dad. The police are here."

I sprinted to the Mustang, talking. "Kat, I'm on my way." I barreled off in the car. "Tell me what happened."

More of her heavy breaths sounded before she spoke. "I got here about twenty minutes ago. Parked where I usually do. In the lot. I came in the building and was going to take my first exam, and . . ."

"I'm with you, baby." I scooted to the edge of my car seat and shoved the accelerator. "And then what? What happened, Kat?"

"We heard a loud noise. Thought the building was exploding. Everybody started running." She breathed hard. "People screamed to look out. Then somebody yelled, 'Kat, it's your car!' "

"Oh, sweetheart."

"Smoke was all over the parking lot."

Traffic made me brake. *Come on, come on*, I urged drivers. "Kat, I'm heading there and—"

"I have to go. The police want to talk to me again."

"I'll be there in a minute. Hold on, sweetheart, you hear me?"

The clog of vehicles seemed like sludge on the freeway. I veered off to an exit. City streets slowed me down, but I willed myself to be there with Kat. What happened? Who'd want to harm her? Why?

Her little secondhand car surely wouldn't attract anyone's envy. Roger had bought that car two years ago. He'd fine-tuned the motor and knocked out the body's kinks. Kat's summer jobs at the rec center helped pay for it. She kept that Chevy in shape with weekly washings and much polishing. She was so good at polishing, I thought, feeling a tense smile when I considered her skills. But who'd want to hurt the car? Or Kat?

Grim thoughts made my teeth clench. Did this have anything to do with Grant Labruzzo's murder? Was he murdered?

Potentially deadly circumstances connected to Kat's school were startling. Labruzzo died. A woman who'd subbed was shot. Another, with hair like Marisa's and wearing denim like her that day, was hurt by spilled chemicals. A beaker broke when someone slammed my classroom door. Was the door locked? Why and how? Was Marisa Hernandez attracting killers? Or was she a killer herself? Did her lure endanger Kat?

I tore through an intersection, my scalp tightening with questions, my heart racing in my chest. A blasting horn made me glance out my door window. I'd cut in front of a car, its furious male driver giving me the finger. Ignoring him, I spied unlit stadium lights ahead leaning forward like tall bug-eyed creatures. I careened around a corner to the school.

Vehicles rushed toward and away from Sidmore High. The parking lot made my stomach churn. Police cars with swirling lights surrounded the half-empty lot. Sirens screamed with squad cars and fire trucks pulling up. Firemen were already hosing a smoking car that I couldn't see in the middle of the lot. My granddaughter's car.

Hot tears blurred my vision. My body convulsed with

trembles. I gripped the steering wheel, overwhelmed by a feeling of losing control.

Where was Kat? How could I find her with all this confusion? I kept telling myself she was okay. The reminder wasn't working.

Roadblocks had cut off the street in front of the school. Adults wearing worried faces were pulling up all over the adjacent road near the stadium, where people scrambled to cars and each other. Out of the field house between the stadium and the main building came a large policeman with a black Labrador. Police dog. Bomb-sniffing dog.

I parked in the stadium lot and ran with swarming parents who shouted their fears to each other. They hollered names of their children, relief flooding faces when they found kids unharmed. A sense of the surreal washed ever me. Police, teachers, and students everywhere. People sobbing. They spoke into cell phones, telling others they were okay. Many rushed away from the scene, the new crime scene.

"Kat!" I yelled, my head whipping from side to side as I darted through groups, skimming faces. Some I recognized, most I didn't. I moved through swarms of frantic people and called Kat's name, asking if anyone had seen her. Teens and adults shook their heads, running past me. My mouth was shaking, my jaw aching from my teeth hitting against each other. The sea of people was thinning, the walkway to the school ahead of me blocked off with tape and adult guards.

I spied a familiar woman. "Anne. Anne Little!" I called, rushing toward her. She didn't seem to hear my voice between the sirens' wails and shouting voices, and headed into the field house.

I ran in behind her. The stench of urine and stale body odor made me bite back the instinct to gag. People were talking loudly beyond the locker room.

In what must have been a coach's office, I saw Anne Little. She sat at a table with other adults. And Kat.

"Gram," Kat said, shoving herself up to her feet. She came to me, and we gripped each other.

"It'll be okay," I murmured, rubbing her back and feeling her trembles matching mine.

"You must be Katherine's grandmother," said a man seated at the table. He was bald and wore a sports coat. The police officer beside him had freckles and looked too young to be wearing a uniform. Anne Little gazed at me with sad eyes and shook her head. Kat and I wiped off our tears and sat.

"Yes, I am," I replied. I held Kat's hand and faced this person, who rubbed his hand back and forth under his fleshy chin.

"I'm Captain White," he said. "Katherine wasn't hurt. And nobody was in the parking lot, as far as we know, so we were lucky. It doesn't seem like anyone was injured."

I breathed relief. Then I said, "Who did this?"

"We don't know yet." He peered at me from beneath bushy eyebrows. "We're securing the school and trying to keep everybody safe."

I squeezed Kat's hand. Kissed her forehead. Saw her expression relax into one of gratitude.

"Captain White," I said, voicing what I'd just surmised, "it probably wasn't a bomb. Maybe something went wrong with Kat's car. I'm sure she told you it's old."

"Mrs. Gunther, it was a bomb," he said, his statement settling hard in my chest. "Katherine said she had no idea who might have done this."

He faced Kat. "Have you offended anyone? Have you caused anyone to be embarrassed?"

"Kat doesn't have enemies," I snapped.

Captain White looked at me. He left his wattle alone and peered at Kat.

"I haven't hurt anyone," she said, "that I know of."

"Did you see anyone around your car when you left it this morning? Or when you drove up?" he asked, and Kat shook her head.

Roger rushed through the doorway. "Kat!"

"Dad." She bounced up, and they hugged. Clung. The pain in Roger's face mirrored all the sorrow he'd borne while watching Nancy die.

Tears stung my eyes. I yearned to stop all this suffering in my son and grandchild.

"I was checking out the motor in a car," Roger said to all of us, "and just got back to the shop and received the message. I can't believe this happened."

Captain White spoke to him. "I'll need some information and then you can all go." More questions would come later, at the station. Anguish remained in Roger's face while he gave answers and held Kat. She looked more peaceful by the time we left, with her father's arm still secure around her shoulder. Kat seemed especially frail, held by the gaunt man at her side, my grown boy.

We were out of the building when Roger glanced at me. "I'll take care of her, Mom."

"I could help."

He shook his head. "I'm taking Kat home. She needs rest." They both thanked me for coming, and Roger said he would keep in touch.

I watched them sag against each other. I had to keep my feet planted to keep from grabbing them and forcing them to come with me. I'd take them straight to the airport and shove them in a plane. We'd fly far away.

I walked across the grass to my car, peering over my shoulder to keep the two of them in sight until they were gone from my view. Few people remained in the area. I slid into the Mustang and sat slapping the steering wheel, cursing whoever had caused my family such anguish. I peered out, saw a brilliant, clear sky and cursed that, too.

Vehicles were inching by, the people inside them staring at the school parking lot. I drove away, my inner eye viewing the grief I'd just witnessed. I wanted to be with Roger and Kat. But my son had taken charge. Could he find sudden power?

The image of Gil's shoulder came, the cushiony space where I had often leaned my head. I could curl up on his lap and let him hold me. Tell me not to worry.

I gave my head a shake. Strength had to come from inside me now.

Captain White had told Kat, Roger, and me that we'd have to go to the station as soon as possible to give more information. For me, this seemed like a good time.

I drove there and walked in without concern about the place or its people, but noted the strong odor of a sweet cigar. Maybe the fruit trays weren't working. The man I had spoken to before wasn't here today. He'd probably gone to the school early this morning to question John Winston.

Detective Sandra Jones led me to her office. The dark-skinned, petite woman told me to sit, and I did. She sat at her computer.

"Who could have had a bomb?" I asked. "That should tell you who to arrest."

"Anybody with computer knowledge and a little sense could have learned how to build a simple pipe bomb. We'll check with places that sell the parts and see if we can find out who bought them, but they'll probably be hard to trace."

My mind rummaged through people from Sidmore High. No student in my first day's classes could have figured out how to make a bomb. But all of those kids were in that construction class. They learned how to build things. Did all kids today have expert computer knowledge?

"When you went to Sidmore High School to sub," Detective Jones said, "did you antagonize anyone? Would any student have it in for you, Mrs. Gunther?"

I made rapid eye blinks. "You think somebody did this to Kat because of me?"

"Kids do all sorts of things to get even."

Her comment dumped a crushing weight on my chest. I had decided to do something about Kat at her school. And *I* could have caused her death. I slapped a hand over my mouth to keep from vomiting.

Slumping back in the chair, I tried to force away all my trembling. My pulse throbbed in my head, and I leaned toward this young woman. Words tumbled from my mouth. Anything. I had no idea what information the police might be able to use. Sandra Jones wrote, her fingers seldom slowing on her keyboard. I told about Sledge. Roxy, who was probably okay, but she'd once pulled that knife on Kat. My head reeled. "Kat likes this teacher." I talked a little about Marisa Hernandez, waiting to see Jones's intense expression change. It didn't. "I heard that Miss Hernandez has been a prime target in your investigation of Grant Labruzzo's murder."

Jones stopped typing. She stared at me. "He was murdered? Do you know that for a fact?"

I shook my head. "Uh-uh, but I thought—"

She typed more while I told my concerns about murderous-looking Coach Millet and tiny red-faced Miss Gird. Jones's eyes scrolled down to mine. "Are they connected to Katherine? Did either one of them threaten her?"

"No. But Miss Gird teaches her now." I considered. "Oh, and Roxy said the police should be questioning a teacher named Abby Jeansonne."

"Why?"

I was blank. "Roxy just said." I raised my shoulders. "Your killer could be anyone in the office or driving those trucks and Jeeps and cars."

"Again you say we have a killer. Are you sure of that, Mrs. Gunther?"

Air left my lungs with great sound. "I'm not sure of anything."

Of course Detective Jones knew about Mrs. Peekers. She was fine, Jones said, when I asked of the woman's condition. Went home from the hospital Saturday. "Anything else you can give me?" Jones asked. "Anything that seemed threatening? To you or your son or granddaughter?"

"Roger only fears having Kat leave him soon for college." A recent concern sprang to mind. "Do you know if anyone from your office questioned a student named John Winston today?"

She didn't know. I told her everything that transpired with the boy. She typed, stopped, and with big brown eyes peered at my face. "Any threats to you?"

My eyes rolled up. Which events to tell? Anything that might help Kat. I looked at Jones. "Well, my Lexus was keyed and kicked in when I parked with the students."

She nodded, making notes. "Kids do stuff like that all the time. Rebelling against adults."

"And somebody wrote on my mail truck."

Her head jerked back. "You drive a Lexus and a mail truck?"

I certainly wasn't going to tell her about the Mustang parked outside. "When I fly into a city, I like to rent different kinds of vehicles."

"Why? Most people rent the same kind of cars."

"I try to match what I drive to my mood. Variety keeps me from stagnating."

She turned to her keyboard. "What was written on the mail truck?"

" 'Leave or die, bitch.' "

Jones peered at me. "Did you talk to anyone in the office at school about that? Did you ask if anybody was seen around your mail truck?"

"The staff was all busy. A kid pulled the fire alarm that day, and everybody had to go outside. Then they had to get the kids back into classes."

Jones made notations. "Okay," she said, glancing up, "anything else done to you? Anything that might have scared or concerned you?"

I didn't like the way some kids looked at me, or that time Abby Jeansonne whipped her body around and gazed at me. Didn't like the looks of some people in the office. "Nothing was done to my Mustang convertible," I said without thinking.

"Convertible?"

I'd goofed. With a shrug, I said, "Let's see, what else? I was locked in my classroom, I believe. Not long before Mrs. Peekers was locked in the custodians' room. And then somebody shot at me."

Jones blinked rapidly. "Maybe," I amended. I took the bullet out of my purse and gave it to her, explaining that I wasn't sure it was new. And someone may have tried to run me down at a curb, but again, I wasn't certain. "The driver probably just cut the corner too sharply. And he—or she—drove through a red light. The person could have trouble seeing colors."

Little sighs sounding like exasperation came from Jones as she typed all I told, and as I considered all those small events together, they seemed like a mountain of trouble. Eventually Jones stopped. "Were any of the kids jealous of Katherine?"

"Jealous?"

"Your granddaughter's popular at school. She makes good grades."

I asked how she knew, and Jones reminded that deputies had been around Sidmore High. They'd gathered information about many people. Some of the teachers. People they were close to. She asked lots more questions and when we were through, I felt as if I had taken an all-day exam and hadn't studied nearly enough.

How would Kat do on exams if she had to go through anything like this inquisition? And then, of course, the police had quizzed her. They would ask more questions. Prod her about enemies. How could anyone not like Kat? I wondered, leaving Detective Sandra Jones, who said she might contact me again for more information. She kept my bullet.

I restrained my grandmotherly instinct that told me to rush to Kat. Instead, I phoned her house while I drove.

Roger answered. "She's exhausted from queries. And what happened." He was fine, he said. His voice did sound strong. Fear for Kat must have invigorated him.

"You try to rest, too," I said.

"I'll want to inspect Kat's car. And find the bastard who made that bomb."

I liked hearing Roger take control. I told him about the police station.

"Locked your room?" he asked, incredulously. "And somebody shot at you?"

"I'm not sure. Wish I would be." Of course he was shocked to learn that I'd even gone to the school.

"Why didn't you tell me? Mom, I'm your son!"

The power in my child's voice commanded my tears to come. They seared my cheeks, their salinity finding my lips. "I love you, Roger."

"And I love you, Mom. Never forget that. Come to me whenever you have a problem. Please."

My hand clasping the phone quivered even once we clicked off.

I gripped my steering wheel, wanting to speed to their house and hold Roger and Kat. They needed to rest, needed some time alone.

I needed someone to lean on. I couldn't help myself. My car closed in on the last remaining blocks to Gil's restaurant.

CHAPTER 21

I rushed inside Cajun Delights, not pausing to think. I only felt. I felt a need to find comfort on Gil's shoulder. Felt a need for him to love me.

He met me as soon as I entered. "Cealie." Gil's face showed a mixture of joy and surprise. He was walking past the entrance but came to me, his arms outstretched.

"Gil," I whispered from my secure place against his chest, welcoming his arms around me. I clasped his back and felt its power. Lingering in his embrace, I ignored voices of hungry patrons who entered, the strength to meet Kat's problems seeping back to me.

Gil took my hand and moved me from the crowd gathering near the door. "What happened at Kat's school?" he asked, sounding worried. "I just heard and was about to call you. A bomb blew up in the parking lot?"

Hearing Gil say the words brought back all the images. The intensity of his gray eyes when he turned them to mine swamped me with emotions. I fought the sting surging up behind my eyes and nodded.

"Kat didn't get hurt?"

"No, thank God, at least not physically."

His shoulders relaxed. "Do the police know anything? The news didn't say much, only that Sidmore High had been evacuated."

"Nobody knows what happened yet." At least nothing the

police were sharing with me. I hadn't considered the media. They obviously hadn't announced that Kat's car had been the one targeted.

I was ready to tell him all about it. I'd tell Gil all of Kat's problems and even share with him the news that I'd been subbing. Sticking my nose in police business and Kat's, trying to make her take exams and show up for graduation. I'd pour out my woes to this man who had stood by me through turmoil in the past. I adored Gil, I realized while his firm hand clasped mine, guiding me toward the back of his restaurant.

We passed tables filled with people eating stuffed flounder and bacon-wrapped shrimp. I'd tell Gil all and share my fears and my theories. Tell about threats that had, or might have occurred with me.

He glanced at me, his breath blowing out relief. "At least Kat's all right. We'll have to talk more in the office." He was leading me toward a door in the rear when my peripheral vision caught sight of mega cleavage above a woman's tight black shirt. I glanced at Gil's table, where Legs sat, watching us.

Ramrod stiffness gripped my back. My hands grew cold, my neck muscles rigid. While I'd be pouring out my miseries to Gil, she would sit here to wait for him? And then after I left, she would ask him to tell her everything I said.

My feet stopped abruptly. I pulled my hand away from Gil's. "I don't have time to visit," I said.

His eyebrows shot up. "Why not?"

I knew his girlfriend was staring at my back. Refusing to give her a direct look, I replied to Gil in a cold, accusing tone. "You have a new friend." I tilted my head to indicate that young woman.

Gil grinned. "Cealie, you and I have been apart for a while."

"I only came in for one thing," I said, my fury-blurred gaze managing to spy a passing waiter's plate and giving me the idea.

I needed to stop Gil's upcoming spiel about an unattached man needing a lover. "I want French fries."

"You don't even like French fries," Gil said.

My fingernails bit into my palm. "I do now. Could you get me an order?"

He asked a waitress to fix me some. "And I want them to go," I added. Gil stared at me, and I clenched my lips to pause my inner squirm.

"Sorry I missed you last night," he said. "I heard you came here with Kat and Roger."

"I figured you wouldn't be here." Was that a lie? I wasn't certain anymore. I only felt the female eyes boring into my backside.

"If I'd known, I might have been able to change my plans."

"No problem. We ate. The food was good."

Gil's expression turned bland. Were we strangers? Acquaintances? People who'd known each other once but no longer?

"I'm sure the school will close for a while," he said.

I nodded. "I guess the police will check everything out and make sure things are safe before anybody goes back there."

"Graduation might be pushed back."

I hadn't thought about that. Didn't really want to. "Maybe so."

"I'll be invited?"

My mind and body all felt stiff. "I'll ask Kat."

Gil narrowed his eyes. "Cealie, can I help with anything? Don't you want to sit down and talk?"

I had already talked too much. "We're all right. Thanks for asking." I accepted my bag of fries from a waitress and gave her the same polite thanks. I held the bag up toward Gil. "Your treat?"

His face was stern. I turned and rushed out with my eyes

focused straight ahead.

At the condo I pulled on running shoes and used them to pound the cement. I ran so hard that my heart pumped harder than I could remember it ever doing. Not so good for a mature woman who hadn't stayed in shape. But I needed to dump out every inch of fury coiling through my lungs. Every ounce of fear. Every concern I had for Kat and Roger. Forget Gil and counting on him.

Where was my upbeat attitude? I wondered.

Lost, it seemed, when my grandchild became threatened.

I was panting when I returned. I didn't feel like talking to Minnie. She leaned sideways in the pot. My fault for sure. Just like Kat's problem. She hadn't been in danger until I came around, shoving my nosey self into her school.

I threw the French fries in a trash can and slammed the cover. Slumping across the couch, I heaved guilt-laden breaths. I needed to stop thinking of the restaurant, stop all the worry. Being angry at myself wouldn't help me find answers to help Kat. I inhaled and exhaled slowly to purposely calm my breathing.

Detective Jones had mentioned jealousy. Could Kat have taken away another girl's boyfriend?

Hardly a reason for planting a bomb. But how would I know? I'd seen some of those female students who looked fearsome. Their tiny tops and bottoms. Some girls showed tremendous cleavage. And skirts almost to their panties, if they wore any. Some of those females were surely fooling around with young men. Who knew what they would do to keep them?

Hannah Hendrick also had huge boobs. Anne Little had huge gold hoops on her ears. Cynthia Petre had small braces and mismatched clothes. Harry Wren had many cacti. Grant Labruzzo killed one of them. Tom Reynolds missed school. He hurried from the warehouse church after he saw me.

I reached my arms out and stretched. My calves were tight. I'd run hard and hadn't stretched before or afterward. My view of the ceiling took in the chandelier's glistening teardrops. No spider in sight, but a piece of web clung to one of them. A deadly web . . . like the one Kat was caught in. I needed to set her free.

Worry cluttered my mind. Of course, the detectives and Roger were doing all they could to help Kat now. But I'd been in different situations connected to her—or maybe some weren't. I needed to sort things out.

Detective Jones had suggested that another senior might've worried about Kat's final average beating his or hers. Maybe that person would lose an important scholarship because of Kat's grades. But if Kat didn't show up for finals . . .

The detective's suggestion had pointed toward a good student going after Kat. With all of those apparent punks in the school, we also had to analyze those who weren't? The good kids.

Where had I heard of someone losing out on a scholarship?

Sledge, caught in a compromising situation with a female student. Grant Labruzzo had turned him in.

Now I was back to considering the bad kids. My head reeled, and I imagined Legs at Gil's side, asking about the girl he wanted to watch graduate. What would he say? That he'd almost married her grandma? No, he wouldn't tell that. But Legs would want to attend graduation with him, if he went at all.

If Kat showed up.

My head lolled back. Roger was taking control. He had attended college for two years. His choice to quit. He wanted to keep working on cars. Loved his job, built up his own business. My son had been enthusiastic about his occupation, until Nancy took sick.

Nancy. Her image and soft voice swirled. She didn't graduate. And even while we assured her it didn't matter, to her it always did. She appeared the perfect wife and mother, yet never seemed to feel as important as other people. Only because she'd missed receiving that one damned piece of paper.

Kat would be safe. I imagined Nancy's voice telling me that and felt her assurance. The police would protect all the students.

I hopped to my feet. Yes, Kat would graduate. I didn't need Gil. I didn't need anyone's help any longer.

I rushed across the den for my cell phone, and it rang. The incoming number showed my Cape Cod office. "Cealie!" Bud Denton cried when I answered.

My heart jumped to my throat. "Bud, what's wrong?"

"Isn't a semicolon's main job to replace a comma and *and?*"

"Huh?"

"I wasn't totally certain, and Jena's out for vacation. Sue Ellen isn't sure either."

"Bud . . ."

"It is, right?"

"Don't you have a nice grammar book or two or five?"

"My glasses broke. And Sue Ellen needs to get some."

I took a deep breath and exhaled. "Yes, you're correct."

"Ah, thanks, Cealie. So how are things going for you?"

My eyes rolled up. "They're going."

"Great. See you."

I clicked off. Soon I was going to have to fly up to Cape Cod and have a little instructional talk with Bud and Sue Ellen. Did I have the right people running that office? Should I move there and run it myself?

I shook my head. I didn't want to settle down. And I couldn't think about it now. Much more critical concerns swirled through my head. Kat. Roger. Gil. Legs. Exploding automobiles.

The explosion grew in my mind, its flames and racket and blown-up fragments drifting toward the school building and trickling inside. Nearing the auditorium, filled with graduates in caps and gowns.

An explosion on stage?

"What?" Kat asked once I reached her on the phone.

I repeated my statement. "Kat, don't graduate!"

Her small snicker came through the line. "Gram, you've been pushing me like crazy to attend graduation. And now you're telling me I shouldn't go?"

"Warning you, honey. Wherever they hold graduation, don't go there. Forget that school." I paced in and out of my condo's rooms, clasping the phone to my ear, an ache in my heart from wanting to hold Kat.

"We'll talk about it later," she said. "I had to talk so much to those police and everybody, and now I'm really tired."

"I know you are, sweetheart." My hip bumped the bathroom counter. I twirled and sped toward another room. "What's your dad doing?"

She sighed. "Same as you, worrying about me. But I'll be okay, Gram. I just have to—"

"Rest, Kat."

"I'm trying."

"Just one more thing. Who else in your class has a real high average?"

She grew silent. Probably wanted to ask why. Probably didn't have the energy. Finally she said, "I guess John has the best grades."

"John, your boyfriend?"

"We broke up, remember?"

"I remember. He wanted to get serious."

"And started to get jealous. I'm really exhausted, Gram."

I reminded Kat that I loved her and she said the same. We hung up. My heartbeat had quickened. John Winston. I jabbed in the number of the police station and asked for Detective Sandra Jones.

She wasn't currently available. I asked whether the person I was speaking with could give me any information. Had they learned anything new about my granddaughter's car that blew up at school?

No, sorry. But Detective Jones would have a note to return my call. I hung up and tried Sidmore High. Heard the busy signal. Tried again. Still busy. "Damn." I threw my cell phone across the den, and it clattered along the floor.

I yanked open the door of the console that hid the television and flicked it on. Scrolling through channels, I searched for news. Finally found a local reporter. "So decisions haven't been made yet about when classes at Sidmore High School will resume."

A close-up of the school snapped up on screen. Then a distant shot showed the blocked-off parking lot as I'd last seen it. "This is where a bomb, apparently a small pipe bomb, blew up beneath a student's car. All we've been able to ascertain is that the car was an older model red Chevrolet." The female reporter returned into view. "We'll continue to break into regular programming whenever we receive more information."

I was grateful that they weren't naming the student whose car exploded. I still couldn't believe it happened.

Later in the evening, Gil came by. His face showed concern when he entered.

I led him through the den. "Can I get you anything?" I said without emotion. "Water?" I opened the frig and peeked in. "Cranberry juice?"

"I don't want anything except to find out what's going on with you." Gil's eyes were piercing. He stepped close, moving into my space in the kitchen.

I slid away from him. "Nothing's going on. I'm just waiting to see what'll happen at school. I'll attend graduation, if they have it. And then move on."

He shifted, and his hand settled on the counter. It nudged my cactus's pot, making him notice the plant. "That's Minnie," I said. "My new traveling companion."

Gil's eyes appeared darker while they gazed at me. I stayed across the room. "I see," he said, his expression telling me he understood more than the words I had spoken.

"Cealie, if I can help you with anything. . . . Or Kat. Or Roger."

"No thanks, we'll be fine." I gave a small smile to show him.

His shoulders seemed lower when he walked to the door. Gil stopped and turned. "Even if we aren't together anymore, you'll always be important to me."

Gushy flutters rushed around in my chest. I was tempted to dash across the room and knock him down, stripping off my clothes and his.

I lowered my head. Forced deeper breaths and purer thoughts before I answered. "Thank you. And you'll keep being important to us." I made certain to include the others, couldn't tell him all he meant to me. I almost ran to the door to give him a parting hug. But letting Gil go would prove too difficult. There was no more Cealie and Gil. "I saw your new girlfriend," I said.

"You did?"

"At your table. At least twice."

He nodded slowly, wearing a small grin. "Now I really understand."

"I'm glad you found someone else." I forced my voice steady while I opened the door for him. "And I appreciate your concern. That's what friends are for."

He gave me a steady gaze. I turned my head away and opened the door wider.

"Thanks for coming over. Goodbye," I said, locking the door after he went out.

I walked straight to the sofa, trying to swallow the knot and keep my shaky arms still. I sat, staring at the television. Faces and motion came and went. At some point late in the evening, I heard the breaking news.

Sidmore High School would reopen in the morning.

CHAPTER 22

I trembled through most of the next day. Kat was at school, taking her final exams.

"The police said they thoroughly searched the school and surrounding parking areas," Roger said when he phoned me sometime during the morning. Many officers would remain at school for security. He had dropped Kat off, and she'd get a ride home with a friend. "Kat's fine," he said to me in an uncertain tone.

"I'm sure she is," I blatantly lied. "And how about you?"

"I'm good. Kat said she'll give you a call when she gets home."

She did. I rushed to their house. My gaze skimmed over her, and she looked okay. At least physically. "So you decided to go," I said.

"Yes. The tests weren't too bad. Being at school was kind of scary. But I guess I did all right." She had avoided the parking lot. Some teachers told her that her average was high enough in their classes and she wouldn't have to take their finals. But now she needed to study for her last exams that she would take tomorrow.

"You don't have to," I reminded.

Kat gave me a look. "Gram, I know how much Mom wanted to see me graduate. And Dad might not say it or show it, but he'd be crushed if I didn't finish school." She sighed and sat down. "And I'd be disgusted with myself if I gave up now."

Roger came back from work early, and we visited a few moments. I left, knowing they needed their lives to feel as normal as possible.

Detective Sandra Jones returned my call. I told her what I'd learned from Kat about John Winston. "He makes top grades. He was jealous." I also made sure she knew what the girl from the warehouse church said. "Last Thursday John wrote a note saying Miss Hernandez was being arrested, and he passed it around class to reach Kat. Of course, Miss Hernandez was at school the next day, so he'd just made up a lie to antagonize Kat."

Jones thanked me for the information and said she'd get back to me with any new developments.

I pondered over what I'd told her. Who knew what else John Winston might be capable of doing? And just because Marisa hadn't been arrested didn't mean she was no longer a suspect. My brain felt frazzled, as though it had been given the frizziest perm.

Early the next afternoon, Kat phoned. "I'm through, Gram."

"With that school?"

"Yes."

Enthusiasm filled me. "Woo-woo-woo! That's terrific!"

Her tone was less enthusiastic. "I'll be sending out my announcements late because I hadn't decided if I'd go to the ceremony." She exhaled loudly. "But I will."

She had no choice but to let me come over and get her. Kat needed a change of scenery.

When I reached her house, she was holding the panda. She showed me her graduation pictures. Kat in a lagoon blue cap and gown, smiling, her happy green eyes peering straight into the camera. Kat with her head tilted, her look pensive. Her reddish hair blurred with my tears. She autographed a large and a wallet-sized picture and gave them to me.

We hauled everything over to my condo. There we sat at the

table with her pictures, announcements, and a list of people to send them to. What scared me the most was that the announcements said commencement exercises would be held at Sidmore High School. "Why there?" I asked.

"Since the explosion, some people thought about changing the ceremony to the Community Center. But the seniors voted. They still want to graduate from Sidmore." Concern showed in Kat's face.

"Nobody believes that's too dangerous?"

She shrugged. "There weren't any signs of explosives or other sabotage. It seems that whoever did it was just after me. Or my car. For some reason." Her gaze shifted toward the floor.

"Kat, you really don't have any idea why that would have happened?"

She stared at me, shook her head. "Miss Hernandez called," she said, voice still dull. "She wanted to see how I was doing."

"What a nice lady. But I still get creepy feelings about you going back to that place."

"I know. During the exams I kept looking around, wondering. . . ."

"I haven't quit wondering either. Who did it? Why?" Kat's eyes clouded, and I added, "Some of the other kids are jealous of you, too, aren't they? You make great grades. You're beautiful."

She gave her head a small shake. "I'm no better than anybody else."

I grinned. Took her hand. "Are you scared to return to Sidmore?"

"Of course."

We clasped hands. Stared off but saw only inside ourselves. We drew our hands apart. "Now let's invite people," I said. "Let 'em know you'll be commencing the new and probably the best phase of your life."

Our gazes met and reflected. Kat's new phase, her going off, would mean more worries for her father. And that worried Kat.

"You haven't considered going to a college around here?" I said.

She shook her head. "I suggested that to Dad, but he knows I always wanted to go off and feel independent. He says I can't stay around here now just for us to baby each other."

She addressed envelopes and I stuffed them with announcements, adding pictures to those she indicated. We talked about some of the relatives. Kat wrote little notes to a few of them and suggested I do the same. I jotted a few sentences, telling people I knew how brilliant and gorgeous my granddaughter was.

I only questioned two of the announcements she was sending. "On your note to my cousin Stevie, absolutely do not tell her I'm here. She lives so far away, and there's no need to tempt her. So don't send her a ticket either, just a picture and the announcement, okay?"

Kat agreed, and I quickly mentioned Gil. "Send his to the restaurant." I considered, one ticket or two? "And I'm sure he'd like a picture of you with his ticket." He would only receive one.

I stuck stamps on the envelopes after Kat finished writing, and she drew up her knees and cocked her legs sideways on the chair like she used to do as a youngster. She created a slight oval, elbows at her knees, hands cupping her face. Her unfocused eyes watched my hands.

A few days ago I wanted nothing more than for her to strut herself in a colorful robe across a platform in a large auditorium. Now I was dreading that scene.

How was she seeing herself? As one of the graduates who'd walk up to that stage and . . . hear an explosion?

"Kat, you really don't have to do it."

She didn't seem surprised or ask what I was talking about. "I know, Gram."

We gathered her things and then left. Kat ran into the post office with her stack of envelopes. She came out swinging her arms. "I just sealed my fate. I'm about to become a graduate."

We rode in silence. Kat, like me, probably trying not to think. We picked up the mail truck from the last repair shop. I crossed my hidden fingers and told Kat some kid had scribbled *I hate you* on its door, so I had to get it painted. I shivered, recalling the threat the person really wrote. She seemed too weary to question anything.

She drove the Mustang while I returned the mail truck to the dealer. I no longer felt adventurous.

"I'd like to go home now," Kat said, scooting over so I'd have to drive the Mustang. "I'm meeting some friends tonight to get ready for our senior trip to the Bahamas next week." She gave me a small smile. She'd been saving the money for quite some time.

Kat, lying carefree on a tropical beach, sounded terrific. If she survived until then.

A thought came. Frightening thought. "Will Sledge be going? And Roxy?"

"I'm not sure about Sledge. But Roxy won't have enough credits to graduate."

Kat promised to call me in the morning. Maybe we'd get together. Do something.

I was lonely all evening. Until the doorbell rang. Gil's gray eye was at my peephole.

"Hi," I said, letting him in. I backed away from the door and from him.

"Cealie, I have to explain something. You are so—"

Behind him, the doorbell chimed again.

"Mr. Gil," Kat said, coming in and sharing a warm hug with him. The three of us sat in the den, making chitchat about the restaurant and graduation. Kat was returning from meeting with friends and had stopped by to show me her brochures. Gil and I raved about them and her upcoming trip. Gil asked about the bomb at school, and Kat and I gave general comments, neither of us mentioning that her car had been the target. Kat's eyes became fearful.

"Kat," I said, shifting the conversation, "I want you to open one of your graduation gifts." I retrieved the box from my bedroom.

She and Gil made anticipatory remarks while she loosened the fancy wrapping and then Kat shouted, "A Twister!"

"I've never played," Gil said. "Anybody want to show me how?"

I spread out the plastic sheet and spun the arrow. Kat hopped up from the sofa. "Oh, a video camera," she said, spying one on the floor. I'd purchased it to film her graduation and afterwards planned to give it to her. "You two play. I've got to film this." She giggled like a young girl.

Soon the den was filled with all our laughter. Gil's big socks covered whole red, green, blue, or yellow circles where I sometimes wanted to put down my foot. "Shove it over, buddy," I said, nudging his side with my hip.

He keeled over, purposely tumbling to the floor. "She cheats," he said, pointing a finger at me for the camera's benefit.

Kat laughed, teased me, and kept filming. Gil got back into place, his foot allowing space for mine. Our bodies were twisted, his left hip jamming against my butt. *Mmm, comfy,* I thought. His next move seemed impossible. Gil revealed his agility. He spun on one foot and somehow maneuvered his body to reach his next circle. The move left his body bent over mine, with little air between us.

I fought my torso's rising heat and was hoping Kat wouldn't notice. The doorbell rang. "I'll get it," she said, scooting away to the door.

Gil murmured in my ear. "Nice being so close to you again."

I scowled. "But soon you'll be going back to your young lady friend." I forced on a wide smile. "I've been watching Miss Long Legs. And she's been eyeballing me."

Gil's grin looked smug. Or maybe it appeared that way because I was peering at him upside down.

"Mother!"

My knees folded, and my torso fell to the plastic sheet.

"And Gil," Roger said, coming in the door with a plant. He stared at Kat, who again aimed the video camera at us. "And you're filming this?"

Roger's shocked expression made me peer around, until I determined what this might look like. "We weren't making a porno movie," I said.

Gil sat back on the mat, grinning.

Roger yanked the camera away from Kat. He glared at me. "I was coming to bring you a plant, and I'm glad I did." He thrust the camera and the plant on the sofa and then gripped Kat's arm. "Let's get out of here. I think I have enough misery without your grandmother creating even more."

"But Dad—"

"Go on, baby," I told Kat, seeing Roger tremble. "Your dad needs you now. You can explain later."

Kat stared at me. She swallowed. Went out the door ahead of her father. He slammed the door.

I took breaths and finally turned to face Gil, sitting close to me on the mat. "I would have explained to Roger," he said. "But it seems the three of you have things on your agenda that I don't know about." Gil cocked his head to the side. "Want to tell me?"

I peered at his concerned eyes. Watched the rise and fall of his sturdy chest, where I could surely rest my head. And those powerful arms that could hold me.

But he'd said he came over to explain something. I didn't need explanations. I didn't need to hear about how and why he'd met Legs. And I didn't need to depend on him. "No," I said, "I'd rather not talk about family concerns. And I think it's best if you leave, too."

"Are you sure?" He watched me. Waited.

"I'm not sure about anything. But please go."

Gil pressed his lips to my forehead on his way out.

Roger phoned early the next morning. "Mom, I'm so sorry. Kat explained what was going on over there last night."

"I understand."

"No, I can't believe I didn't even think. I wanted to call you right away. But Gil was there."

Oh. He'd thought we were having hot sex.

"No problem," I said. "You've been upset." I recalled what he'd carried into my condo. "Thanks for the plant."

"I wanted to get you something, kind of a thanks-for-coming gift. I thought a peace lily might be appropriate."

My eyes warmed. "Glad I could be here."

Roger needed to get to work. He asked me to apologize to Gil for his behavior. I told him I would, and we hung up. Maybe I'd speak to Gil again. Maybe not.

I mentally flailed myself. I should have butted out. Gil had suggested that the first time I mentioned Kat's indecision. Now I'd only made matters worse. Somebody bombed her car. John Winston was mad at her because of me, maybe even wanted to get even. That ruffian Sledge hated me. He'd know Kat was my grandchild. Maybe he tried to hurt her to get back at me. Would one of them go after her again?

Dragging myself into the den, I spied the camera and the plant on a sofa. I turned away from the camera. The plant looked healthy, with long shiny leaves and spiky white flowers. I'd seen such plants in offices.

I carried this one into the kitchen, trying to sound perky. "Look, Minnie, you have a new friend." I set it down beside Minnie. The flowering thing overshadowed her. I shoved the lily farther away. "You two can keep each other company," I said, wondering who'd be company for me. More gloom set in. "We'll have to come up with a name besides peace lily." I left them alone, hoping they'd know how to get acquainted. I was scoring pretty low on making friends.

Pulling on running shoes, I duckwalked to activate endorphins to determine what I must do. I neared the corner, remembered a truck had run over it and shied away. Where had the bullet I'd found come from? Chicago had outlawed handgun purchases some time ago, but what about people who already owned guns? The bullet on my patio wasn't shiny the last time I saw it. But it probably hadn't been there for long, unless it was hidden beneath something.

I gave up walking in my neighborhood. The only thing I absolutely had to do was help keep Kat safe through Monday night. She'd graduate. And then I would leave.

I dusted the stove and a coffee table, uneasiness still skittering around my stomach. Leaving the condo, I drove toward Sidmore High. Paused a block away but couldn't make myself go closer. I could see numerous vehicles parked on its lot. Undergraduates still in classes. Police cars visible, with officers continuing to make themselves known.

Sounds and faces from the school returned, making me shove the gas pedal. Shuddering, I veered away. I passed Cajun Delights and ate at the next restaurant I found. Wondered if Gil still wanted to attend the graduation.

I had little to do but shop. I moved in and out of stores, buying things for Kat and having them wrapped. I considered driving into downtown Chicago but couldn't muster enough interest. While I drove, I spied other shops, pulled in, and bought Kat more stuff.

When the day ended, my car held lots of pretty, wrapped packages. None of them lifted me out of the doldrums.

So many unpleasant events had taken place while I was around Sidmore High. So many enraged faces. I wanted to meditate but wasn't sure how. My mind needed to wrap around one specific incident out of all those that had transpired, one that should have alerted me to knowing the real killer. Yes, I was certain now. Someone had murdered Grant Labruzzo in that place.

I slept through the night and awoke mulling on faces from the school. Something had seemed especially out of place at Sidmore High. I was forcing my mind's eye back there, recalling people's voices, hearing their words, when the phone rang.

"I checked with the police this morning," Roger said once I answered.

"And what did you find out?"

"They don't have any real leads yet." He sounded as disappointed as I felt. "And Mom, I went to see Kat's impounded car."

"You did?"

"Yes. And I suggest that you and Kat not go."

I had no happy report to give either. "Could I do something with her today?" I asked. "Take her some place?"

"She wants to spend most of the day alone. Cooking."

"Cooking all day would make me severely depressed."

"I know, but cooking calms Kat. She wanted me to invite you for dinner. You can ask Gil to come if you'd like."

I drew in a breath. "I'll be coming. But not Gil."

"Oh," he said, but he didn't ask questions.

The day seemed extra long while I waited to join my family. I pondered Kat's situation, dusting pieces of furniture that didn't have dust, straightening things in rooms that were already perfect, and found no solutions. By mid-afternoon I wandered out the door. Taking off in the car, I headed toward the opposite side of Sidmore High.

A sign near the school announced that undergraduates would start final exams Tuesday. By then seniors would've graduated and been long gone. Heading for their futures. Enrolling in college summer classes. Taking off for the Bahamas.

Would Kat reach its beaches? Today was Friday. She'd graduate Monday. Unless an explosion blew across the stage.

The more I considered, the more my mouth dried. I swiveled around the next block. Headed back to Sidmore. I wasn't sure what I'd do there, but I needed to get some answers.

I approached the road where I'd parked after Kat's explosion, jitters quaking through my stomach. I wouldn't go in, couldn't make myself go inside that gray building. I recalled the frightening sound of the fire alarm breaking into the classroom's silence. Relived hearing terrifying screams and sirens after the bomb's explosion in the parking lot. Firemen hosing Kat's car. Black, acrid smoke flooding the air.

I couldn't go back there. But solutions to keeping Kat safe drew me closer.

School buses were parked side by side in a small lot near the school, suggesting a happy place, a safe environment. No one was outside that I could see. Everybody inside the school, learning.

I eyed the parking lot. Cars and trucks jammed together as when I'd first seen the area. I drove through the lot, rounding each row, searching for one vehicle in particular.

My spirits sank when I didn't find it. I was heading out the lot and glancing to the side. My pulse raced. A black truck was parked in front of an outdoor building where I'd counted room numbers while on duty. It was mid-sized, fairly new. No bumper sticker.

Was it the same truck that had come near my condo? If I got closer, maybe I could tell. I whipped around the corner near the school's indoor swimming pool and started down the block again.

A teenage girl was dashing alongside the street, away from the schoolyard. Agitated movements, stringy blondish hair. "Roxy," I cried, pulling over. "Get in. I need to talk to you."

Her navy eyes flitted toward the school. Roxy hopped in the car. "Can't let 'em see me. I cut out of my last class."

"Shut the door. I'll take you home."

"I ain't going home yet, and I ain't staying with you." She leveled her gaze at me. "How's Kat doing?"

"I'm not sure. Roxy, nobody would tell me what they know. What have you been hearing at school?"

"The kids all like Kat."

"All of them?"

"Maybe not everybody, but most of 'em. They're sorry about what happened to her. The teachers are, too."

"When I asked you about the custodian's death, you mentioned Ms. Jeansonne and Coach Millet. What about them?"

Her look said she was sorry she'd told me anything. She shrugged. "Hardly anybody knows. They're lovers."

"What?" I couldn't envision those two together. "Are you sure?"

"I saw 'em getting it on between the bleachers in the gym." Roxy shoved her door open and slid out.

"But why would that implicate them in a murder?"

"They didn't see me peeking through some doors. But Grant Labruzzo walked in on them." She shut the door and ran off.

I drove, glancing at her retreating figure in my rearview mirror. Could I trust Roxy? Could I believe her? I never would have paired up the teachers she mentioned. And how horrible, that a student would have seen those adults making love. Of course Roxy didn't look too pure or innocent.

If the custodian really did walk in on that couple, had he told anyone? Reported their indiscretion to administrators? Or kept what he saw to himself? What would have happened to those teachers if the school staff found out?

I made a quick turnaround in a driveway and caught up with Roxy. I called to her through my open window. "How long before Grant Labruzzo died did that happen?"

She gave me a snippy look. "Two days. Now leave me alone."

"Do you know who drives a black truck to school?" I yelled, but she dashed off, cutting through a yard, scrambling away from my view.

My car crept through streets, my mind in a whirl. Had that couple killed the custodian? To keep from being embarrassed or losing their jobs? And even if they had, how would that death connect to Kat's car exploding?

I drove closer to the school. Could I go inside and ask the office staff those questions?

I made a small laugh, not a happy one. Of course no one in there would tell me all. I continued past the high school, trying to sort through information I'd just heard and my experiences in that place. I imagined Abby Jeansonne shoving little Miss Gird away from Coach Millet's side and taking her place, envisioned Abby's red-black bangs draping across Coach's furious face. Did she make love to him and take his anger away?

Making a sound of disgust, I thrust off that image of them. I had taken to the freeway. Driven a distance and begun to slow. I pulled in at Gil's place. He'd help me think.

I rushed to the front door and yanked it open.

Ten feet in front of me, Legs leaned over, talking with seated customers.

"Can I help you?" A young man held menus and stood beside me. His question made me realize how I must look, peeking inside.

I drew back my head. "I was just checking . . . the décor."

"Oh." He scanned the restaurant's interior as though checking it himself. He looked at me. "Do you like it?"

"Sure do. Thanks." I took off. How could I have thought in that building? Seeing Legs had immediately sent all my ideas away. My one consolation was that Kat was fixing dinner. Now that I had inhaled the scents in Gil's restaurant, I wouldn't be satisfied with anything else except Kat's cooking. She was keeping herself busy in the kitchen. And she might know who at school drove that black truck.

I returned to the condo, gathered Kat's gifts, and hauled them out to my car. It was still too early to go to their house. I sat out on the patio awhile, thinking but getting no answers. Returning inside, I set water flowing in the Jacuzzi, threw off my clothes and sank into the tub.

Warm bubbles streamed against me, but I entertained no sexual ideas. I didn't read or get sleepy. I needed to know what happened to Grant Labruzzo. Had someone gone after him? Why had they gone after Kat's car? And would that person, or persons, go after Kat on stage Monday night? If I told the police what Roxy said, they'd certainly want the information directly from her. And she certainly wouldn't want to tell them.

I lit chunky candles and tried to meditate. I pondered about threats—written and oral—and people. So many scary faces from that school. Frightening voices. Mrs. Peekers and I unable to get out of rooms. Accidents, or real attempts to kill us?

One attempt succeeded, on the custodian. And another, on

Jayne Ackers. But she had been shot near her home. Murderers ordinarily used similar methods. Nothing the same here. I drew in a sharp breath. I'd been shot at on my patio. Maybe.

I gazed at Minnie. I'd brought her into the bathroom but probably shouldn't have. Too much humidity. Her stem slumped against the side of her pot. Nancy used to lean like that toward the end. My chest tightened. I had to admit it—Minnie was dying. I was killing her.

I tapped the side of my head and spoke to me. "Stop feeling sorry for yourself. *You're* not the victim here." I needed to refocus my thoughts. I envisioned the faithful from that warehouse church, all victims of their beliefs and that preacher. All slumped across benches and the floor. Grant Labruzzo, found slumped across chairs. Who had access to the auditorium? Who might have keys?

I eyed the bubbles flowing from my tub's walls. Felt my hips floating up. Saw my stomach rise. Not nearly as flat as it had once been. Mature women don't need flat tummies, I told myself, trying not to pass judgment on mine. I needed to remain centered on the problem at hand. Meditation, I'd once heard, could be brought on by the repetition of some meaningless sound. I shut my eyes. "Ah-umm." I felt the last part of my sound vibrate in my throat. "Ah-ummm. Ah-ummm."

Feeling really silly, I let my eyes open. My face towel had floated above my thigh. The towel bubbled up in the center and felt pleasant where its edges rested. My skin looked pale, the towel, dark pink. When dry, my towel had been the same light shade as Minnie's head.

One of Harry Wren's cacti looked like Minnie. Pink tufts on its head. Most of his other varieties had different flowers. Black stockings, black truck. Yellow feathers. Red lights. Red skirt with pink blouse. Ink stains. The hues of people's hair and clothes—

"That's it!" I said, scrambling out the tub. It wasn't a face I'd seen or a warning I'd heard. What tipped me off to a possible killer was a color.

CHAPTER 23

It was 5:46 p.m. when I clutched my steering wheel, nearing Sidmore High. No cars or trucks remained on the parking lot. No Friday afternoon practices or games.

I rounded the block and slowed, passing the school. It had been only a few days since I first came. I'd expected high ideals. My senior sweetie, about to graduate. Kat, wearing a gold band across her gown, symbolizing an honor student. I had arrived in town with fluffy dreams of happy days with my granddaughter and pleasant hours with my son. I'd tried to keep from seeing Gil, but in my mind's recesses, always knew I wanted to. I hadn't planned to search for a killer.

I eased up alongside the stadium. A blue truck and a white compact car were parked beside the field house, a goodly walk from the main building. Coaches? Lovers? People from town who'd located a spot to leave their vehicles?

I drove behind the school, where a small recessed area snuggled beyond the addition for the swimming pool.

There it sat. The black truck.

No one was at school. Except whoever owned that truck.

Its owner would have had an opportunity. A motive to hurt Kat? I wrangled with scenarios and came up with few ideas. Parking near the truck, I scanned the area. Didn't see anyone. I slid out.

Mexican music came from my purse. I jumped, already spooked, and yanked out my cell phone. "Yes," I said, voice low, gaze steady on the building. If that truck's driver came out, I'd see the person.

"Mm, nice husky tone," Gil said. "Did I catch you at an inappropriate time?"

My pounding heart slowed its thrusts. Somehow, hearing his voice made me feel more secure. "I'm about to catch a murderer," I said.

Gil chuckled. His laugh abruptly froze. "You're not serious?"

I left my car but didn't lock it. If something happened with the individual inside, I didn't want to be chased out here and not be able to jump in this car and take off. My first plan, though, was to use my phone if I decided I needed help. "Dead serious," I said, creeping toward the stairs, clinging to the phone. "It's good to hear from you."

"Cealie, where are you?"

I reached the entrance doors. "Getting a higher education."

I could handle life alone, but felt comforted by having him sound so near. It seemed he would come with me through those heavy doors into the school's dark bowels. But he was across town. Probably at the restaurant. With a friend. "I need to be quiet now," I whispered. "See you."

Hanging up, I turned off the phone's ringer. I didn't need Gil phoning back while I was trying to creep up to check on the person inside. Of course I would've wanted him here with me. But if I had explained what I was doing, he'd tell me to let police do all of the investigating. And maybe he'd be right. Maybe I should tell police what I'd surmised. But what proof would I give them to make them investigate this person? That I had a woman's intuition? I was almost positive about who did it? No, if I needed assistance, I had this cell phone, fully charged. And I could run.

I tried a door. Locked. The second door opened.

Creaking sounded as I slipped in with as little opening as

possible. My purse vibrated against my side. Gil, calling back? Or my arm shaking?

I scooted past the enclosed swimming pool. Its water reflected off the darkened room's pale blue walls. The next door was open, bringing me into the main corridor. I paused. An eerie quiet claimed the space, cavernous now without students' noises and bodies. Their smells lingered. Schoolbooks, liniments, and sweet body lotions. The small wall lights probably stayed on. I craned my neck and listened.

Breathing seemed to come from my right—the mathematics hall.

I waited, my legs tensed. Was someone nearing?

I wished I'd gone to the bathroom before coming. My heart began counting out seconds. Minutes. Numbers pushed through my head, growing louder. I needed to move before my knees gave out.

I dashed to the math hall's doors and yanked.

Locked. Glass panes revealed darkness down the hall, with darker shadows fabricating black pictures on a rear wall.

I scanned the main region again. A click sounded. It came from . . . somewhere I couldn't fathom in this large space. No one moved that I saw. Maybe a clock? I hoped so.

Scuttling down the main pathway, I tried other doors. The English hall was locked. So was science. Gym doors wouldn't yield, nor would the ones to the office. Lights inside the office remained on. The secretaries' desks bore scattered papers beside their computers. Cynthia Petre's desk held her calendar and picture of John Winston. New posters on the glass panes shielding the office announced dates for exams. The spirit stick was gone.

I scooted to the cafeteria hall. As I figured, one auditorium door wasn't locked. A man I hadn't known was murdered inside this room. I clasped the door handle, my body trembling. *Cealie, you're a concerned person but usually not stupid,* my mind warned. I could leave here and do as I'd planned. Attend graduation. Then go on with my life.

But Kat needed help. Maybe to stay alive.

I darted into the auditorium, scrambled up a short flight of stairs, and reached the deck. Staring in a doorway, I eyed an absolute black abyss. *Do you think you're Super Hero?* flashed inside my head. I forced my mind to shut up. Stop thinking about me. Take care of Kat.

I wanted Gil. Roger. The police.

But Roger would also tell me to leave everything to authorities. And those authorities might arrest me for trespassing now. Detectives might discover who killed two people and then bombed Kat's car, but would they do it before Monday night? Before another explosion might occur in this room during graduation?

A small light played up from the stage.

My quivering body made my purse shake against my hip. From the main landing, I peered down at the backs of rows of chairs. The auditorium, dark except for the stage's tiny spotlight, could seat hundreds. This rear hall was circular. Other doorways back here led down to more seats. The molded chairs' seats were folded up, except for the broken ones. Cracked seats hung, creating odd geometric shapes. Chairs that alternated the blue and yellow school colors resembled a tremendous checkerboard. The yellow ones stood out, looking friendlier than the darker ones. Metal strips connected all of them. Between each wide section of chairs, concrete steps led down toward the stage.

Cougars had been painted on the walls outside it, facing the audience. The big cats appeared fierce, poised to charge. An American flag stood on the stage beside a podium. Up there was where Kat would soon make her grand crossing. I hoped.

My eyes adjusted to the dark, and an oppressive quiet pressed against my eardrums. I clutched a chair's rear. Rubbed my palms dry against it. "Someone's upstairs," my mind or throat whispered while my heart drummed. I stood on wobbly legs, feeling the doors closed behind me, encasing me in this tomb. *Upstairs,* my thoughts ordered.

My knees bumped against each other as I moved. I glanced at chairs stretched along the room's rear. On which one did that young man die?

I backed out and darted to the stairs leading above. If I stopped, I'd turn around and dash away from the terror. I wished I'd worn running shoes instead of pumps. My shoes click-clicked on concrete while I made my way up the sinister stairwell, sliding my palm along the handrail for support.

I paused on a stair. Steadying my breaths, I glanced down through metal strips that supported the handrails. They resembled prison bars. I could see the entrance door. It was still shut, nobody coming inside. I wanted to run out.

Entombed in the tiny black cell, I inched up the stairs, the growing pulse in my throat tasting bitter. My scalp tingled as I neared the balcony, the glow from the stage below getting brighter.

Finally up, I paused. I was standing on a balcony.

Being up here wasn't so awful, I told myself. Nobody was going to lift me up and pretend to toss me down, like my big cousin had. Satisfaction sprinkled through me. I'd done it. I had stood up to my anxiety about balconies.

Still, the air was scant, my legs feeling jelled. I made them take me down steps toward the handrail.

Scanning the area, I saw no one. But felt I wasn't alone. A person could be hidden, stooped in the shadows behind those rows of chairs with raised seats. I peered at the stage, trying to center myself. Calm my breathing. I couldn't believe I was really up here.

I forced new thoughts. Many people must have keys to this place. Band director. Office staff. Coaches. Some teachers. Custodians. They all had reasons to be here at different times.

The person here with me now had a purpose.

The single light on stage created a spotlight on its center.

I glanced back across the balcony. Three rear doors were left open. I had come up on the left, but this wasn't the area where I thought I needed to be. With eyes trained on my surroundings, I crept toward the central section.

Nothing seemed unusual, I thought, moving all the way down to the rail, struggling against my body's tremors. I scanned the rows of chairs I passed before exposing my back to them. A backward glance told me no one had come through a door.

Needing to stop my shuddering, I clutched the railing. Stared down across the dark auditorium. Focused on the stage. It looked ready for a performance. Someone would cross that platform. Maybe speak. Do another activity that would take center stage. The production might call for an encore. I envisioned it. Shoved the scene from my mind. Other lights surrounded that platform, I noticed. Small lights below it, some above. But only the single light shone, spotlighting the shiny wooden floor. I heard footsteps.

They came from behind me. Soft steps, slowed for my benefit.

CHAPTER 24

I gripped the balcony's railing. The feet moving behind me stopped. My hearing shot into high gear. Once again the person moved.

"Inspecting the stage for graduation?" a voice asked from the black void to my rear.

I didn't turn. Forced my voice strong. "I was just wondering how Kat is going to look out there."

"I'm sure she'll look pretty, as always."

Breathing came closer. To my left and behind me. The darkness seemed to close in. Tapping sounded. The slightest *tap-tap* of something hard against flesh.

My eyes swiveled down and toward the left. Fringes of lagoon blue swept down. They rose. Swept down again. The spirit stick was tapping against an open palm.

"You probably owned a pistol," I said without looking, "but it would be long gone by now." If I faced the person, I might force a physical confrontation. I didn't want that. What did I want? I asked myself again.

I wanted answers. To keep Kat safe.

No reply came from behind me. "Maybe a thirty-eight," I suggested. "That you probably tossed in the bottom of a river."

"You must have one yourself."

"No, a gun would make my purse too heavy." My fingernails pinched my right palm. So stupid, standing with that weapon tapping behind me, admitting I was unarmed.

But my purse held my phone. And my purse might become a weapon. Sometimes it held bulk.

I shifted my shoulder. Damn, I'd cleaned out my purse to make it lighter. *Forget the phone, too, Cealie. Not much good against a long heavy spirit stick Unless I could get a quick call off.*

"My gun is in a full cereal box. Stuffed in there after I shot at you." I swallowed. More explanation came. "I was driving to the grocery store the day I spotted you walking to that corner. I tried to hit you with my car. Then later you were such a nice target, lying on your patio. I guess I'm not a very good shot."

My mouth zapped dry. I forced words out. "Cereal box, that's clever."

"I thought so. I taped the box shut and then shoved it in the middle of a large bag filled with trash. That's gone too."

"And I imagine you'd seen Jayne Ackers and thought she was Marisa Hernandez and instinctively pulled out your gun."

"They were both tall and slender. Blond hair down to their shoulders." A pause. "So many young women today seem tall and blond."

But not you and me. "And after you'd killed once, it got easier."

A loud sigh sounded. "You have no idea of the exhilaration."

"Sure, getting a good adrenaline rush would cause anyone to murder."

My opponent seemed to ponder. "You're pretty smart. For an older woman."

I flung around. "You have gray roots yourself."

Her free hand touched the base of her hair. She smiled, her humorless smile looking especially wicked with her lips shut.

"And that spirit stick you're holding probably has that man's blood stains on it," I said. "That young man, your lover."

"I didn't want you around this school anymore," she said, taking purposeful steps down the stairs toward me, "after I realized I would go after Katherine."

My breaths stopped. I hated this woman. Fury gave me strength. Hatred was replacing my fear. "Why would you go after Kat?"

A half-grin smeared the woman's lips. "I was after Marisa Hernandez."

"I figured that." I wasn't totally sure why. "Grant Labruzzo always kept her room clean," I said to prompt a reason.

Her gaze swept out toward the dark cavern below. "Grant became obsessed with Marisa. He started to watch her, and he watched Kat too, since she's Marisa's good friend. He was furious when Marisa asked him to hang her students' things from her ceiling." The woman looked at me. "As though he were just some lowly janitor."

"But he thought of himself as someone Marisa admired," I determined. "A man she might love."

My opposition's throat tightened with her swallow. She was about half a foot taller than I was, so I could easily view her neck. Absently, she tapped the stick. "But I'd also become obsessed. I made another mistake. I thought Sue Peekers was Marisa."

"The teacher you locked in the custodians' room."

"A stupid blunder."

Peekers and Hernandez, both blond, both wearing denim that day. I'd seen Peekers from the rear that morning and also mistaken her for Marisa Hernandez. "You saw her in the custodians' room and saw that the boxes of cleansers had been left near the door." A smile responded to my musing, and I said, "No one else was in the hall, so you poured the chemicals under the door, then hurried back to your office."

Hannah Hendrick's eyes flittered toward mine. "Cealie, you're even cleverer than I figured. You might have even guessed that I locked you in that classroom, changed my mind, and unlocked it before anyone came near."

"You kept Grant Labruzzo here even though he didn't do his job well. And when he spurned you, you killed him."

The principal studied me as though she were assessing me as a job applicant. "Before Grant, I hadn't had a man in so long." Hannah gave me a friendly smile. "You're an older woman. Surely you understand."

I held back my heated response. "The police are certainly figuring out some of these things," I said, trying to sound more assured than I felt. Of course no one would be bothered by the principal's vehicle being here at school after hours. If anyone even noticed her hidden truck.

"Nobody saw me do anything. And the kids here get into trouble all the time. I call the police regularly," Hannah said, grinning. "Sledge pulled the fire alarm that day you were here. I knew you'd driven that ugly mail truck, and nobody was in the parking lot right after everyone went inside, so I wrote that warning on your door. One way to get at Kat was to scare you."

Anger swelled up in my throat. Since it wouldn't help Kat now, I forced it down. "What happened between Sledge and Grant Labruzzo? Sledge's buddy suggested that Sledge had done something."

Hannah's smile faded. "They got in a fight after school one day. Sledge thought he'd won."

"Is that it?"

Hannah turned up the palm of her empty hand. "That's it." She seemed relaxed about answering my questions.

Before her mood changed, I hurriedly asked more. "Did you mess up my Lexus?"

"I don't know anything about that. I'm sure you can thank some of our delinquents. We have a few."

"Abby seems to believe Grant was interested in Anne Little."

Hannah smirked. Her shoulders drew up higher. "Lots of women worried about who Grant was interested in. He was a handsome man. He spent lots of time in the office. But not to see Anne. Or Cynthia Petre."

My heart hammered while I considered the most important question. "Why did you blow up Kat's car?"

Hannah moved so close I felt the stick's blue fringes sweeping my arm. The full-figured woman stared out at the stage. "Kat had become like Marisa's daughter." Hannah quieted, apparently going off in her thoughts.

I pushed to learn more. "They'd often talk . . ."

Hannah nodded. We might have been two friends, sharing our experiences.

Clacking sounded. Her stick was striking the rail, working harder. "And what's the worst way to harm parents?" Hannah asked.

I knew the answer. "Hurt their children."

She peered at me. "So I went after Kat, at first thinking I'd just scare her. If her grades dropped, if she didn't come to school for exams and got all F's for them . . ." Smiling as if she had told me the best story, Hannah said, "Then she'd lose everything she had worked so hard for all those years. Kat wouldn't become an honor graduate." Hannah's shoulders jerked while she seeped more into the tale. "And then—then I thought, suppose I didn't only scare Kat away from exams?"

Hannah grew so excited her eyes sparkled. She said, "If I scared Kat enough, then she might even not even come to graduate. That would get Marisa for sure."

And me, too.

Hannah's empty hand clapped against her hand that held the rod. "But even better, I could kill Kat."

My heart stopped.

"Yes, I could kill her. And then Marisa would be devastated."

My throat only managed to squeeze out a small sound.

Enthusiastically, Hannah continued. "I learned to make a

bomb. I'm a speed reader, you know, and have an extraordinarily high IQ." I couldn't speak, and she went on. "I set the timer and placed the device under Kat's car while everybody was inside, listening to Anne make announcements. But I rushed so much that I set the timing device too early. I had planned for it to blow up right after school, when Kat reached her car. She is so punctual."

My granddaughter's principal smiled at me. "Now I'll have to wait until summer to find a way to kill Marisa. Too much security around here now. But summer's just around the corner. And, of course, I'll be absolutely certain it's Marisa this time." Hannah grinned at me as if waiting for applause.

My grim face must have sobered her. Hannah said, "How did you know?"

My gaze dropped to her skirt. Her suit was tan. "Where your blood stain was the first day I came here. You hadn't started your period. You're probably too old to still be having them."

Hannah snickered. "Not quite. I still have a few." She looked smug. "So that's it?"

"I knew you might still be having periods. But the place where that dark red spot was. I remembered for myself. Sometimes I bled through, but no stain ever came to the location of yours, that close to your hip."

Hannah's hand went to where the stain had been on her cerise suit skirt.

"You should have packed your skirt in that cereal box, too," I said, "because it'll incriminate you. Just like the stains that are certainly somewhere on that stick you're holding. Those are Grant Labruzzo's blood stains."

"I cleaned them off." She shook the spirit stick and made the fringes sway. "Pretty, isn't it? Colors of the Fighting Cougars."

"You knocked him down with that stick. And probably went downstairs, checked to make sure he was dead, and unknowingly brushed your skirt against him." I considered and said, "You wore the same outfit for his funeral. Nostalgia maybe?"

Hannah grinned. She pointed with the stick. "Grant hit those chairs right down there." She bent her head, the bob of her chestnut-colored hair rising from her neckline. "You must have some killer instinct yourself," she said, not looking at me. Her next words were more sinister. "Or you're stupid." She drew back and peered at me.

"Sometimes both," I admitted.

Hannah's stick rose and lowered, its fringes falling over the rail. *Plunk. Plunk. Plunk.* She beat the rail faster, harder, her nose starting to flare.

I needed to keep her in conversation. Needed to think. Plan a defense. "You probably made out with Grant Labruzzo here at school," I said.

"Oh, lots of places. On my desk. In classrooms."

I grimaced. Hannah's bare butt had been everywhere. No wonder that young man hadn't been interested in emptying trashcans.

She continued. "The gym's center circle. On tables in the teachers' lounge."

I pictured Deidre munching on food at one of those tables, and an utterance of disgust left my throat. I pointed to the stage. "And down there?"

"That was to be the next place. See that wooden circle in the middle? It would have been lovely." Her heavier breathing filled the air surrounding us.

I kept my tone low. Tried to make it friendly. "You might have thought of yourselves as performers. Putting on your love scene for a filled house. You. Him. The spotlight."

She faced me. "Cealie, I knew you were a romantic, too."

I couldn't punch her. The spirit stick was blocking her face. I reeled in my emotions and spoke calmly. "Grant only did a good job of cleaning the office. And Marisa's room. You had him meet you here before your planned center-stage performance. And carrying that stick, you confronted him."

Hannah's face turned stormy. "He admitted he loved her."

"Did she love him?" Marisa was about to lose my respect if she did.

"She didn't know he existed. Except as a person, a man who kept her room clean."

"And you knocked him down."

"I caught him off guard, striking him with the stick. He tripped over his dust mop, so when his body tilted, I shoved." Hannah's mouth remained open, her vision seemingly far off. "Grant's head hit the third chair, seventh row up."

She breathed hard. And smiled at me. "You can see where his leg caught on the chair. That one."

I pretended to glance down to where she pointed.

"His head cracked on the concrete. Must've been at the same place where I hit him." Hannah smiled pleasantly. "They didn't suspect anything but the fall. His back was cracked too, you know."

My jaw clenched as I faced this person who'd once looked attractive. Now she personified evil. Considering the depravity that had built inside her made my brain numb. I became aware of the slightest sound and hoped it wasn't urine dribbling to the floor. Hannah couldn't witness all my fear. She had no idea of my inner trembling from just being up on this balcony.

I glanced at her shoes. Straps around the ankles, three-inch heels. My pumps had low heels. I could slip out of them. And if I could get past her, I could probably run much faster down those rear stairs. I slipped my hand into my purse and tried to open my phone and press a number in Memory but couldn't.

Dip dip dip, the noise sounded. I watched fringes rise and fall. Hannah knocked the stick against a chair behind us. "And now you know," she said. "What a shame. You could have kept teaching for us, Cealie. You seem a bright person."

Bright enough not to stand here and let you bludgeon me to death. Hannah could toss me down like she did her lover.

She slammed the heavy metal against a chair. Then using both hands, she swung the spirit stick up above my head.

If the person attacking me were a man, I'd know what was open to aim for.

Still I tried. My knee went up to Hannah's groin. She twisted her hips. Groaned when I only kneed her thigh.

Raising both arms higher, she had the Cougar spirit stick coming down toward my head.

I reached out for what she'd exposed. With her arms up, Hannah's breasts became huge targets. I grabbed her nipples and pinched.

"Ugggh!" she howled, her arms flinging down as she tried to protect body parts. But she didn't release the stick. Its weight slammed against my shoulder. Pain shot through my arm, but I held on, squeezing tighter. Hannah screamed, and her throat made sadistic yowls. She writhed, her free hand shoving my arm. She hit against my back with the stick.

I felt welts rising. She cursed, squirmed, and thrust out her hips, trying to disengage me. I concentrated on pinching boobs. "I was right," I said, fabricating a statement to taunt her. "They're fake."

Our faces were close to each other, and her huffing breaths felt hot. A grimace contorted her features. "You won't get away!" she shrieked, striking me across the back, the end of her stick nipping my hip. My only consolation was that her blows would've been even harder if she wasn't using one hand to try to pry my fingers loose. Hannah shoved my right hand away. "Ah," she sighed.

I reached out and caught her boob again.

Hannah yowled, hunching her shoulders and coiling her torso. My knees hit the cement floor. She stood above me, and I covered my head with both hands. She struck my hands and part of my head. Dark spots sprinkled through my eyes. She could easily knock me out and then shove me over that rail. Crack my spine and neck. Pain shot from every spot on my body where she whacked. Thickening spots danced across my vision. Soon I'd black out.

I thought of not getting to see the babies Kat would have. And my family's misery from having me die, especially since I'd so stupidly hastened my demise.

Hannah grasped her weapon with both hands. She raised the stick straight up above my head and cried, "You're dead, bitch!"

With every remaining fiber of my strength, I stretched up and pinched tits. I squeezed so hard I could feel my fingertips against each other through Hannah's skin. I pulled and twisted. She sounded like a wounded wild creature. Hannah toppled, coming toward the floor with me, slamming the stick down.

"No!" a male cried.

The voice of God? I was lying on my side, seeing the bottoms of chairs. *Could I already be dead?*

The stick's fringes touched my shoulder. Aches let me know I still lived. Through widening dark circles, I saw Gil. He knocked the spirit stick away. It clattered against chairs. "Don't lose that stick!" I cried. "It's got blood stains."

"So will this poor lady if you don't let go of her. We were down in the hall and could hear her yelling." Gil made his gentle chuckle. Obviously, he hadn't seen her hit me. He placed his fingers inside mine to pry them apart, and my numb fingers came off Hannah's bosom. She folded over, her fingers fluttering above her breasts. She didn't touch them but scrunched over, whimpering like a small puppy.

My shoulders and scalp ached. Pounding came, probably

from inside my head. Gil glanced toward the stairwell. "Police," he explained. "I called them and said another murder was probably about to be committed here."

"I could've beaten her without your help," I said.

He kissed my forehead. I winced and tried to smile. "You came up on a balcony," Gil said. "It wasn't so bad, was it?"

I didn't even try for a grin.

Hannah cocked her head toward the sound of feet running up the stairwell. She hunched like a wicked witch, glaring at me, still protecting her chest.

"How'd you know this would happen?" I asked Gil.

"Cealie, I know you." His eyes wore that sparkle I adored. Lines of kindness creased their outer edges.

God, I liked him. I rolled to my back, a cool floor beneath me, Gil's face above. If he and I weren't in this place—with this woman squirming with her nipples, and policemen scuttling toward us—and if my head wasn't doing all this throbbing. . . . No, I'd been sniffing his after-shave. I did enjoy its woody fragrance.

I put my hands out, and Gil helped me to my feet.

Dizziness struck, making my knees wobble. Gil wrapped an arm around me. "I knew that with your persistence, you'd find something. And someone. And that person would probably need protecting." He peered at me with a slight smile until I stood steadier. Footsteps reached the landing. Changes in their sound let me know people in uniform were about to run in through the doorway.

"Bitch!" Hannah called to me. She'd hunched herself down to half my height. I wasn't about to lower myself to trading names with a murderer. But mainly I couldn't think of a better name to call her.

Male voices exchanged shouts, while my world busied itself with painting spots into a solid circle. My mind picked out a few of Gil's words: "better read her her rights . . . a stick back there. . . ."

"Oh," I said, resuming some mind control, "and look in her closet. A nice suit has blood on it. Not hers." People in uniforms held Hannah between them. "And by the way," I said, leaning closer to her face, "cerise really isn't your color."

Hannah spat. I drew back, barely missing her spittle. I couldn't stop myself. "Whore!"

She whipped toward me, but handcuffs stopped her from striking out. Hannah was only able to nudge her arms closer to her chest. Continued protection.

"Ouch," Gil said, glancing at her departing figure.

I grinned. Things started swimming beneath my breastbone while Gil stood back, allowing me to walk out in front of him. The swirls in my chest swept up, reaching inside my head. My knees gave way, and I sank.

Gil caught me as I fell. "Too much excitement," he said, laying me straight on the floor. He sat on a step beside me, and I heard someone phoning for an ambulance.

"I think," I told Gil, "she might've hit me."

Worry lines creased his face. "I didn't see that happen. Oh, Cealie—"

"It's not bad. I think here," I said, indicating the rear of my head. Numbness had spread, but I pointed down. "Maybe bruised there."

"Do you want me to check?" Gil touched my back much lower than where I'd felt pain.

My grin was weak. "Maybe some other time," I said. After that, I knew nothing.

CHAPTER 25

I awoke in the ambulance. Again in the hospital. "Concussions come and go," I told Kat when she came to visit. The child looked so distraught that I tried to amuse her. I knew she'd be frazzled. Her granny had been hurt. Her principal had murdered people.

Hannah would destroy the faith of all those high school students. While I drifted off again, I saw their faces. Roxy and Sledge and all the other kids. I wished I could've told them. The only person you can control is yourself. Most of them would learn it someday. But today's teens were tough. From all they experienced in their young lives, I knew the kids at Sidmore High could handle what happened.

Kat was gone when I awoke later. Gil still sat near, stroking my arm. Having support people in your life is nice, I would tell all those teens, if I ever saw them again.

"Roger's been coming in and out," Gil said. "You have had one worried son." Gil kissed my cheek. He placed a gentle hand where my shoulder hurt. "You have lots of black and blue marks, starting from here."

I remembered that a doctor had told me so. I fought to keep Gil's image, but my eyes scrambled him. "Hmm?"

"They'll just watch you. So will I."

"Good." I let my head sink deeper into the pillow.

"They want to be certain of no internal damage. I think you're one lucky little chicken," I believe Gil told me while my eyelids fluttered him in and out of view. Chicken Boy's image grew in his place. Chicken Boy waddled down the school's dark stairwell. He saw a threatening woman wearing a bloody skirt. Without a second thought, he jumped up, landed on her head and squashed her.

"We're taking care of everything for the graduation tomorrow," Roger told me when he came to visit. He was relieved to learn doctors had ruled out internal problems.

"Well, there may be some problems in here," I said, tapping my head on the natural sienna. "But that's nothing new."

My son gave that warm genuine smile I recalled. Sometimes I'd envisioned it. How good to see his happiness start emerging. Kat was more content, he said, because Miss Hernandez had been cleared of all suspicions. She and Kat had been talking.

Later in the evening, the hospital released me, and Kat drove me to the condo. Roger needed to work late, but Gil came over, bringing Cajun food. In the hospital, Gil had massaged me with lotions, and whether they were medicinal or not, I'd enjoyed the rubdown. I'd held the front of my gown against my breasts when he'd once tried to rub down there. We had both laughed, and I hadn't asked about his girlfriend. Didn't need to be thinking about her.

"I brought enough plates and silverware," Kat said at the condo. She'd also brought her fettuccini that I'd missed eating. Gil's seafood-stuffed eggplants from the restaurant were still steaming. With salad and breads, we filled our red plastic dishes.

The three of us laughed and ate. When we finished, Kat said she'd clean up, but Gil nudged her. "No, let me wash the dishes like Cealie always does them." The duo exchanged winks. Then Gil carried the plates, matching silverware and cups to the trash can. He tossed everything.

I carried Minnie to the den to join us while we all sat to visit.

I showed Kat my high school report card. She admired some grades and giggled at others. Roger arrived, and I had him and Gil get all the packages from my car. "Happy graduation," I told Kat. "Open your gifts."

She happily unwrapped one outfit after another. Summery clothes that she could wear to the Bahamas, other outfits for college. She opened a short set, and Roger raised an eyebrow. "Isn't that kind of skimpy?"

"She's grown up," I said. "Get over it."

Roger laughed with us. Gil handed Kat a gift from him. The lovely card bore beautiful sentiments and enough cash to probably pay for her entire trip. Kat thanked us. She giggled at my last present. An Easy-Bake Oven.

Roger had already given Kat his gift, a fairly recent model Jeep that he was fixing up. I had asked him about letting me get her a new one, but he'd declined. I understood. After all the gifts had been opened, Roger spoke hesitantly. "I didn't really get to see that game you all wanted to show me the other night. What was it?"

Kat set up the Twister. "This is an intriguing game," Gil said. "Come on, Roger, try it." Roger protested, but soon all four of us were tying our legs about each other's. We walked our hands backwards. Kat started chuckling first, or maybe I did, as she later proclaimed. Anyway, we fell down, Gil first. Me next. Roger and Kat stayed up, both saying they were the winner. We all were, I thought. Everyone was smiling.

I felt dizzy when I lowered my head. My shoulder still ached. My visitors left, saying I needed rest. They were right. I slept hard through the night and most of the next morning.

Graduation day had arrived.

In the evening I was walking out the condo door with Roger when "The Mexican Hat Dance" played. I kicked my feet a little and answered my cell phone.

"Well?" a young male's voice said.

"Who is this?" I asked.

"You don't recognize my voice? I thought you'd know it real good by now."

"Chicken Boy!"

He mumbled about being bored. "And you come up with fun stuff to do and all."

Ah, he needed someplace to go. I had Roger make a call to locate an extra ticket, and then we picked up Chicken Boy, who told us his real name was Derek Owens. He looked handsome in dressy casuals, and his face didn't appear quite so lean with his recent shorter haircut. He rode in the back seat of the Mustang beside Marisa Hernandez, whom Roger had just met. I noticed Roger's smile. As time progressed, his smile widened.

In Sidmore High's parking lot, Roger wrapped an arm around my shoulder. "Are you okay, Mom? Do you want to leave?"

"No-o." I clasped a hand over my mouth. Took deep breaths. "I'm all right."

Gil pulled up next to our car, and then he and Roger walked on either side of me. The long brick building appeared more ominous in the dark. I glanced away, at all the people talking as they headed for the well-lit doors.

I didn't look up at the cougar while we walked inside. Pulsing in my head brought renewed aches. Gil touched the small of my back. I hadn't realized I'd stopped walking. I unglued my feet and trudged on. Gil peered at me often, studying my reactions. Seeing if I needed to get out. I prayed I wouldn't.

Vice-principal Anne Little had reserved seats for us on the right side of the auditorium, close to the stage. She sat onstage now, in the chair beside the podium. I was grateful for the lights flooding the auditorium. Instead of silence, I found people creating happy noises. "I'm fine," I said to Gil's brooding face when we reached our row. He sat beside me. Derek took the next seat. Marisa sat, and then Roger.

Gil rubbed my arm. With closed lips, I tried to smile at him. No use.

Marisa looked especially pretty in her amber suit. She could have sat with other teachers but I had invited her, and she'd chosen to come with us. I understood why Kat liked her so much. She had told Kat she'd avoided her at school lately because she had somehow become suspect in Grant Labruzzo's murder and didn't want Kat to get hurt. Today we learned Hannah had fueled that rumor about Marisa. I'd also discovered Tom Reynolds had been ill for days during the time I saw him in that warehouse church. He'd been pale and often needed to dash out of a room to reach a restroom in time, as he'd probably done when I saw him disappear from Grant's church.

Roger fidgeted with his tie, looking insecure seated beside Marisa. While she'd ridden in the back seat with Derek, she had chatted with the boy about school. We discovered Derek had dropped out in twelfth grade but now wished he'd finished. Marisa offered to help him do that. Now she was speaking to Roger. A hint of pink colored Roger's cheeks.

Gil touched my arm. "You said you don't try to control situations," he said, nodding toward Roger and Marisa, "and you didn't have a hand in trying to start something here?"

I smiled. "They are a cute couple, aren't they?"

I heard Roger's laugh. Gil made small rubbing motions on my arm. "Hey," Derek said, leaning across Gil to speak to me. "You promised me some fun tonight." His face grew more pointed with his frown.

"Listen," I said, hearing the first strains of music. "Here it is!"

Strings of seniors held their heads erect as they entered through every rear doorway. Kat came in fifth, in her lagoon blue gown and cap, the gold ribbon of an honor graduate draped across her chest.

Pride swelled inside me. I saw only Kat. She did as the senior adviser, Abby Jeansonne, had ordered. Abby had warned all the seniors to keep their faces solemn and eyes straight ahead during this procession. Kat followed the instructions, until she passed us. Then she twisted around and, with both hands, threw our entire group big kisses.

We blew kisses in return. I shouted Kat's name. Some time during the evening while people gave speeches, I realized Gil was holding my hand. Roger was wiping his eyes. Marisa watched the stage. Our de-feathered Chicken Boy appeared semi-interested.

A school board member introduced Anne Little as acting principal. She stood at the mike, and without mentioning what occurred in this room, said, "I want all of you to remember. Sidmore High, home of the mighty Cougars, will always be a winner!"

Cheers resounded. People whispered. Surely most of them knew what had transpired. Their former principal had killed. But the school's tragedy appeared to add to the event's poignancy.

Anne thanked parents for all their help during these seniors' school years. She praised and thanked teachers, asking them to rise. Coach Millet smiled as he stood up beside Abby Jeansonne.

I applauded, seeing these and all other teachers in the universe in a new light. Those professionals would forever keep my utmost admiration.

Soon Kat strode to the stage. "Yay, Kat! Yay, Kat!" I called, clapping until my hands stung. Anne Little handed Kat her diploma. They hugged each other a long time.

I didn't notice much else that transpired. I did know Nancy

remained with me all evening. Nancy's hot tears rolled down my cheeks. When I told Kat later, she said she'd felt the same way.

The end was drawing near. Gil saw me glancing at Roger and Marisa, who spoke happily together, and *tsk-tsked* at me. I smirked.

Anne Little congratulated all the graduates. "We gave out most awards at Class Day," Anne said, "but saved our finest ones for last." She named the salutatorian, and John Winston strutted on stage to receive his trophy. "And now our valedictorian," Anne announced. "The best of your class, Katherine Gunther!"

How little I recalled after that. I jumped. Cheered. Stomped my feet.

Kat glowed on stage. She still beamed afterward, running out from the crowd of caps and gowns toward us. Roger's outstretched arms caught her, and he swung Kat around, both of them chuckling. She fell against me and whispered, "Thanks for being here, Gram." We squeezed each other. Gil and Marisa kissed her. Derek then told Kat, "You did pretty good." She grinned and thanked him.

I would be flying away from these family members soon. Right now, Gil was bringing us to dinner. My shoulder muscles tensed when I considered that Legs would be there.

We reached Cajun Delights, the voices inside me persisting. This was *our* night, the night for celebrating my baby girl. I peered at Gil, entering beside me. I liked him there. At the moment, I didn't want to share him. But what must be . . . "Here's our guest of honor!" Gil announced to his friends working inside.

Everyone applauded. Kat did her little shy thing, that slight hang of her head. But soon she was kidding back with people who were asking for her autograph. She signed a few of their napkins.

I chuckled. My laughter wore off when I began searching. We sat at Gil's table.

"Hi," Legs said, popping up behind me. I glimpsed her cute face and turned away.

"Everyone," Gil said, "this is Margo Conners."

"Hi, Margo!" our group said. We were a happy bunch. I raised my hand over my head and waved backward at the woman who also had a cute name. We had filled every chair at the table, but I imagined that a waiter would soon shove in an extra chair between Gil and me.

He told Margo about Kat's award, and Margo's voice oozed sweetness as she congratulated Kat. Again I decided I hated her. Gil must've known what I was thinking. He gave me a clever grin. "Cealie, don't you want to meet Margo?" he asked loudly.

"Of course," I said through clenched teeth. Forcing a smile, I watched the short black skirt coming around me.

"Oh, I remember seeing you. So nice to see you again, Mrs. Gunther," she said. She stood almost eye-to-eye with me. And I was sitting.

My neck folded. "Where are your legs?" I said.

Margo giggled. She patted chubby knees beneath her dark stockings. "They're not much to cover."

I jumped up and stood facing her. "Look, I'm a nose taller."

Everybody at our table laughed. Margo hugged me. "I like her," she told Gil. She pulled a pad out of her pocket. "Are you ready to order now, Mr. Thurman?"

Gil gave me a smirk.

My fingers covered my nose tip. Beneath my hand, I was grinning. Gil let the others give Margo their orders while he quietly spoke to me. "I tried to tell you a couple of times, but you stopped me. Cealie, you really look enticing wearing that jealous streak."

"She's your table's waitress," I whispered. "And you aren't having an affair with her?"

"Only in your mind." Gil's mouth widened with his smile.

Lord, he had pretty teeth. And beneath them, a right clever tongue.

The others in our group insisted that I ride back with Gil. He and I stood beside the Mustang, where Kat slipped in to take my place. She and Roger said I'd make them too crowded. I could have squeezed in. If I'd really wanted to.

While we'd all been eating, I had done a mental scroll back through the times I'd been in the restaurant, concocting the idea that Margo had extra-long legs. Each time I'd thought she was sitting at Gil's table or leaning from somewhere to watch us, she had actually been standing up straight.

The Senior Prom had been postponed because of fear of sabotage at the school, but now Roger was driving Kat home to change. Then he would take her back to join friends for the dance about to be held in the gym. Derek said it might be kind of fun to hang around there a little while. Kat sat with him in the back, making certain Marisa would sit in front, near her dad. They promised to take lots of pictures.

I smiled, watching Roger looking freer with Marisa. *Did she ever put on underwear?* I wondered. Maybe my son would soon find out.

Gil drove me to the condo. He walked me to the door and stood, gazing at me. "Should I come in?" The overhead light forced a glitter from silver strands in his hair. Gil's eyes looked like new charcoal. A murmur came from deep in his throat.

I touched that area of his neck. My hands stroked his familiar skin. This man was a wonderful lover. Such fun to be with. Did

I want to renew our relationship?

I ordered up a vision of mounds of dirty dishes. Hampers of clothes to wash, me waiting around for repairmen. Being stuck in one house. Long grass outside, wanting to be mowed. Social Security checks now or later?

I moved my hands off him. I adored this man. But now I needed freedom. Self-discovery. "Not tonight," I said.

Then why didn't I move back? Step away from him. I clasped him within my arms. "See you, mmm, later," I said.

Gil backed me through the doorway. "Yes, see you."

"Ummm." I don't know who pulled off the other's clothes first. Gil probably shut the door. We fell to the floor. Peeled off garments. Felt remembered curves and swells. Drank in of each other. The still-open Twister mat beneath us felt slippery. It made squishy sounds.

Satisfied, we moved to my bed. Clutched each other. Renewed smells and heat and passion.

Gil would stay with me. So would the intense satisfaction he gave my body. Most of all, I'd miss Gil Thurman, the person. He knew I needed to complete this mission of renewing me. Some fortunate woman might take Gil one day. I'd keep his memory.

I left two days later. I had to. If not, these cozy homey feelings I'd been experiencing would settle in and remain.

I dusted the stove before I left the condo. If I didn't leave now, I'd have to keep dusting things. I wanted to stay with Kat and my son. But their lives were moving on. I needed to get on with mine.

Family meant permanence, I told myself, and one thing I knew. With life came change. Kat would be leaving for college. Roger would explore a relationship with Marisa Hernandez. What could I do? Stay around Gil and lean on him for support, as I'd done with Freddy and my relatives? I had no idea how many years of life I had left, but surely they weren't meant for dependence. I needed to find my evolving life's purpose.

"Let's go find Cealie," I said to me right before opening the condo door for Roger and Kat to come in and get my things.

All three of us cried at the airport before I boarded the plane. My cell phone played its music. I answered and then heard, "Hi, Mom."

"Hi, Tommy." I smiled, hearing my son in Alaska. Tommy hadn't been able to come in for graduation, but now he and his family all wanted to talk to Kat. Then Roger and I each took turns chatting with them. I clicked off, overflowing with more emotions. Missing more of the people I cherished.

"Don't forget to call us as soon as you reach Acapulco," Roger said to me, giving a final wave. "I love you, Mom."

"Love you, Gram," Kat yelled, blowing kisses.

Tears trapped in my throat only allowed me to wave back at them. I walked into the plane and located my seat. Peered out the window. Wished I could still keep them in view. Wished I'd let Gil come to see me off too.

No, I couldn't have handled that parting. Our final goodbye at the condo had been difficult enough. "Whatever you want, Cealie," he'd murmured into my hair.

How great of him. What did I want? "That's what you're trying to find out," I told myself. The Asian man seated beside me peered up from his newspaper. Our plane rolled down the tarmac. From the plane window, I waved. Probably Kat and Roger were watching from that large window, doing the same thing.

It had been great to be near Kat and Roger, but being around relatives caused confusion. Just look at what I'd just been through, I reminded myself, wiping my damp cheeks and branding my mind with my purpose. Family was most important. But I'd want to keep them all around me, and I couldn't. I had to go off and discover my current purpose.

My life was totally mine now, and I was headed into the sunset. Or almost, I saw as my window framed the orange-blue evening sky.

I'd lightened my suitcase and my life. What I carried instead were the people. I tightened my inner view of cherished ones, wrapping them into my heart. My sons, their families. Gil. I wiped my eyes. I needed to do something.

Unzipping my carry-on bag, I took out Minnie. "We should find some of your relatives in Mexico," I said, pressing more of the dirt against her side. "I'll do better now," I promised before setting her back.

Our plane was airborne. Besides loved ones, I'd left behind some of my nicest outfits. Maybe the lady who dusted and mopped the condo could use them or know another person would might. I had also left the plant Roger gave me. I'd kill that big peace lily. And I hadn't felt close enough to it to even give it another name.

Poor Minnie wouldn't have a friend with her. I sniffled and wiped my nose. Peered at the Asian man. I pulled out my laptop and checked e-mail.

HELP!!! CEALIE, I NEED YOU. IF YOU BELIEVE IN FORGIVENESS AT ALL, CALL YOUR COUSIN STEVIE.

I read the next message: *DAMMIT, CEALIE, I'M GONNA DIE IF YOU DON'T COME TO GATLINBURG!*

I hit the reply button and then wrote in all caps—*I'M FREE! NOW IS THE TIME FOR ME!* I was about to push *send.* But didn't want Stevie to know I'd received her messages. I shut down my computer. Slammed its cover shut. My muttered oaths made the Asian man glance up. "Sorry for my language," I told him.

Why hadn't I read my cookbook from Belgium instead of checking e-mail? Why hadn't I left the damned laptop in the condo?

Dammit, I could probably make a brief stopover in Gatlinburg.

Gatlinburg. Hmm, okay, I was going after me. But I could check in with my cousin first. I wouldn't stay with Stevie long, only see what she wanted. Get that psychic danger stuff out of her mind. And after that, I'd definitely try to refrain from being around most relatives.

I uncrossed my tensed arms. Of course while I was in Stevie's area, I might want to check out the restaurant that would be opening soon. I believed they'd be serving something Cajun.

CAJUN DELIGHTS

EGGPLANT SUPREME À LA BOB

(Since Cajuns don't measure anything, measurements are approximate. What's definite is that this is a scrumptious dish.)

Ingredients:
4 eggplants
1 lg. onion chopped
½ lg. bell pepper chopped
2 cloves garlic minced
2 T. cooking oil
1 lb. crabmeat
1 lb. small shrimp
1 c. seasoned breadcrumbs
salt and pepper to taste
melted butter or margarine

Heat oven to 350°. Cut eggplants in half and parboil 25–30 minutes. Carefully remove pulp of the eggplants with a spoon so as not to break the skin. Set the skin aside on a shallow baking pan. Mix cooking oil, eggplant pulp, onions, bell pepper, and garlic in a heavy pot and sauté about 20 minutes. Add crabmeat, shrimp, and salt and pepper. Cook about 20 minutes more. Fill eggplant shells with the cooked mixture. Top with bread crumbs and drizzle melted butter on top. Bake until topping is brown. Will serve 8. Yum.

SMOTHERED POTATOES À LA BOB

Ingredients:
5 medium potatoes
3 lg. onions
½ lg. bell pepper
⅓ c. cooking oil
1 t. salt
1 t. black pepper

Peel potatoes, or if desired, leave peelings on half of one potato. Chop potatoes into very small rectangular pieces. Chop onions and bell pepper. Place all ingredients in a heavy pot. Cook over medium heat, stirring constantly for approximately 30 minutes, scraping bottom of pot continuously, until mixture is softened. Then eat—and pat your happy belly.

BASICS OF GROWING CACTI
AND OTHER SUCCULENTS

First, don't do anything Cealie did with these low-maintenance plants except give them love. Next, decide on one or a few plants you like. Succulents enjoy hot, dry conditions and need good drainage. Most are shallow-rooted and do best in small pots. Line the bottom of the pot with gravel. A good potting mix is three parts sterilized, fibrous soil, one part washed grit, and one part peat moss, although it's simpler to buy prepackaged cactus soil. Top the soil with a layer of pebbles.

Work with your plants carefully, being careful not to break their stems. Place them in an arrangement you like, using a pair of tongs to handle small prickly ones or rolled-up newspaper for large ones with spines, unless you have one like Minnie that's been shaved. Give your plants a couple of days to settle into their new environment before watering them.

Fertilize your plants lightly during their growing season. During winter, water them sparingly, and keep them at 50° F or above. In spring you can return them to a sunny window or outdoors as soon as the weather begins to warm and new growth starts on the plants. Be careful of direct sunlight. Succulents can get sunburned.

You can easily propagate new plants after yours grow a bit. Most succulents reproduce by sending off shoots. Separate the shoot from its parent plant and stick it into the mixture you used for your other succulents. Protect it from excessive jostling while it forms roots, and soon you'll be proud of your growing new plant!

*Note: Links to sites explaining much more about cacti and other succulents can be found at www.juneshaw.com.

ABOUT THE AUTHOR

June Shaw, award-winning novelist and screenwriter, lives along a lazy bayou in south Louisiana, where she sometimes fishes or plants flowers. She's always happy being surrounded by loved ones, especially her large family. Please visit her at www.juneshaw.com.